about the authors

KATE FORSYTH's first book was published in 1997. She is a direct descendant of Charlotte Waring Atkinson, the author of Australia's earliest known children's book, and has a doctorate in fairy tales. She writes for adults and children. This is her fortieth book.

KIM WILKINS's first book was also published in 1997. She has a PhD in English and is a researcher and lecturer at University of Queensland. She writes fantasy under her own name and historical fiction as Kimberley Freeman. This is her thirtieth book.

The
Silver
Well

The Silver Well

Kate Forsyth
and Kim Wilkins

illustrations by Kathleen Jennings

introduction by Lisa L. Hannett

For our children: Astrid, Ben, Ellie, Luka, and Tim

The Silver Well by Kate Forsyth and Kim Wilkins

Published by Ticonderoga Publications

Designed and edited by Russell B. Farr
Typeset in Sabon and Sudbury Book

A Cataloging-in-Publications entry for this title is available from The National Library of Australia.

ISBN 978-1-925212-50-1 (limited hardcover)
      978-1-925212-51-8 (trade hardcover)
      978-1-925212-52-5 (trade paperback)
      978-1-925212-53-2 (ebook)

Ticonderoga Publications
PO Box 29 Greenwood
Western Australia 6924

www.ticonderogapublications.com

10 9 8 7 6 5 4 3 2 1

The authors would like to thank Lisa Hannett (who was there) and Kathleen Jennings (who captured our ideas so beautifully). We also offer our gratitude to Russ and Liz, who were so enthusiastic about our madcap idea. Thanks, too, to the owners of Old Gaol Cottage, Cerne Abbas, who unwittingly hosted the fantasy writers sleepover. Finally, we want to celebrate each other for 20 years of friendship, creativity, champagne, and travel. Kindred spirits always.

Contents

Introduction

Lisa L. Hannett

OME PLACES IN THIS WORLD SIMPLY brim with magic.

There are the obvious places, of course, the ones where supernatural encounters are so often sought and so often expected to be found. Stone circles and fairy rings, ley lines and dolmen, whispering woods and graveyards. Tor-topped hills. Haunted houses. Cathedrals with cloud-piercing spires. Humble Romanesque churches. Open-air temples overlooking quiet barrow downs. Ancient sites drenched with sacrificial blood.

And then there are the *really* magical places.

Places where history is so thickly layered, time becomes irrelevant. Places where light falls differently; it's softer and paler than everyday light, as though each beam has been sifted through a veil of centuries. Places dense with ghost trails and drifting memories, where you swear the firm earth underfoot is packed with more bones than dirt. Places humming with shadow-wings that can only be glimpsed from the corner of your eye. Places of the heart.

These are the places you immediately recognise—places you *know*—even though you haven't visited them before. Though you've never felt the July warmth of this particular sun nor filled your lungs with that particular Dorset breeze. Though you've never seen that once-Benedictine abbey with its rustic guesthouse and its lichen-encrusted stone walls. Though you've never meandered through the cemetery beside those enclosed ruins nor read the names on old headstones aloud with your friends. You've never strolled out through the wall's arched gate nor followed the gently sloping path down to St Augustine's blessed well. Never before have you dipped your bare toes into those healing waters nor enjoyed the dappled green shade of the surrounding trees, all those lindens with their vibrant heart-shaped leaves.

And yet.

Even so.

Truly magic places like these convince you that maybe, once upon a time, you have done such things. These places make you believe in past lives, if only for a while. For a few whimsical, beguiling moments. While you're there you can't help but feel a sense of return. A sense of belonging.

It feels so *right* discovering these places for the first time, again.

Despite any physical or factual evidence to the contrary, once you find yourself at the saint's well at Cerne Abbas—whether in person or through the pages of this lovely book—you're *positive* some part of you has already heard the clatter of tiny wish-scrolls (hundreds and hundreds of them!) strung in the boughs overhead. Some part of you has already reached up and tightly tied your own quickly scrawled ribbon to a perfect, low-hanging branch. Some part of you has long taken comfort in this sort of dreaming, this secret sort of hoping, in this very place.

Call it the soul, if you will. Call it the spirit. Call it the essence we all carry inside our ribcages, the ineffable core that instantly connects with myth-rich places like this one. The part of us that yearns for and cherishes stories.

This is exactly the sort of place that has inspired—and has been beautifully captured in—*The Silver Well*.

"It was said that the well was a portal to the Otherworld," Iona tells us in 'The Giant', "that if a mother dipped a newborn baby in it at dawn then good fortune would follow, that the faces of the soon-dead appeared in the water at nightfall at Samhain.

"It was said the well could grant wishes."

The Silver Well is just such a portal—and it certainly is enchanting. One tale at a time, Kate Forsyth and Kim Wilkins immerse us in the fabled waters of Cerne Abbas, plunging us deeper and deeper into the lore of this village, further and further into its past. Here we meet a cast of characters whose lives span two millennia—charming artists and shopkeepers, forsaken lovers, cunning-women, severe Puritans, proud warriors, shell-shocked soldiers, bereft parents, fierce and fragile children, and many generations of Brightwells. Across the ages we hear their carefully hidden thoughts. Their worries and fears. Their hopes and losses.

Perhaps most of all, we're swept up in their desires. Longings that eventually—inevitably—call us all down to that sacred well, that magic place where the light falls differently and words become powerful spells. And there, at the beginning and end of each story in this collection, we'll pause for a breath, turn the page, and make brand new familiar wishes together.

September 2017

The Wishing Tree

March 2017

I WISH HE WAS DEAD.
Or hurt.
Or humiliated.
Or, worst of all, pitied.

Rain smeared the glass of the bus window. Beyond were patchwork fields, sodden with water. Mist drifted in pale veils across a twisted skein of green downs.

By rights, I should have been lying on a beach in Honolulu, on my honeymoon. I had bought a new bikini and a hibiscus sarong in preparation. It had been unbelievably painful to return them. I'd boasted to the sales girl about how I was about to marry the love of my life and how he was taking me to Hawaii. Slinking back to the shop, I'd been unable to meet her eyes. I'd spun some lie about losing too much weight, but then would not let her find me a smaller size.

I could not confess that he had jilted me.

I'd sold my wedding dress on Gumtree, for a fraction of what it had cost me, and swapped two return plane tickets to Honolulu for a single one-way ticket to Europe. I'd never wanted to go to Hawaii in the first place. That had been his dream. We've got plenty of time, I had told myself. I'll go and lie by the pool and drink Mai Tais for him, and one day he'll tramp through bluebell woods and explore ruined castles with me.

What a fool I had been.

The bus passed through one charming village after another. Lyon's Gate. Minterne Magna. Minterne Parva. I saw a road sign for Cerne Abbas, and my heart quickened. I thought of my grandmother, and all the stories she had told me of growing up here. Watching badgers snuffle around a beech wood in the twilight. Helping bring in the harvest, as hares leapt for freedom from the stands of rustling corn. Walking through the fields, gathering the wild fruit of the hedgerows to make jams and pies and summer wine. Singing and dancing on the top of Giant Hill on midsummer morn.

"If you take a peek out the left-hand window now, you might get a glimpse of the famous giant," the bus driver announced over the microphone. Of course I turned and pressed my face to the window, trying not to fog up the glass. A glimpse of faint white lines carved on the hillside. A giant man held a club high above one head. The other hand was lifted as if in warning. The lines were so deep they cast shadows across the turf, making him seem as if he was about to surge forth into motion.

A frisson of excitement shivered my skin. I wondered how old the giant was, and who had carved him, and why. How strange and mysterious this landscape was, with its tumbled circles of stones and fairy hills and devil's chairs. The green folds of the downs, enclosed within dark hedges and bare trees hung with rooks' nests, sang to me in a way no other landscape ever had. I had grown up in a small terrace house in Melbourne, with a few weeds growing in the cracks of the concrete, and the dull roar of traffic always thrumming in my ears. Power lines overhead, graffiti on the walls, cigarette butts in the gutter. How I had longed for fields and meadows and wildflowers, for the countryside of my grandmother's stories and my favourite childhood books.

I'm here now, I told myself. Maybe it was all for the best.

But there was a lump in my throat like dry bread.

It had been just over a month since Zac had told me he didn't want to marry me anymore. I'd been to Italy, to France, to Germany, to the Czech Republic and Slovenia, to Poland. I'd spent my days in cathedrals and museums and art galleries. I'd walked till my feet throbbed. I'd taken a thousand photos with my iPhone, and posted them on Facebook with false squeals and lots of exclamation marks. I'd unfriended all his friends, and forced myself not to stalk him on Twitter.

What an adventure I'm having, I told myself. All my dreams come true, I told myself.

Yet I was numb with pain. Grief, I suppose. Embarrassment. I felt like a recovering alcoholic. Knowing the danger, yet unable to help longing for it.

Last night I'd been so tired and lonely, I'd gone and checked out his status. Stupid, I know. And there he was, grinning like a goon, fondling some skinny bitch, smoking like a chimney (Although he'd promised! He knew how I hated it!).

My carefully rebuilt dreams were smashed in a moment.

Today I felt shaky and fragile. The juddering of the bus seemed to bruise me right through, as if I was seventy-seven and not twenty-seven. I pinned all my hopes on the village I was about to see. The place that had offered my grandmother refuge from the horror of the war. The place that had, she said, taught her to be happy again.

We turned down a narrow road. I saw cottages with thatched roofs, and quaint shops with bay windows. A tree foaming with pink blossoms. Duck Street, the sign said. A flash of memory. "The main street flooded so often, it was a heaven for ducks," my grandmother had told me. "That's why they called it Duck Street."

If Zac had been here, he would have sneered and said something disparaging.

But I smiled. I couldn't help it.

I got out near the pub, dragging my cheap battered suitcase from the bowels of the bus. How I wish I'd travelled lighter, but I had not known how long I'd be away. I'd not known what I'd need. I had never left Australia before.

Across the road from the pub was a B&B, and so I went there straightaway. I was in luck. A single room, clean and fresh. A heavenly soft bed. A view on to a garden. I dumped my bags and went out walking, even though it was drizzling. My shoes were useless. Far too thin. My feet were damp and cold in minutes.

On the footpath beside the Royal Oak, a pub that proudly proclaimed on its shingle that it was built in 1540, a trestle table had been set up under a striped, pop-up gazebo. The woman under it wore a green all-weather coat and had steely grey curls under her beret. I was far too tired and dazed to pay much notice, but she called me over.

"New to town, love? Care to buy something to aid the Historical Society?"

I politely looked at the display of locally published books and bookmarks, at the jam drops in cardboard trays, the hand-printed shopping bags, and the pretty watercolour postcards.

"These are nice," I said, picking up a packet of postcards.

"Local artist."

I looked at the paintings more carefully. I had loved art once. I was always sketching and painting. Zac called them my "little scribbles". One too many times, I suppose, as I had eventually stopped. "They're very good."

"Three pounds. What do you say? It's a good cause."

"All right then. Yes." I fished in the pocket of my jeans and pulled out three one-pound coins.

As she slid them into a brown paper bag for me, she said, "You're Australian, then?"

"Yes," I replied. "No pubs that old in Australia." I pointed to the Oak.

"Barely any history at all, I should think," she replied.

"Lots of history. Just not ours. White people, I mean."

"Ah yes. Of course. And are you staying long in town?"

"I'm . . . not sure."

"Well, if you're interested in Cerne Abbas's history, you could come along to one of our talks. Here." She pushed a pamphlet into my hands. "You'd be very welcome. I'm Isobel."

"Rosie," I said, tucking the postcards into the back of my waistband and hoping they wouldn't get ruined in the drizzle.

I was three steps up the road when she called out, "By the way! The local artist is me."

I turned and smiled at her, and she grinned proudly in return. She looked so happy, carefree. I bet her husband never told her that her painting were little scribbles.

I soon tired of walking with wet shoes and stopped to eat at one of the local pubs. Thick slices of dry roast lamb with tasteless brown gravy and vegetables so mushy they were almost unidentifiable. I should offer them my services, I thought. Teach them how spring lamb should be cooked.

All the time a low buzz of anger and misery. How could he? Why? What did I do wrong?

I wish I'd never met him, I thought.

I pulled out Isobel's postcards and studied the pictures. A kissing gate in fine ink lines surrounded by watercolour trees. A meandering stream in sunlit patterns. The ruins of an old building, surrounded by yews. I flipped one over, pulled out a ballpoint pen, but could only draw a picture of Zac standing next to his wretched BMW, with a piano about to fall on both.

Satisfying, but not my finest work.

After dinner, I was so tired I could barely stagger across the road to the dear little B&B. Or perhaps it was the red wine. I could not remember how much I'd had. Never quite enough to fill the void.

I dropped my keys with a clatter, and stumbled over my suitcase. Could only hope no-one would hear. I fell into my bed and tried to comfort myself with my grandmother's stories. "We lost everything," she had told me. "Not just our home and our parents. All faith, all hope, all love. Yet we found it again. In that little grey village cupped in the hollow of the hills. And once lost and rediscovered . . . well, you never lose it again . . . "

I spun away into sleep.

I woke some time later, my heart pounding, my chest compressed so I could not breathe. Don't worry, I told myself. You're safe, I told myself.

It did no good. After a long while, I got up and dressed. I let myself out into the street.

The rain had passed, but everything glistened in the silvery pre-dawn light. I saw a church steeple, and walked towards it. My grandmother had gone there to that church every Sunday. It had the most astonishing array of gargoyles, she had told me. As if the builders had tried to ward off some terrible evil. The first time my grandmother had gone there, she and her sister had crossed themselves before the altar, as superstitious as Catholics. It had taken years for the congregation to forgive them.

I walked around the church, the hems of my jeans getting wet and muddy. My feet were cold and wet again, but the air was cool and damp and clean, as though freshly washed. A bird sang. A divine trilling chirp that I had never heard before. A blackbird?

I'd always wanted to hear a blackbird.

I continued on up the road. It was almost as if my grandmother walked with me, pointing out the landmarks. The row of medieval timber-framed houses with their upper storeys jutting out over the street. The thatched cottage with daffodils flying defiant flags of sunlight. The village pond, dappled with lily pads and overhung with willows, their tendrils budding with fuzzy catkins. Abbey House, with tall hedges and mullioned windows, that my grandmother had always wished was hers.

My breath puffed white before me. I pulled up my hood and shoved my hands deep into my pocket.

An archway set in a high stone wall. Beyond, an ancient graveyard. I hesitated, feeling like an intruder. But the gate stood ajar, and the street was empty. Everyone else in the world was asleep. Slowly I pushed the gate open and stepped within. Mossy headstones, sunken slabs of lichened granite, a row of little evergreens, and—along the edge—an avenue of tree skeletons. I tiptoed that way.

A sunken path led down to a hidden dell, protected by high stone walls. There was a miraculous spring of water somewhere here, I remembered my grandmother telling me.

All was quiet. Frost silvered the grass, sharpened the breath in my lungs. Then I came past the last of the great gnarled trees, and saw before me a small pool of water, enclosed within stone like a garden pond. Hundreds of faded ribbons fluttered from the overhanging twigs. A man sat cross-legged on the ground, his hands resting on his thighs.

I stopped, and caught my breath, and tried to back away. But leaves crunched under my sneakers.

The man opened his eyes.

"I'm sorry," I babbled. "I didn't mean to intrude. I was just . . . "

He smiled at me. "No need to apologise. You've come to celebrate the spring equinox too? Please, join me." Something in my face troubled him. "Please, there's no need to fear. You are safe here."

It was uncanny, the echoing of the words I had told myself only a few hours before. Slowly I came down into the little dell. The water glimmered within its oblong of stone. I tried to remember what my grandmother had told me. The old saint's well, she had called it. A most magical place.

"Are you new here?" the man said. "I've not seen you at the well before. It really is the most magical place, isn't it?"

I stared at him wide-eyed. It was as if he could read my mind.

His thick hair was streaked with silver, but the stubble on his chin was dark. A few laugh lines around his eyes, which were brilliantly blue, making him look otherworldly. He was dressed in jeans and hiking boots, but also wore an old embroidered waistcoat over a flowing white shirt. He had picked a daffodil and stuck it through his buttonhole. A green hat with a feather in it lay on the ground beside him, and a long stick of twisted wood. If I'd had to guess, I would have thought him only a few years older than me, despite the silvered hair.

I realised he was waiting for an answer. I tried to smile, and said, "Yes. I'm new here. But I've heard a lot about it. From my grandmother."

"What's your accent?" he asked. "South African? New Zealander?"

"Australian," I said reprovingly.

"You're a long way from home."

Tears nettled my eyes. "I . . . I don't know where home is anymore."

I wiped my eyes on the sleeve of my hoodie. When I looked up, he was watching me intently.

"Is that what you are here for?" he asked. "To wish for a new home?"

I stared at him blankly.

"You've come to the well at dawn on the spring equinox. That's usually the time for wishing for new beginnings." He indicated the ribbons hung all over the trees by the well. I must have still looked confused for he went on, smiling, "that's what all the ribbons are for. People come and tie a ribbon and make a wish. They have for centuries." He put his hand in his pocket and pulled out a green ribbon. "See? That's why I'm here."

I sat down on the stone seat, pulling my knees up to my chin. "What are you going to wish for?"

He smiled. "You know I can't tell you that. The wish must be secret, else it won't come true." He regarded me thoughtfully. "You really didn't know it was the spring equinox today?"

I shook my head.

"Then it must be fate that brought you here this very morning," he said. "Do you have a ribbon? Would you like half of mine?"

"Oh no. That's all right. I couldn't . . . "

"Yes, you can. Here." He pulled a small canvas rucksack towards him and pulled out a small flick knife with a beautiful white bone handle. He cut the ribbon, then passed me one half.

"Thank you," I said, wrapping it about my fingers.

"Be careful what you wish for," he warned me. "Do not take this place lightly. It is a sacred spot, filled with power."

I frowned at him suspiciously, afraid he was having a go at me, but his face was serious. "Do you really believe that?"

"Oh, yes," he answered. "My family have lived near here for centuries. There are many tales about this old spring. My grandma said it has three purposes. It's a well of prophecy. You're meant to be able to see the face of who you are to marry, or have visions of who will die, or glimpse those who are far away or long gone. It's a wishing well, as you can see by the coins in the water and the ribbons in the twigs. And it's famous as a healing well. My grandmother used to make all kinds of potions and lotions with the water and various herbs, and if one of us boys ever twisted an ankle we were sent here straightaway to bathe it." He laughed, his face warm with the memory. "Oh, yes, and we were all dunked here as newborn babies. A kind of pagan baptism, I suppose. It's supposed to bring long life. Certainly my grandma lived till she was a hundred."

"You were lucky to have her so long." Despite myself, my eyes filled with tears again. I tried to wipe them away surreptitiously but he was observing me closely.

"You've lost your grandma? Recently?"

I shrugged. "Almost a year ago. It's just . . . well, she raised me, you see. My parents died in a car crash when I was eleven. My grandmother took me in, looked after me, taught me everything I know."

"So you're an orphan."

I nodded.

"That's sad. No brothers or sisters?"

I shook my head.

"Any cousins?"

"Maybe here in the village. My grandmother and grandfather

came from here. I know my grandmother had a sister. I don't know about my grandfather. He was a man of few words, unlike my Baba. Besides, he died when I was fifteen. Lung cancer."

I don't know why I was talking so much. I realised it had been a while since I'd had a proper conversation with anyone. Not since I'd fled Australia.

"There's been a lot of death in your life," he said. "Maybe that's what drew you to the silver well today. When you lose enough people you love, it draws you closer to the veil."

"The veil?"

"Between life and death. Known and unknown."

I hugged my knees tightly. "Maybe."

"Or maybe loss has given you a taste of life's impermanence. You're here for something new. A fresh start." He stood up and stretched, his shirt lifting to show an inch or two of well-toned stomach muscle. "I must go. I need to get to work."

"What do you do?" I asked, not wanting him to go.

"I manage the garden of an old manor house, and run a small nursery business from there, selling seedlings that we've grown on the premises. It's a beautiful old place. You must come and visit if you like gardens."

"Oh I do. Particularly kitchen gardens. I'm a bit of a foodie, you see."

"Then you'll love it. There's a restaurant on site, built in the old dovecote. All the food is grown using our own produce, except for the meat and fish which are locally sourced."

"It must be some garden, if you're growing all you need."

"Well, it is, if I say so myself. Built on the foundations of the original medieval walled garden. Espaliered apple and pear trees, and lots of herbs and vegies."

"It sounds just wonderful." Hearing the wistful tone in my voice, I added brightly, "I don't suppose you have a bluebell wood at your manor house?"

"We do." His voice was warm with understanding.

"I've always wanted to walk in a bluebell wood."

"Well, you'll need to stick around a few more weeks. The bluebells will be at their best after Easter."

"I guess I will, then."

He smiled, and picked up his rucksack and the tall twisted walking stick. It looked like something a druid would carry. "Well, hopefully I'll see you at Winterthorne gardens one day. Ask for Christopher Beaufort."

"All right then. I'll come see your gardens. Maybe later this week." I scrambled up. "I'm Rosie, by the way."

"Pleased to meet you, Rosie." He held out his hand and I shook it shyly. "What's your last name? If your grandparents once lived here, you might still have family in the area. It's only a small place, everyone knows each other."

"Brightwell," I replied, flushing a little. I'd been teased about my last name all my life. Dumbsick, the kids at school used to call me.

He grinned. "Well, Rosie Brightwell, you're in luck. One of my best friends is a Brightwell too. Her name is Poppy. She must be some kind of cousin, it's an unusual name. She works in one of the little shops on Long Street. You can't miss it. It's called Brightwell Health and Beauty."

His grin deepened at the expression on my face. "You'll like her, I promise. She's a sweetheart. Now I've really got to go. Hope to see you around, Rosie."

Christopher turned and, with no self-consciousness whatsoever, tied his little scrap of green ribbon to the wild rose that scrambled over the stone wall. I wondered what he was wishing for.

Once he was gone, I sat down again on the stone seat and twisted my half of the ribbon around my fingers. I realised I was smiling, and sternly gave myself a lecture. You're meant to be heart-broken, remember?

But my heart was pitter-pattering so quickly, it was clear it was still in perfect working order.

I wondered what I should wish for.

All month, I had been wanting something awful to happen to Zac. I'd wanted him as hurt and humiliated as I had been. I'd imagined all sorts of horrible scenarios for him. Being beaten up by his new girlfriend's boyfriend. Being sacked. Having someone anonymously post something about his miniscule penis online and the post going viral.

But Christopher had said that the morning of the spring equinox was the time to wish for new beginnings.

I wondered, for the first time in a long time, what it was I really wanted.

To love, my wounded soul cried out. To love someone with all my heart and be loved by them.

I had always longed for that, though.

To be loved for who I really am, I thought. To not always be twisting myself into a new shape, to please them, and yet still always be found wanting in some way.

Yet who was I really? I had no idea. When I'd been with Zac, I'd worn the type of clothes he liked, ate what he liked, drank what he liked. Before Zac, there had been Joshua, and before him, Ryan. I'd been a different Rosie for all of them.

Just be yourself, my grandmother had always said.

But I did not know who that was.

I had come to Cerne Abbas on some kind of pilgrimage, I realised, wanting to see where my grandparents had grown up, wanting to feel myself at home in a landscape where generations of my ancestors had lived and loved and died. Perhaps it was meant to be, this journey of discovery, this meeting by the silver well.

My pulse quickened again at the thought.

I couldn't really have loved Zac, if a month after we were meant to be married I was having fantasies about a strange man I'd just met. Or perhaps I was just a silly fool who fell in love with anyone who was kind.

I sat down by the pool and splashed water on my face, trying to steady my pulse. It was icy-cold. How those babies must have yelled, being bathed in this spring water within hours of their birth. Especially in winter.

I smiled again. Had he told me the truth, that blue-eyed stranger, or was he laughing now, thinking of the gullible tourist he had bamboozled with his tall tales?

Above my head, the faded ribbons fluttered in the wind. The sky was flushed now with light, and birds were singing joyously. I stood and tied my green ribbon next to Christopher's, on a branch of the linden tree. I had a sense of history pressing down on me, thinking of all those sad pilgrims who had been here before me. Had my grandmother made a wish? Her grandmother? The well surely represented a history of longing. I felt connected to all those wishes in that moment, all those people who had felt the absence of something in their lives, and the feeling was too big for my chest.

I whispered, "I wish I knew who I really was."

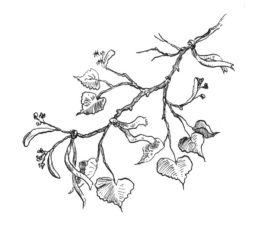

The Blessing

August 1944

I T WAS A BLESSING, MY MOTHER SAID, that the baby had died.

No-one need know.

I hunched over the hollow within me, arms crossed.

I could not think any of it was a blessing. My lover shot down in the mud of Normandy. His mother touching her eyes with her handkerchief in the next church pew, dressed in the blacks I was denied. The night sky full of the rattling drone of doodlebugs, the glare of bombed towns. Each day a weary round of digging up potatoes, knitting khaki socks, listening to the ladies of the church read out one blaring headline after another.

If only there had been time for us to be married. George had made me a ring from the curling binds of honeysuckle. He'd promised we'd elope to the registry office the next time he was home on leave.

His mother would come around, he had said. Once she had grandchildren.

Except George had never come home.

I had known him since we were kids together, peeking at each other over the back of that same church pew. He'd not gone to the same school as me, of course. He'd gone to one of those schools for toffs. At the beginning of each term, he'd been driven to the station in his stiff white collar and top-hat, his trunk strapped to the back of the Daimler, the chauffeur looking very proper in his peaked cap. George would glance at me, standing outside Pa's grocery store in my old gingham dress, socks falling down, shoes dusty from playing in the lane.

Once he had winked at me.

Our paths did not cross in the normal course of things, even though we lived so close. Then one night he and some of his other smart-set friends came to a dance at the village hall. He looked so handsome in his black tie and tails, and didn't care one bit for the dirty looks cast at him by the village boys in their shabby tweeds. He asked me to jitterbug. I didn't know how but I took his hand, anyway, and let him lead me out on to the floor. Soon we were breathless and laughing, leaning on each other. He gave me his silver flask to sip from. I think it had gin in it. I'd never drunk anything but a little sherry when the vicar came to call. The gin made the world seem so dazzly and bright.

He walked me home after the dance, and tried to kiss me by the front door. I wouldn't let him. I knew Ma would be looking out for me. She'd be so angry if she saw me keeping company with George Atwick-Sellick. Ever since the Affair of the Kippers, my mother and Mrs Atwick-Sellick had refused to acknowledge each other's existence. It all seemed so silly now, with the world at war and George dead and my brother Kenneth in some filthy camp in Poland.

But back then it had seemed so important.

"Mary! Stop your wool-gathering. It's time to go." Ma shook my shoulder roughly. I got up and collected my prayer book and my gloves, and stood waiting as the congregation filed down the aisle. Mrs Atwick-Sellick drifted past, one gloved hand at her throat. Everyone moved aside, murmuring condolences. She did not spare me a glance.

Yet I knew George had told his mother about us.

Or at least, he said he had.

I did not know any more if I had been played as a fool, or if George was the one true love I had longed for all my life. Once I had been so sure. I was sure of nothing now.

Outside the congregation stood in the churchyard, chatting to the vicar and exchanging news of the war.

"I'm going for a walk," I told my mother.

"But, Mary . . . the vicar's wife is coming for tea . . . "

I didn't answer. With my hands shoved deep in my pockets, I walked up Abbey Lane, past the medieval cottages of the Pitch Market, with their crooked timber framing and mullioned windows and battered wooden carvings. A black cat lay in the middle of the road, washing its hind leg. I crossed to the other side of the road.

I didn't need any more bad luck, you see.

I came to the old abbey wall, with the iron gateway into the graveyard, and pushed it open. Its hinges squealed. I kept my eyes on the path, not looking down the avenue of linden trees towards the old well where I used to meet George. Instead I went out the far gate. Past the signpost that said "Giant's Hill". I did not turn that way either.

Everywhere hurt.

I walked till I was bone-tired, my mind grinding the same deep rut. If only George had not died . . . if only it had been a ring of gold . . . if only Kenneth was home . . . my twin would not say that it was a blessing that my baby had died . . .

It was all so stupid. As if I had tears in my veins instead of blood. As if my eyes were wounds that would not stop weeping.

"Ah, Mary, my love, what's the matter?"

I jerked around. It was Violet Brightwell, the village eccentric. She never went to church, but spent Sunday tramping the hills, picking nettles and weeds which she made into murky-looking potions she was always thrusting upon people. Her hair was long and loose and wild and white, and she wore a battered man's hat with feathers and twigs stuck into the ribbon.

"Nothing," I said.

Violet came and clapped me on the shoulder. "Oh, my dear, I'm so very sorry."

I couldn't breathe. The world blurred.

"When did you lose the babe?" Violet asked. "It can only have been a few days ago, you were blooming last I saw you."

"What baby?" I said, fast and high. "I don't know what you're talking about. I . . . I'm fine. I'm just worried about my brother."

"You're white as a ghost, my dear. Did you lose much blood? Motherwort is what you need, and angelica root. I'll mix you up a brew . . . "

"No!" I jerked away, began to walk. "I'm fine. I'm just a little tired . . . not sleeping well . . . I'm sorry, I must go. The vicar's wife . . . "

Violet called my name, then strode after me. "You must take care . . . you need to clean out your womb . . . "

I walked as fast as I could without actually breaking into a run. I reached the graveyard, but Violet was still following after me, calling out advice in her foghorn voice. I could not bear it. I scrambled through the bushes and slid down the slope to the shadowy hollow where the old well gleamed between its stones. I crouched down there, my heart thudding so hard I felt sick. Shame was scarlet within me. How had she known? Would she tell?

I heard Violet tramping past, calling my name, and tucked myself lower. Slowly silence returned. The only sound was the music of the water running over pebbles, and somewhere, a blackbird warbling.

It was a peaceful place. Green and shadowy. Above my head, faded ribbons fluttered from the ends of every twig. Leaves shaped like hearts. Light dappling and shifting. I rested my head on my arms. I felt scooped out. The old woman had been right. It had been only two days. Two days since my baby had died.

❄

At long last I heard nothing but silence.

I stumbled to my feet and went to the well. I ached all over, as if I had run a long race. I dipped my hands in the water and drank deeply. Its coldness was a shock. I pressed my wet hands to my face and neck, then sat on the edge of the stone ledge, took off my shoes, and bathed my hot sore feet.

The well was set in a corner of the old abbey wall, with a simple flying buttress of cobbled stone. Once there had been a chapel here, but it had long ago fallen into ruin. The well was made from a natural spring, but had been enclosed into a long oblong pool with a channel that led the water away under a heavy capstone. It burbled away over pebbles, and wound its way towards the village duck-pond.

Above the pool, hundreds of ribbons had been tied to the lower branches of the linden trees. Many were tied about little scrolls of paper. Wishes and prayers. Me and George used to leave notes to each other here, mine tied up with twine, his with scraps of bright embroidery silk filched from his mother' sewing basket.

At first they had been a joke.

I wish Mary, Mary, quite contrary, would be at the dance on Saturday night.

I wish Georgie Porgie could come out and play.

It was not long before the tone of the notes changed.

I wish you would let me kiss you. I promise not to make you cry.

I wish you would kiss me again. Meet me at the Abbey gate at sunset?

I wish you did not have to always go. Damn all mothers.

I wish we could be together always.

Then one day I tied a secret note to the branches of the wild rose, using a white ribbon I had drawn from one of the little cardigans my mother had knitted for me when I was just a newborn babe. On it I had written shakily, *I wish I could have his baby.*

Surely then he would marry me?

All the girls of the village knew what you must do if you wished to have a child. You drink the water of the well in springtime from a cup made from a laurel leaf, face south towards the church and make your wish, and then take the man you want to be the father to the carving of the giant on the hill. There you must lie with your lover on the Giant's enormous ding-dong.

So this is what I'd done, the night before George left to go back to his regiment. There were rumours that the Allies were to invade France, and indeed there were soldiers everywhere in Dorset, Yanks as well as Tommies.

It had been a mild night in late spring, the sky overhead swarming with stars. We might have been alone in the universe, no chink of light escaping the blackout curtains, no headlights lancing along the roads. The Giant himself was invisible, hidden beneath brushwood by the Home Guard so no enemy aircraft could use him as a landmark. George had laid down his coat on to the soft turf, and I sat there, slowly unpinning my hair, unsnapping my stockings and rolling them down, lifting my dress over my head, listening to his breath quicken. George laid me down, and kissed me. I clasped him close, closing my eyes.

He is mine now, I thought. *Nothing will ever part us.*

Six weeks later George and his regiment had landed on the beaches of Normandy. I could hear the bombardment from far away over the sea. A dull red bruise on the horizon. The taint of smoke. I already knew I had a child growing inside me. I was sick each morning, and half the day too, and my breasts were so sore I could scarcely bear the touch of my brassiere.

I went alone to the church, and knelt in the dimness, and prayed to God to keep George safe, and this tiny new life inside me too.

God did not listen.

A few weeks later, I was walking home from the Women's Institute meeting when I saw the telegraph boy cycling along the lane to Atwickthorpe, the beautiful old house where George and his mother lived. I'd known at once. I had to grab on to the lamppost to keep from falling to my knees.

Somehow I got home.

I had been sobbing on my bed when I felt the sudden rush of blood between my legs. All night the baby seeped away, staining my nightgown and sheets, horrifying my mother.

I could not bear to remember. I scrambled up and ran to the wild rose that clambered all over the ancient stone wall, I dragged at the ribbons tied to the briars, I tore the little notes to shreds.

There was no point in wishing.

✻

It seemed the war would never end.

I had stopped listening to every news broadcast on the radio, or following the shifting tides of battle across the map of the world. I found it hard to have much interest in anything. Ma was cross with me, and told me to buck up, and get on with things. "People will start wondering what's up with you, Mary, if you're not careful."

I looked down at my clenched hands and managed a little shrug.

"You may not care what people say, but we're at centre of the village here and need to keep appearances up. Things are hard enough as they are, what with the rationing and the difficulty of getting decent meat . . . "

She pressed her lips together and turned away, banging dishes in the sink.

"Now, now, Mum, leave the lass alone," Pa said, picking up his newspaper and unfolding it. "You know she's all cut up about

Kenneth. She must be missing him sorely, you know what twins are like."

My mother did not answer, which was not like her. My Pa did not know about the baby, though. He did not know about George.

And I could not bear the thought of him knowing.

I wanted to creep away somewhere quiet and dark, and curl up there, my face pressed down into my arms, like a little girl thinking she was invisible, like an injured creature deep within the hedgerow.

My father suddenly exclaimed. The newspaper shook in his hands. "Gladys, listen to this," he cried. "There's been an uprising in Warsaw."

Both my mother and I rushed to lean over his shoulder and read the newspaper report.

The Polish Home Army has begun a battle to liberate Warsaw, the first European capital to fall to the Germans nearly five years ago.

At 1700 local time, the code signal 'Tempest' was given and there was a wave of explosions and rifle fire throughout the city. Reports from Poland say the timing of the uprising was chosen for maximum effect as the Germans appeared to be about to withdraw from Warsaw.

"Do you think that means the prisoner-of-war camps will be freed?" my mother asked in a shaky voice.

"Maybe, maybe," my father said. "Don't get your hopes up, lass."

My eyes flew over the page. The Polish Home Army had taken the Germans by surprise after nearly five years of occupation. They had re-captured many key buildings and services. In retaliation, the Germans were burning the city.

"What will the Germans do with the prisoners-of-war?" my mother whispered. "Will they take them away? Will they . . . " She couldn't say it.

I felt sick. Kenneth's plane had gone down over Poland. He had been captured and taken to a camp in Warsaw. We had tried to reassure ourselves that he was safer there than up in the sky.

But I had the most terrible dreams. Of boots and fists and barbed wire. We had always felt each other's pain, my twin and I. Once he had broken his arm falling out of an apple tree. Back at home, sullenly hemming sheets, I had cried out in pain and clutched at my wrist at the exact same moment. Another time I had sprained my ankle on the hillside. Kenneth and I had both limped home, supporting each other.

That night I dreamt again. I saw a sky aflame, a city in ruins. I heard screams and shouts and gunfire. I ran through a maze of broken walls, piles of rubble, shattered arches, broken spires. Men in heavy boots chased me. I ran and stumbled and fell and crawled and ran again, my breath sobbing. A stitch in my side. Sweat stinging my eyes. Still they hounded me. An explosion. Fire blasting. Debris hailing down. I crouched in a hole. Long dark shadows looming over me.

Sweating and shivering, I forced myself to wake, telling myself it was only a dream. But my heart was pounding and I could not catch my breath.

I felt my brother's presence clearly in my bedroom, as if he still slept in the other narrow bed, as if I could reach out my hand and touch his shoulder.

"Kenneth," I whispered. "Are you there?"

But there was no sound but my own rapid breaths.

I was so afraid that I had felt his ghost, reaching out to me to say goodbye. I did not think I could endure it if Kenneth was dead too. I hardly know how I got through the day.

That night I dreamt of him again. Awful as the dream was—all fire and black smoke and screams—it gave me hope that my brother still lived.

Each night, the dreams grew more intense, more real. I both feared going to bed and longed for it, wanting that tiny glimpse into my twin's life.

One night I dreamt I was drowning. Black water. A weight on my back, dragging me down. My arms and legs thrashing. Too deep.

I woke with my nails clawing at the air above me. "Kenneth?" I whispered into the darkness. "Are you there?"

I felt his terror.

"Kenneth! Kenneth!" I flailed my arms and legs as if I was swimming, as if I could give somehow buoy up his strength and save him from going under.

My screams brought my mother rushing into the room in her nightgown and curlers. "Sssh, sssh," she whispered, rocking me from side to side. "It's all right. Sssh."

At last the horror of the dream left me, but I did not sleep again that night.

The uprising in Warsaw dragged on. The Soviets failed to come to the rebels' aid. They sat outside Warsaw, waiting for the Germans to crush the rebellion. Churchill sent planes to drop supplies to the starving Poles, but it was little use. The Germans demolished the city. Tens of thousands of people died.

My father seemed to get old overnight. He shuffled about in his carpet slippers, his receding hair ruffled, his spectacles smeared, pipe ash on his cardigan. He would go into the shop and stare at the empty shelves, his hands hanging by his side. When people spoke to him, he gave a vague smile and did not answer. My mother, meanwhile, scrubbed out every cupboard and drawer, and ironed every tea towel and handkerchief into crisp folds. She would not rest. And I could not.

One day we saw the telegraph boy puttering up our street on his old motorcycle. Women came out to watch, wiping their hands on their aprons. He pulled up outside our shop. I heard my mother sigh. She sat down on the stool. I put my hand on her shoulder, and she put her hand up blindly to grasp mine. The boy shoved his goggles up on to the top of his helmet and came into the shop, the bell above the door chiming.

"Mrs Jones?" he asked. He can't have been more than fourteen.

My mother nodded.

"Telegram for you." He held it out.

My mother would not take it.

He looked at me. "There ain't no cross on it."

I stared at him blankly.

"No cross means no death," he said, and gave me a sudden grin. "It means the news ain't all that bad. Here. Take it. It's a glad day we don't have a cross on the envelope."

I took the envelope and tore it open.

FROM AIR MINISTRY 73 OXFORD STREET W1
REFERENCE OX/5589
THE NAME OF FLIGHT LIEUTENANT JONES
CH 968401 IS INCLUDED IN LIST OF PRISONERS
OF WAR ESCAPED WARSAW HE WILL BE
REPATRIATED ASAP.

I could not believe it. I read it again.

"Mary?" my mother quavered.

I bent and kissed her powdered cheek. "He's coming home, Ma. He's coming home."

❈

It was raining hard. Bucketing cats and dogs, as my Pa liked to say.

We heard the bang on the front door as we sat around the wireless in the kitchen. Ma ran to fling it open. Kenneth stood on the doorstep. So thin and haggard. I gasped at the sight of him. He had an army greatcoat flung over his head and shoulders, to keep off the rain. As Ma went to embrace him, she stepped back in surprise.

Two small girls sheltered under the coat.

"But . . . who?" she faltered.

Wearily Kenneth stepped inside, and shrugged off the greatcoat. "Hi, Ma," he said. "Hi, Poll." He smiled at me, though it obviously cost him an effort, and hung the greatcoat on his hook. "It's good to be home."

I tried to hug him, but the little girls would not let go of the hem of his jacket. I had to reach over their heads. He was frighteningly spare under my hands, the jut of his bones bruising me. I took his arm and tried to lead him down the hallway, but the two little girls still clung to him, getting in my way.

Small white faces, with flaxen hair that straggled out from underneath badly knitted scarves wound about their heads and necks. Widely-spaced eyes blue as cornflowers. Fading cuts and bruises.

Ma was babbling greetings and questions all at once, and Pa had shuffled out to the hallway to pump Kenneth's hand. "Welcome home, lad, welcome home," he cried.

Kenneth dropped his kitbag and sat down abruptly. "Sorry. Not very strong yet."

The girls leant against his knee, gazing at us with enormous frightened eyes. The younger one clutched a grubby rag in one hand. She lifted it to her mouth and began to suck on one corner.

"But the children?" Ma demanded. "Who are they? Where did they come from?"

"Warsaw."

The two girls at once looked up, their faces lighting with eagerness. The larger of the two said something rapidly in a strange language. Kenneth looked down at her and shook his head. "Nie. I'm sorry. Nie."

Her face fell. She looked down at her shabby boots.

"They helped me escape," Kenneth said. "Without them I would have died. I could not leave them there."

"No, of course not," I said, taking a step closer so that the girls would not see my parents' faces. I knelt down before the smaller of the two girls. "I'm Mary. What is your name?"

She did not answer, or even look at me, but sucked more frantically at the rag.

"This is Agnieszka," Kenneth said, "and her big sister is Katarzyna."

"Well, they are welcome, very welcome." I got to my feet again. "You must be hungry. Can I get you something to eat?"

"A cup of tea would be good," Kenneth said. He struggled to his feet again, leaning on the back of the chair for support. "Can you believe that's what I missed most? And bangers and mash."

"I'll put the kettle on," Ma said, and bustled away down the hallway. Pa followed, one arm around Kenneth's back. The two little girls followed close behind, hands clasping the hem of his coat tightly. The elder one shot suspicious looks all around her. The younger one kept sucking away at the dirty rag, which was now all twisted and wet.

In the kitchen, Kenneth unwound the children from all their shawls and scarves, and we could see just how shockingly thin they were. It smote my heart. Both Ma and I rushed around, boiling potatoes and frying sausages, while Pa and Kenneth fumbled for pipes and tobacco.

"It's good to be home," Kenneth said again, looking around the shabby old kitchen with a strange look of bafflement on his face.

Ma was full of questions and Kenneth did his best to answer them, though as time went on he grew more and more terse.

"What was the camp like?"

"A hell-hole."

"Kenneth. Language!"

"No other way to describe it, Ma."

"And did they feed you enough? You're so skinny."

A wry grimace. "Not really. We were glad when the Red Cross parcels came through. Though there was never enough."

"And . . . the little girls? Did you really bring them all the way from Warsaw?"

Kenneth nodded. "Had to. Couldn't leave them there. The whole city is in ruins. I owe them my life, Ma."

"Those tiny mites?" she said incredulously.

He grinned. "Katarzyna was a courier for the Polish resistance. She carried secret messages and rifles right under the noses of the Jerries. Even little Agnieszka did her part. She helped make dozens of home-made hand-grenades. Stuffed them full of nails and pieces of shrapnel, and gunpowder made from their own piss."

Ma was too shocked to protest at his language. We all stared at the two little girls. They stared back.

"But what are we meant to do with them?" Ma said at last.

Kenneth looked up at her pleadingly. "For now, just foster them. Look after them, feed them. They have ration cards and all the proper papers. I looked after all that before I came. Then . . . after the war . . . "

He jerked his shoulders into a crooked shrug. "Who knows what will happen when the war is over? Perhaps they will want to go back to Poland. If Poland still exists. Perhaps we could adopt them." He voice rose a little at the end, and he gave Ma the kind of look he had done when bringing home stray puppies when he was just a kid.

"No need to rush into anything," Pa said, in his usual calming way. He puffed on his pipe, filling the tiny room with fragrant smoke. "For now, let's get some food into them. They look ready to faint."

As soon as the plates of food were put before them, the two little girls began to gobble as fast as they could. Hands grabbing at bread and sausages, cheeks bulging.

"Manners, please," Ma said, but they paid her no heed.

"They don't speak any English," Kenneth said. "Just let them be. They've eaten nothing but spit-soup for months, poor kiddies. And nothing but Spam since we were picked up."

I cut them some more bread and slathered it with homemade blackberry jam. The expressions on their faces when they tasted the sweetness brought a lump as hard as a pebble into my throat.

Afterwards, the little one just lay down on the floor, put her head on her arm, her thumb and the soggy corner of the rag in her mouth, and fell asleep. The older one sat beside her, licking her fingers and glowering at us. I didn't know quite what to do or say, but I could see Ma was upset. Already worrying about what the neighbours would say.

"Well, let's find them some beds," Pa said, getting to his feet with a groan. "They'd better have your room, Mary, with the two little beds. You can go in the spare room."

Ma made a small sound of protest. The spare room was kept nice for visitors. Not that we ever had any.

Kenneth carried the little one to bed, the older girl shadowing him. We put them to bed in their ragged underwear, having nothing else for them to wear, and left a nightlight burning so they would not be frightened.

"They've had a hard time," Kenneth said, as I shut the door.

"And you too?"

He nodded.

"Can you tell me about it? Later?"

"When the old folk have gone to bed. Meet me at the well. I don't want them hearing our voices."

So, when all was quiet and dark, I crept out my window and down by the rose trellis, as I'd done so many times before. The rain had cleared, but the ground was wet. I could see clearly enough by the light of the stars overhead, but could have made my way there in pitch blackness if need be.

Kenneth was perching on one of the two old stone gateposts next to the pool. He was smoking in silence. I spread out my mac on the other gatepost, and sat down. As I reached out one hand for the cigarette, he passed it to me. No need for any words. I took a few deep drags, then passed it back to him.

We sat in companionable silence for a long while, till the cigarette was gone. I heard him fumble for his battered tobacco tin, then the whisper of the papers as he rolled another.

"So you know my old ship was a flamer?" he began.

I made a little encouraging noise.

"I had to bail out, right over Warsaw. Thought I was a goner for sure. Ack-acks going off everywhere, and searchlights . . . "

My own imagination filled in the gaps. The terror of the freewheeling dive over Poland, the smash of his plane into the forest, the sick lurch of his stomach at the sight of the German soldiers and their guns and dogs, his helpless fear as he was dragged away to the prisoner-of-war camp in Warsaw.

"It used to be the ghetto where they kept the Jews," Kenneth said, then bent his head to light the cigarette. "They built this great wall around a few street blocks of the old city and crammed them in there. Hundreds of thousands of them, packed in like sardines in a tin. They were all gone by the time I got there though."

"Gone where?" I asked.

He hesitated. "Don't know. Nowhere good, by all accounts. The place was nothing but a ruin by then. We PWs were set to tidying the place up. Hauling rocks around, really. Bloody Jerries kicking us along every step of the way."

In early August, the Polish resistance had risen. One group had driven a stolen German tank right through the wall and into the camp. Kenneth and three hundred-odd other prisoners had escaped, with the help of a swarm of dirty children armed with broken knives and rocks. It was then he had met Katarzyna.

"But she's only a child." I just could not believe it.

"She's twelve."

I stared at him in the darkness. That was only eight years younger than Kenneth and me. "But she's so small."

"Malnutrition will do that to you."

"And the other one? Agnes . . . " I could not pronounce the rest of her name.

"Nine."

"And they're all alone in the world?"

He nodded. "Saw their mother shot."

"Oh how awful. The poor little things."

"I had to bring them back with me, Mary. I couldn't leave them there. It was hell."

"How did you get out?"

"We fought for almost a month," Kenneth said, his hands clenched on his thighs. "But it was no use. There was no food, no water, no guns. We had to get out. The only way was through the sewers."

I remembered my dream. The suffocating darkness. The feeling I was drowning.

"We had to go in single-file. It stank. You can just imagine. Only the leader was allowed to carry a candle, to show if the air was bad. So it was virtually pitch-black. We put our hand on the shoulder of the person in front of us, to try and make sure we did not fall. The girls were not tall enough. They clung on to my coat."

I remembered the white-knuckled grip of the sisters as they followed Kenneth down our dimly-lit hallway.

"We took turns in carrying the stretchers of the wounded. No-one could make a noise. The Jerries were listening. If they heard even a rat squeak, they'd lob a grenade down into the tunnel. Then we'd all die."

I imagined the deathly procession of silent shadows, creeping through the filthy water, the injured biting back their groans of pain. I imagined the hungry eyes of rats.

"The Jerries tried to flood the sewers so we'd drown. I had to carry Agnieska on my back. I was so weak . . . so tired . . . I almost didn't make it."

I blinked back tears, nodding my head. I knew. I had dreamt it.

As Kenneth lit up yet another cigarette, the flare of his lighter illuminated his face. He was looking at me with a wry grin on his face. "I heard your voice, Mary. Calling to me. You gave me the strength to go on."

I put out one hand. He took it in his own.

"I'm so glad you're home," I said, choking with grief. "Thank God you're home."

"You've had a hard time of it too, Poll?" he asked, using my old childish nickname.

I nodded, unable to speak. He let go of my hand to pull a leather-wrapped flask from his pocket. He drank, then passed it to me. I wiped away my tears, took a slug, and then another. Fire spread through my belly.

"Tell me?" he said gently.

So I did.

He did not think it a blessing my baby had died.

※

In the end, we called the girls Katrina and Agnes, our tongues simply unable to shape the sound of their real names.

It was like having wild beasts from the zoo in our house. They stole food and hoarded it under a floorboard they prised up. They spoke only in wild gusts of a strange language we could not understand. They snarled if we came too close, and once I had to snatch my arm away, sure it was about to be bitten.

No. That's not quite true. It was not both of the girls who snarled and stole and bit. Only the eldest girl, Katrina. Little Agnes never spoke and hardly moved. She crouched under tables and behind furniture, sucking on her rag, watching with those blank blue eyes. Occasionally I could coax a reaction from her, by tempting her with food. The little hand would snatch it from me and cram it into her mouth, and then she would turn away, hunched over, chewing and swallowing with indecent greed, the filthy tattered cloth twisted about her fingers.

Ma tried to get her to stop sucking the soggy scrap of material, but the child gripped it tightly between her teeth and we could not get it from her without hurting her.

"It can't be hygienic," Ma complained.

"It's obviously a comfort to her, poor little mite," I said.

"But think of the germs!"

"I'll try to wash it."

But when I approached Agnes with a bowl of warm soapy water, trying to show by sign language that I wanted to wash the rag, she huddled it close to her, baring her teeth and growling at me like a dog. When I persisted, she struck at the bowl with her hand, so soapy water went everywhere.

At least I knew now that her muteness was not due to some problem with her voice box.

"Have you ever heard her speak?" I asked Kenneth. "To her sister, perhaps?"

He shook his head.

My brother had spent all his strength in getting himself and the little girls home. He could barely manage to wash and shave himself in the mornings, or get himself down to breakfast. I put an armchair out on the back terrace for him, so he could sit and enjoy the late summer sunshine and listen to the bees humming in the garden. The two girls crouched behind the chair, trying to hide from sight. I called to them, trying to coax them out, but they only stared at me from behind the tangle of that silvery-white hair they would not let me brush.

The language barrier seemed insurmountable. But then I hit on the idea of labelling everything so that the girls might learn some English.

Bread, I would write in my neatest handwriting. "Bread," I'd say, picking up the loaf and holding it so they could see it. Then I'd show them the written word. "Bread."

"Chleb," Katrina answered one day. I repeated the word questioningly. She jerked her head up and down. "Chleb."

I passed her paper and pen, and painstakingly she wrote the word.

"Chleb," I said.

"Bread," she answered in her stilted accent.

A brief gleam of a smile.

My mother got out some old dresses for them, and I measured them against the girls and pinned up the hems.

"Frocks," I said.

"Suknia," Katrina said.

I wrote the word down in the little book I was turning into a Polish-English dictionary, then practised saying the word as I took up the hems. To my surprise, Katrina took up a needle and deftly threaded it. She sewed with tiny neat stitches; someone had taught her well.

Each day I tried to gain a little ground with the girls. I showed them how I brushed my own hair, and then mimed brushing theirs. Eventually they allowed me to gently tease out the knots and snarls in their fine blonde hair, and plait it neatly with bows on the end. I marvelled at the corn-silk colour of it. They made my hair look mousy-brown.

As their hunger and fear abated, they stopped gobbling their food quite so greedily, though Katrina kept hiding crusts of bread and heels of cheese around the house.

"We'll get rats," my mother complained. "I'll ask your father to put a lock on the pantry door."

"Please don't," I begged her. "It's just that they're afraid of going hungry again. They don't mean to be dishonest."

I gave Katrina a little tin box to store food in, so she did not need to secrete it in in her drawers or under the floor. I had to draw her a series of little pictures to explain. My rat was rather lifelike, I thought.

"Rat," I said, and made a squeaking noise.

"Szczur," she answered, and squeaked back.

My tongue had great trouble getting around that word.

Day by day, the sisters grew less like frightened wild creatures and more like normal little girls. I taught them to say "please" and "thank you" in English, and Katrina taught me how to say the words in Polish. They remembered how to use a knife and fork, and helped wash up after dinner.

On Sunday, I stayed home with Kenneth and the girls while Ma and Pa went to church. It was a particularly beautiful morning, and so I put on my hat and gardening gloves and went to work in our tiny vegetable plot, which had once been my father's prize rose garden. Kenneth sat in his chair, a cigarette smouldering in one hand, and the girls sat close by his feet as always, playing with some paper dolls I had cut out of an old newspaper.

"Katrina," I called. She looked up. I beckoned her. "Come and see."

She did not move. I plucked a fat strawberry and showed it to her. When she did not come, I tossed it into my mouth. "Mmm, delicious." I rubbed my tummy in an exaggerated show of pleasure. Then I beckoned her again. "Come! Come and pick some for you and Agnes."

Katrina got to her feet and looked all around, then up at the sky which arched overhead, clear of any cloud or trail of smoke. Cautiously she ventured into the garden, her body ready to run at any sudden sound or movement. Agnes watched her from behind the chair leg, sucking hard on her grimy rag.

At last Katrina stood by my side, and bent to see the ripe red strawberries lying on their bed of straw. "Pick one," I urged her, smiling. "Eat." I tried to remember the Polish term. "Jeść."

She bent as warily as if the fruit was an adder, then plucked one and put it into her mouth.

"Good, yes?" I said, and rubbed my tummy enthusiastically.

Katrina flashed me a smile. "Yes. Good." Then she turned and called her sister's name, and Agnes ran to her side, the little rag dangling from her fist. The two girls gorged themselves on the berries, staining their mouths red. I smiled triumphantly at Kenneth who gave me a thumbs-up.

It was a small victory.

The next day was Monday, which was wash-day. Sitting up at the kitchen table, drinking their milk, the two girls watched with wide eyes as Ma and I dragged out the dolly tub and put it in the centre of the scullery. She set water to heat in the old copper, while I sorted the dirty clothes and sheets. Then we set to work, swishing the sheets about in the tub with the dolly peg, then wringing them dry in the mangle. Then we rinsed them clean in the sink, then put them through the mangle again. By now, both Ma and I were hot and red-faced, and the scullery windows had steamed up.

I beckoned the girls to help me hang out the washing. "Smell how nice," I said, and lifted the damp cloth to my nose. Solemnly Katrina and Agnes copied me.

Soon they were helping swish the clothes about, and scrubbing Pa's cuffs and collars with soap on the washboard. They loved the froth that lathered up, and I showed them how to blow soap bubbles. Agnes held one huge quivering rainbow bubble on the end of her finger, then blew it into the air. As it sailed away, she smiled for the first time.

By the time the washing was done, the water in the tub was grey. I poured it out, then beckoned to Agnes.

"Do you want to wash . . . " I mimicked scrubbing and rubbing and swishing, then pointed to her little rag. Not knowing what to call it, I hesitated, then said, "wash your lovey?"

Katrina said something to her in rapid-fire Polish. Agnes clutched the grimy cloth closer to her.

I poured some warm water into the tub and held out the squishy yellow soap. "You . . . wash."

Agnes stood for a moment, drawing with her toe on the ground, her lower lip pouting, the rag all tangled up in her fingers. Then she took a step forward and then another. With great care, she lowered the rag into the tub and rubbed it with soap. Froth lathered up. She smiled and played with the soap bubbles, swishing the little rag about.

Soon the water was mucky but the rag was much cleaner. It had tiny blue forget-me-nots on it. I helped Agnes rinse and wring it dry, taking care not to tear the cloth. It was stained here and there with brown splotches, but I dared not try and scrub them away.

Katrina had been watching from her stool. To my surprise, she looked sombre. I glanced at her enquiringly.

"Suknia matki," she said.

"Suknia," I repeated, trying to remember what it meant. Then I remembered. It was the word for a dress. I glanced back at the rag. It looked like the kind of fabric that a frock might be made from.

I wondered idly who might have worn the dress, then—with a sudden shock of insight—I realised what Katrina must have said.

"Your mother's dress?" I asked.

She stared at me blankly. In the steamed-up window, I rapidly drew a stick-figure mother holding the hands of two little girls. I touched the triangle of the mother's skirt. "Suknia matki?" I tried to say, my tongue stumbling over the strange syllables.

Katrina nodded. "Tak. Suknia matki."

I looked back down at Agnes, lovingly washing this torn fragment of her dead mother's dress, and felt the familiar choke in the throat and sting in the eyes that was never far away anymore.

"Come, little one. Let's hang it out to dry." I took her damp, soapy hand and led her out into the garden. I pointed up to the washing line but Agnes's brows contracted and her lip began to pout. She clutched the rag close to her.

I thought for a moment, then fetched her stool. She climbed up on it, pegged out the little rag, then stood there, holding it against her cheek, her thumb in her mouth.

I dried my hands on my apron, watching her. Katrina came and stood beside me, then leant her head against me. I slipped my arm around her.

Agnes stood there all morning, as the sun moved overhead, clutching the little rag. When it was dry I unpegged it for her. Then she stroked its thin fabric, looked up at me, and smiled again.

❈

News of the two Polish girls staying with us had slipped out, of course. My mother loved a good gossip.

"I hear you have visitors," one woman of the village asked me one day, as I served in the shop.

"We do indeed," I said cheerfully, stamping her ration card.

"Polacks, I heard. Can't speak a word of English," said another woman.

"Their English is better than my Polish," I replied.

"How can you be sure they aren't spies?" Mrs Cunningham, the President of the Women's Institute, demanded. She was a thin, sour-faced woman with a narrow-brimmed black hat.

"They're only children," I said coldly.

"Trained up from birth, those Krauts," she said.

"They're not German, they're Polish," I said. "Their father died fighting against Hitler. Their mother was shot for helping the Resistance. Katrina risked her life carrying secret messages during the Warsaw Uprising. Even little Agnes did what she could."

Mrs Cunningham sniffed in disbelief.

"Poor little mites," Violet Brightwell said from the back of the queue. "What they must've suffered."

I smiled at her in real gratitude.

The next Sunday we all went to church, all five of us. There was a little stir as we walked in, then—when Katrina and Agnes dropped a curtsey to the altar and crossed themselves—a hum of surprise and outrage. Ma went red, but tilted up her chin and guided the two girls down the aisle to our pew. Mrs Atwick-Sellick cast us a single disdainful look through her black-spotted veil, before returning her gaze to the front.

I smiled at the girls and twitched one of Agnes's plaits straight. Her thumb had crept into her mouth, but not, thankfully, her lovey.

After church, I took the girls for a tramp on the hills, gathering blackberries and rosehips to make jam.

"Tree," I said, pointing at a big old chestnut.

"Drwezo," Katrina said.

"Really? That's the Polish for tree?"

There seemed no links between her language and mine. I knew a little French. "Arbre" had its echoes in arbor and arboreal. "Drwezo", however, seemed like a made-up word.

Katrina nodded her head vigorously. She pointed at one thing after another, unfamiliar words spilling from her lips like discordant music. I could not keep up. "Slower," I cried.

I saw the disappointment and frustration on her face.

"One at a time," I said, and held up a finger. Then I touched a daisy growing in the ditch.

"Flower," I said. I touched the blooms of the wild carrot and the angelica. "Flower," I repeated, pointing to every bloom I could see.

Katrina repeated the word till she had it right. Then I looked at her questioningly. She smiled at me. "Stokrotka."

I was not nearly so quick to learn as she was.

And still Agnes did not speak.

❄

In early October, the Polish rebels finally surrendered to the Germans.

Kenneth and I had to tell the girls, the best way we could. We could not risk them seeing the dreadful photographs of their devastated city in the newspapers. I was not sure at first that they understood, but later that day, without any warning, Katrina began to smash plates and cups. She threw them down with all the strength of her wiry body. Ma screamed and tried to make her stop, but it was like the girl was possessed. Eventually Kenneth managed to wrap her in his arms and hold her close, shaking and weeping.

I got down on my hands and knees, and began to sweep up the broken china.

"My grandmother's tea service," Ma wept. "Never even a chip."

Agnes had hidden under the table. I could not coax her out. She sat, sucking on her rag, her eyes staring without seeing.

It seemed all the ground we had gained over the last month had been lost.

❈

The news from the Front was discouraging. The Germans were fighting back, the Allies were stalled. All the euphoria after the liberation of Paris had dissipated, and everyone was worn out and anxious. It seemed the war would never end.

One day I heard a commotion in the street. I came out to find Katrina and Agnes surrounded by a mob of village kids, shouting: "Fritz! Huns! Kraut!"

Katrina tried to fight back, but she was pushed and shoved from side to side. Someone had tried to snatch Agnes's bedraggled rag and she was hanging on to it grimly, tears coursing down her cheeks.

Then a tall boy with thick dark hair and vivid blue eyes ran down the street and began dragging the kids away. "They're not Germans, you idiots!" he said scornfully. "Don't you know anything?"

I recognised him. It was Violet Brightwell's grandson. Rowan, I think his name was.

The biggest of the boys said, "Have you heard 'em talk? Can't speak a word of English."

"Can to!" Katrina shouted. She pointed at him. "You . . . stinkeroo."

The boy swung at her with one clenched fist. Immediately Rowan lashed out, knocking him to the ground. "Only cowards hit girls," he said contemptuously. The boy scrambled up, one hand to his nose.

"Anyone else?" Rowan challenged, fists raised.

The children backed away, shaking their heads.

"You ok?" Rowan asked.

"Roger that," Katrina replied, giving him a thumbs-up gesture. A grin flashed across Rowan's face.

I bit back a smile, recognising another of Kenneth's expressions. Rowan and Katrina squatted in the gutter together, Agnes leaning against her shoulder, her lovey hanging from her mouth.

"Do you know how to play conkers?" Rowan said, taking some horse chestnuts hung from string from his pockets. "Here, you can have this one. It's my best."

Katrina took it from him with a glowing look of admiration. I smiled and sighed and returned to the shop. That night I told Kenneth all about it, as we sat by the old well smoking a cigarette and gazing up at the stars through the trees.

He laughed. "Fancy her knowing 'stinkeroo'."

"She's smart as paint," I said eagerly. "She's learning so fast. I've been reading *Wind in the Willows* to them both and she laughs out loud at all the right places."

"They're certainly not the skinny little scraps I picked up in Warsaw," Kenneth said, flicking his ash into the weeds. "I say, have you heard they're giving George Atwick-Sellick a posthumous medal for bravery?"

No," I said after a moment. "That's . . . that's wonderful. His mother will be pleased."

The mention of George's name had pierced me with grief. It had also made me realise, however, that I had not felt so sharp a pain for some time. It was more than six months since his death. Surely I had not forgotten him so quickly? Yet these past seven weeks had been so urgent and busy with the care of the two Polish girls, I simply had not had time to dwell on him.

I put out my hand. Kenneth was already passing me his cigarette.

※

My brother had to go back to the war. The RAF needed every able-bodied man, and he was quite fit now, though still too thin.

It was very hard to say goodbye. Ma did her best not to weep, and Pa kept clearing his throat. Katrina and Agnes clung to him, white-faced and tearless. In the end, I needed to forcibly uncurl Agnes's fingers from the hem of his jacket. I held her close but she was stiff and unyielding in my arms. I watched him walk out the door in his blue jacket and cap, and called after him, with a voice that broke shamefully, "Keep safe!"

He turned and smiled at me. "Bye, Poll!"

Then he was gone.

Ten days later, I was woken by the sound of plane engines screaming overhead. A four-engined heavy bomber, I thought, scrambling out of bed and running to the window. Probably a Halifax V. It sounded like it was going down. A few moments, an almighty boom reverberated down the valley. The dark sky to the east was lit up by flames. It must have crashed near the airfield at Tarrant Rushton, twenty-five miles away across the hills.

A split-second later, terrified screaming rang out from the girls' room. I ran barefoot down the hall and fumbled to switch on the hall light. Agnes was sitting up in her bed, screaming with all her might. Katrina was trying to comfort her, but to no avail.

I took Agnes into my arms, rocking her back and forth, murmuring words of reassurance. Her screams died away, but she was trembling violently, clinging to me.

"She . . . hate . . . bangs," Katrina said in her broken English. "Many bangs . . . Warszawa."

"Yes, Yes, I know," I whispered. "But you are safe now. You are safe and sound."

Pa put his ruffled grey head in the door. "Everything all right?"

"Yes," I said. "She's just frightened by the crash."

"I'll heat up some milk." He went downstairs and I could hear him clattering around in the kitchen. He came up a little later with five cups of warm sugared cocoa, leaving three with me and taking the other two down to his and Ma's bedroom.

I gave Katrina her mug, then settled back against the headboard with Agnes tucked up in the crook of my arm. She sipped the cocoa, her shivers gradually easing. I kissed the top of her flaxen head, and then began to sing an old lullaby I remember my father singing to me:

The rook's nest rocks on the treetop
Where few foes can stand
The martin is high and is deep
In the steep cliff of sand;
But thou, love, are a-sleeping
Where footsteps might come to thy bed,
Hast father and mother to watch thee
And shelter thy head.

Poor little mite, I thought. *She has no father or mother.* I cleared my throat and sang on, very low.

Lullaby, Lilybrow, lie asleep. Blest be thy rest.

When I had finished, Agnes gave a little murmur of protest and so I sang the song again. After a while, I felt her narrow chest vibrating under my hand.

She was humming the tune, very softly, under her breath.

❄

It was a long bitter winter.

Kenneth was dropping supplies to the Dutch who were starving due to the Reich's food embargos. The news was just as bad as could be. The Germans had launched a huge counter-offensive in the forests of Ardennes. Thousands of Allied soldiers had been captured, and there were reports the Nazis were shooting the prisoners-of-war dead. So Kenneth could not come home for Christmas, nor any other of the brave Tommies fighting it out in the snow and the ice.

I busied myself making Christmas pudding, decorating the house and knitting Christmas presents for my mother and father and the girls. I managed to find a new tea set for Ma to replace the one that Katrina had broken, though it took all my savings, and a new pipe rack for Pa. I also managed to find the girls an orange each, and could not wait to see their faces when they bit into the sweet juicy flesh.

At sunset on Christmas Eve, the girls and I went out for a walk in the fields. Hoarfrost glinted on the brown corduroy fields, and birds wheeled in and out of the hedgerows, feasting on the ivy berries. The girls were all rugged up in woolly hats and gloves, their silvery hair windblown, their cheeks rosy.

"Let's go down to the old well," I said on an impulse. I had not taken the girls there before, even though it was only a few hundred steps from our house. Too many unhappy memories.

But my grandmother had always taken me and Kenneth down to St Augustine's Pool on Christmas Eve. It had been one of our favourite childhood traditions.

So I took the girls' hands and we ran through the graveyard and then down the long avenue towards the holy well. The western sky was crimson and molten gold, the bare branches of the linden trees like fragile black lace. Tattered ribbons fluttered in the cold wind.

We jumped over the pool, and knelt on the far side. The stone was like ice beneath our knees, and our breath made frosty clouds in the twilight air.

"Look to the east," I whispered. "Can you see the first star? My grandmother—my *babcia*—said that if you could see the Christmas star reflected in the pool, then it meant you would have a golden future." I tried to translate into Polish, fumbling for words. Peace. Happiness. Love.

Katrina said a few quick words to Agnes, who smiled and leant forward on her hands, peering into the pool. Katrina bent forward to look too, and so did I.

And there it was, a tiny shining star netted in the dark reflection of the twigs.

"Quick, make a wish!" I cried, then clasped my hands together and raised my face to the bright planet glowing on the far horizon, trying to show the children what to do.

"Let there be peace," I whispered.

"I . . . I wish . . . we could stay here," Katrina said falteringly. "With you."

I looked at her quickly, my heart leaping with joy.

Then Agnes whispered, "I want . . . Mama . . . back."

The first words she had spoken in four months.

I felt a rush of hot tears like I had not felt since the days after my baby died. I gathered Agnes into my arms, and pressed my cheek into her hair. "I want that too, little one," I whispered. "I wish I could bring your mama back. But I can't."

Katrina's cold hand crept into mine. "But couldn't you be our mama?" she asked with desperate intensity.

I put my arm about her and drew her close. "I can try. If you want me to."

"Oh, we do," Katrina said fervently

Agnes nodded. "Want," she said with great firmness.

My Sister's Ghost

December 1853

HESE ARE THE THINGS I KNOW.
My name is Jacob Joseph William Wylie and I am nine years old and have blue eyes and brown hair. I live at 33 Long Street, Cerne Abbas, Dorset, England, The World. Our house is at the end of a row of terraces and it has an empty fish pond in the garden. My father's name is Henry Wylie and he is a silk merchant, though he does not go away as much as he used to. My mother's name is Margaret Wylie and she has not spoken a single word since Tuesday the twenty-eighth of December, 1852. That was the day my sister Teresa died.

Christmas is coming again and Mama remains mute.

I sit in the attic with the box of last year's Christmas decorations open in my lap. It is the twelfth of December and I would very much like to put up the tree, but Papa says it will upset Mama. Teresa was very clever with her hands, and she made most of our decorations. Of course we have thrown away the gilded walnuts and the baskets made of orange peel, but there are dusty paper chains, plaited silk ribbons, and a handful of peg figures, dressed as wood choppers and chimney sweeps, and one as a cat. She made him for me especially. I like cats.

There is a window in the attic that faces the street, and I think I hear the rattle of a carriage so I place the box aside and look down. From one side of the carriage, a familiar figure alights. His name is Doctor Paterson and he helped me get better when I had the scarlet fever that made me deaf in my right ear. Doctor Paterson is young but Teresa always said she thought him a bore. He has red hair and mutton-chop sideburns and freckles across his nose. From the other side of the carriage emerges someone I do not know, but I am instantly afraid of him. His face is sharp underneath his top hat, and his beard is full and grey. He wears round spectacles and he looks up at the window almost as if he knows I am standing there. I shrink back and sit on the floor again, but I have lost interest in the Christmas decorations. I slip the peg cat into my pocket and open the attic door. There are voices, but I can't hear what they say. I sit on the stair and peer through the banister. Doctor Paterson and Papa lead the severe-looking man up to the landing where our bedrooms are. There is a knock and a door opening, and I am certain the severe-looking man is here to see Mama.

I stand and hesitate at the top of the stairs for a few moments. I want to know what is going on. Will he fix Mama? I would like to hear her voice again. I have forgotten how it sounds. It occurs to me that Papa will most likely bring Doctor Paterson and the other man into the parlour to discuss things after they have examined Mama, and with this thought I stiffen in anticipation. There is a window seat, quite hidden from view if I pull the green velvet curtain across a little way. My hearing is not good enough to listen at a door, but if I am in the same room as them I should find out who the man is and why he wants to see Mama.

As quiet as I can, I creep down the stairs all the way to the bottom. Our housekeeper, Stanwick, hums to herself in the kitchen.

The house smells of boiling cabbage and dying flowers. My father brings a posy of flowers home to Mama every week; she puts them in a vase then does not look at them again. I slip into the parlour unseen, and sit on the window seat with my knees under my chin. My heart hammers; I know Papa will be angry if he finds me: that weary, sad anger I have seen too many times since Mama stopped talking. It frightens me more than his shouting, which stopped abruptly after he shouted at Teresa to leave the house and play outside and not be *in the way*.

I am never in the way. I am quiet, like a cat.

Slowly my heart's rhythm returns to normal, and I grow bored behind the curtain. I twist around to watch out the window. The carriage is still there, and the driver brushes the two horses. One is black and one is chestnut. I forget why I am behind the curtain and think about running out and asking to pat the horses. I have one foot on the ground when the door opens.

I jerk my foot back into place and hold very still. Very quiet.

"We can speak more freely in here," Papa says, and two sets of footsteps follow him in and the door closes.

Doctor Paterson speaks next. "Your opinion, Doctor Humboldt?"

So the severe man is another doctor. An older, more experienced one perhaps. I turn my head to hear them with my good ear.

"She will never speak again," Doctor Humboldt says. He has a faint accent. His words are clipped, oddly sibilant. "I have seen such cases before. The grief sends them mad. You would be better to put her aside in an asylum and go on living your life."

The words are sharp on my heart. I wait for Papa to rebuke him. Instead he says, "There is no hope?"

"You have battled bravely for nearly a year," Doctor Paterson says. "She is not the woman you married anymore."

"I know of a place free in the hospice where I do much of my research with a colleague. I could send a telegram and confirm it by tomorrow," said Doctor Humbolt.

"Is it in London?" Papa asks. His tone is mournful.

"No, I only have a small office in London. Mercy House is outside Manchester."

Manchester is a long way north.

"What would I do with the boy?" Papa asks. "I cannot continue to neglect my business. Finances are becoming pressing. I need to go away again."

Doctor Paterson answers. "Joseph would do well with your wife's sister and her children perhaps. He is very withdrawn. He needs company."

I want to stand up and shout that I do not like Aunty Ruth, and I certainly do not like my three cousins who are all idle and vain and boring. I do not want to go to Aunty Ruth, and I do not want Mama to go to Manchester with horrible Doctor Humboldt. These words want to spill out of me, the way grain spills from a sack when Stanwick slashes it open. With effort, I hold them back. My blood rushes past my ears with such force that I can hear the men only faintly, making their plans.

I make my own.

❄

Teresa always said that if you tell yourself one hundred times before you go to sleep that you will wake at dawn, then your body will know the moment the sun peeps over the horizon. I wake exactly when I hope to, but it is cold and my eyes are heavy and I very much want to go back to sleep. I draw my legs up under me and slide my hands under my pillow to snuggle into it, when I feel the plaited Christmas ribbon that I hid there last night.

I must get up. If I do nothing, Doctor Humboldt may take Mama away to that place called Mercy House.

I push back the covers and slide my feet into my slippers and pull on my warmest dressing gown and tie it around my waist. The plaited ribbon goes in its deep, soft pocket. As quietly as I can, I leave my bedroom and I'm down the stairs and at the door in a few short moments. The cold hits me with a blast. Frost has come in the night. The leaves of the ivy that climbs over the Royal Oak, which is diagonally opposite my house, are edged with silver. My breath fogs in front of me as I close the door and head to the Silver Well.

I have wished at the Well before. Mama took me one time and we wished for her father to recover from a fall, and it worked. But then after Teresa died, Papa wanted me nowhere near the river, or the duck pond, or even the Well, even though I am very sensible and not likely to go in. Teresa was sensible too, though. A trip. A blow to the head. Face first into the fish pond she went and, unconscious, there she filled her lungs with water and died.

I walk up past the church, through the gate, and down the wooded slope and then I am there. The air is biting. I quickly tie the plaited Christmas ribbon to the lowest branch of the linden tree nearest the well, and I close my eyes and think about what to ask.

Mama was happy when Teresa was with us. Papa was happy because Mama talked and laughed and even sang sometimes, though not very tunefully. I was happy because the three people I loved most in the world were with me. The thought of such happy times makes my stomach hurt, as though ice presses me inside and it is cold but burning at the same time. I open my mouth and say, "I wish Teresa would come back."

Then I scurry back home to my warm bed.

❈

By the time I have slept some more and had my boiled eggs, my memory of making my wish has grown dim and grey, like a dream half-forgotten. I do not think about it as I push my wooden train around the floor of my bedroom. Papa brought the train from India for me, and it has a little brown man in the driver's seat. I hear a knock at the door and ignore it, but then it comes again louder and I remember Stanwick is in the laundry shed and Papa is in the village on business. So I bounce down the stairs, one at a time, until I get to the door and open it.

Doctor Humboldt is standing there, glaring down at me with his flat silvery eyes behind his spectacles.

"Hello, little boy," he says. "Is your father in?"

I want to say something to him, but my tongue won't move. I shake my head instead.

"Where is your housekeeper?"

"In the laundry," I squeak. "I can fetch her."

"Do you have a governess? A house boy?"

"The house boy is with his sick mother in London. The governess . . . there have been several since . . . They don't stay." They are too sad to stay. At least that is what Maria had said. *It isn't your fault, Joey. This house is just so sad.*

"Are you not lonely?"

I shake my head.

"Well. No matter. I only want a message passed on. Do you think you can manage that?" He smiles cruelly, as though he doubts I can manage anything at all.

"Yes," I say defiantly.

"Let him know Doctor Humboldt has a place at Mercy House from the first of January." He smiles, revealing yellowed teeth. "His problems can be solved by the New Year."

I am so horrified by his face (which transforms immediately in my mind's eye into a demonic gargoyle) that I cannot spit out the words that my mother is not a problem to be solved. Besides, I am not supposed to know anything, so I am certainly not supposed to understand his message.

"Will you pass that on, lad?" he asks, and his hand comes out and lifts my chin so I meet his gaze. His fingertips are as cold and smooth as pebbles. I shiver.

"Yes," I say, but I will not. I will do no favours for this monster, especially if it means he will take Mama away.

Doctor Humboldt tips his hat and strides off towards his carriage. I close the door and run to the parlour, kneel on the window seat and watch him leave. As his carriage speeds past back out of the village, I poke my tongue out at the window even though I know he cannot see me.

"Master Joseph!" This is Stanwick, behind me (she's frighteningly quiet when she wants to be).

I jump guiltily. I think she is going to tell me off for poking my tongue, but of course she did not see. Instead, she says, "Did I hear someone at the door?"

"No," I lie.

"Ah, well then. Must be my ears playing tricks." She gave me a fond tweak of my bad ear. "You've only got the one to play tricks on you, so I reckon I'll have to trust you."

I beam at her.

"Right then, young sir. I'm off to the shops. Will you come?"

I nod enthusiastically.

"Shoes, then. And a winter coat. It's cold out today."

✳

We are coming home later, and the sky is grey and cold. Stanwick says we will have a white Christmas for certain, and the excitement in her voice is immediately tempered by sadness. She squeezes my mittened hand and mutters, "It's not right that a young boy can't celebrate Christmas," and whatever vehemence she feels about this notion propels her forward at such a rate that I am almost dragged along beside her. We round the corner past the Royal Oak and I see Camelia Brightwell, the little girl who lives opposite us, in her front garden. She jumps up and down on something and as we draw closer, I see it is a Christmas tree laid over on its side.

"What are you doing, Camelia?" I call.

"This one is broken so my Papa is fetching me a new one!" she replies, her words thudding out of her between jumps.

Camelia Brightwell has two Christmas trees and I have none. I glance up at Stanwick, whose eyes tell me precisely what she thinks of Camelia Brightwell's nonsense, and then we are inside and Stanwick is roughly stripping off my coat, scarf, hat, and mittens.

"Go on, then. Off with you and play," she says, turning to the coat rack.

I run upstairs, tiptoe past Mama's room, then on to my bedroom. From the window, I see that Camelia Brightwell and her father are now dragging the broken Christmas tree outside their gate to leave it on the side of the street. Then they go inside and the door closes, and for some reason I feel terribly sorry for the Christmas tree. Broken. Jumped on. Abandoned.

I return to my trains. I lie on my back with my feet in the air and make animal noises. I draw pictures. I play with my marbles. Between each activity, I stand and saunter to the window and look down at the sad Christmas tree. The sun comes out and the light in the room changes, and carriages and horses come and go, and Papa comes home and life goes on; but the tree lies there still. Nobody comes to take it away.

I open my door and walk out onto the landing. The grandfather clock says three o'clock. Papa will be in his office. Mama will be in the garden. Stanwick is roasting lamb, if the smell is anything to go by. I don't stop to think. I go downstairs and out the door, leaving it open behind me. Outside the Brightwells' gate, I grasp the end of the Christmas tree and I drag it across the street and inside to the parlour. I prop it up against the window seat. The top is broken and hanging by a thread, so I twist it until it comes off. An angel will cover the broken end. There are other broken branches from Camelia's jumping, and I straighten them up by leaning them on other branches. My hands are sticky and smell sharply of pine sap. I stand back and the tree does not look too bad. I run up the stairs, two at a time, and fetch the box of decorations. Then as the afternoon grows dim I wrap the broken, dangerously leaning tree with paper chains and ribbons and peg people, until I hear footsteps behind me and I turn to see my mother.

Mama is very pretty, at least I have always thought so. She has blue eyes like me, but hers are lighter blue and her hair is lighter brown, too. She looks at the tree, and at me, and she begins to cry.

"Mama!" I say, running to her. "Don't cry. I will take it back outside if you don't like it."

Then my father is there, and he holds Mama and he puts his hand on my head warmly, and now I want to cry too but Mama is so much sadder than me so I hold it in.

Mama pulls away from Papa and leaves the room. Papa takes me by the hand and leads me to the tree.

"Will I have to take it down?" I ask.

"No. No of course not. Here." He goes to the fireplace and upends the bucket with the kindling in it on the hearth. He places the tree in the bucket and then packs kindling around it so it stands up straight. Or at least, straighter. Together we readjust the decorations, and his hand never leaves my shoulder.

"I'm sorry I upset Mama," I say.

"Mama was already upset," he replies. "She looks at the world through rainy windows. There is nothing you or I can do."

I think about Doctor Humboldt but I do not tell Papa he came, or that he has a place for Mama in his beastly hospice. I pull the peg cat out of my pocket, where it has been all this time, and I pin it to the tree.

❊

That night I dream I hear my name being called. The voice is female. I am in the front garden of Camelia Brightwell's house, but it is more like a pine forest, dense with trees and the thick silence of a birdless sky. I turn my good ear towards the voice and start to follow it, fighting my way out of the forest and across the street, then through our house to the laundry. Through the grimy little window over the tub I see Doctor Humboldt, bent over the fishpond. It is full again, and he holds Mama's head under the water.

"Mama!" I cry, and try to open the door, but my hand keeps slipping off the knob and her voice keeps echoing in my head from under water: distant, muffled.

Here I wake, with my heart pounding and my hands twisted in my sheets. The echo of the dream has stuck inside my ear, my bad ear that hears nothing at all. A thin, deadened voice calling my name.

It is not Mama's voice. It is Teresa's.

I sit up in the dark, listening hard. My good ear hears nothing but the sound of the ticking clock on the landing, my own blood rushing at speed around my head. My bad ear still hears . . . or thinks it can hear . . .

A hot feeling spreads up my spine and into my scalp. My skin prickles. I stand up and go to the window, but I am not sure why. The voice has gone now, but I am left with a strong sense that I should be outside on the street. I look down and see the gaslights flickering, but no other movement. It must be very early in the morning, for there are no patrons rowdily making their way home from the Oak.

I need to go to outside.

The thought is so forceful that it pulls me to the door of my room like a magnet. The idea of a dressing gown or slippers does not enter my mind. *Outside. Outside. Now.* I open my door and descend the stairs, and I am not careful of my footsteps. I yank the door open and walk out into the street, then stop and linger for a moment, unsure what to do. Unsure why I am here. The thought crosses my mind that perhaps I need to return to the Well, so I start off in that direction but a moment later, a warm pair of hands has me around the shoulders.

"Joseph! You'll catch your death!" It is Papa. I turn and he kneels in front of me, brushing my hair from my eyes and fixing me in his gaze. He is worried and angry at the same time. "What are you doing out here?"

His question is like the tolling of a bell that wakes me. I blink, and I start to shiver from the cold, and I cannot answer his question because I do not know.

"Were you walking in your sleep?"

Behind us, the door of our house slams shut loudly, and we both look around startled. There is no wind.

"Come along, son," he says, standing and tugging my hand. "Your feet will be ice blocks if you stay out here longer."

My feet are, indeed, burning with cold and all the stones on the street seem especially sharp. Papa opens the door and takes me up to my room. He makes sure I am safely in my bed and waits a little while. My eyes are closed but I am not sleeping. I cannot make sense of why I went outside. Was it the dream that made me do it?

Papa's weight shifts off the end of my bed and I crack my eyes open a little. He stands at my window, outlined by the gaslight. His shoulders are slumped.

I close my eyes so I don't have to see how weak and broken he looks.

You mustn't think that because Mama does not talk she does nothing else either. In fact, she lives a very ordered life. When the clock strikes seven Stanwick takes her breakfast in. When it strikes eight, she is up and dressed and reading in our tiny library. At eleven she retires to her room to rest until one. At one, she takes lunch. At two, she goes to the garden and either prunes or weeds or plants or simply sits and looks at the sky. At four, she comes inside and sits in her wing-back chair next to the lamp in the parlour with her sewing. I always know where she is, and what she is doing. I am not alone or even lonely, as Doctor Humboldt said. But sometimes it is like living in the company of a clockwork doll, rather than a real person.

When I come down for supper, the day after I had the terrible dream, Mama is in her wing-back chair, her sewing in her lap. But she has moved the chair so it faces away from the window, away from the Christmas tree.

"Good afternoon, Mama," I say, as I always do. I notice she is not sewing. She stares at the wallpaper, her eyes tracing the gilded vines up and down.

I see something on the floor beside the tree and bend down to pick it up. The peg cat.

"Did you take the peg cat off the tree, Mama?" I ask.

She does not answer.

"Perhaps it blew off," I say, thinking of the door slamming behind Papa and me without a breath of wind to push it.

I pin the peg cat on the tree and watch it for a while, making sure it can't move by itself.

❄

A number of rainy days pass and one evening there is even a flurry of very light snow, but then it is gone and the sky goes blue and clear and it seems, without the blanket of cloud to protect the world, everything becomes unbearably cold.

Papa goes away to London for three nights and Mama resolutely keeps her routine, with the exception of keeping her chair turned away from the Christmas tree. Two more times I find the peg cat on the floor, but by now I have decided that the peg itself is crooked and that is why it will not sit straight. Two more times, I return it to its place, with a nod and a "humph", but I reason that cats are never well behaved.

When Papa returns, he is with a gentleman I know as Uncle

Rugby, which is not his real name and nor is he a real uncle. He is a business associate of my father, and a very jolly and happy fellow with ruddy cheeks and blond curly hair that puffs around his head. He greets me by calling me "Joe Fish" and tickling me until my face is hot and I nearly wet my breeches with laughter. Joe Fish was what I used to call myself when I was very little, because I couldn't say Joseph properly. I have known Uncle Rugby that long.

"What a fine Christmas tree this is," Uncle Rugby says admiring the tree, and I feel pleased with myself.

"I decorated it," I say. I frown, seeing that the peg cat is missing, but then remembered I had been playing with it in Papa's study, and have left it on his desk.

"So your father told me."

For a moment I shine with pride because Papa has talked about my Christmas tree, but then I realise he must have told Uncle Rugby he must compliment it, because it really is very bent and ugly but still it is special to me.

"It's unique," he continues. "I like unique. What do you think, Margaret?"

Uncle Rugby always talks to Mama as though she might answer.

Mama's head turns slightly to take in his face, then the Christmas tree, then back to her sewing.

"Ah, well," Uncle Rugby says.

"Stanwick!" Papa calls, pulling off his gloves and ruffling my hair. When the housekeeper arrives, he instructs her to light the lamps and start a fire in the library, so that he and Rugby can have their business discussions.

"Yes, sir. And shall I be making up the spare room?"

"No, no," Uncle Rugby says. "I'll stay at the New Inn. You have enough to deal with." His eyes linger on Mama's profile.

Stanwick withdraws and Uncle Rugby asks me about my studies and tests me on French words. When I have got twenty in a row correct, he says a word I do not know and Papa says sternly, "Rugby! That's not a word for a boy of nine."

Uncle Rugby chuckles happily, his cheeks pink. Papa laughs too and I try to burn the word into my memory in case I need it one day.

Then there is a sound that I cannot make sense of. A screeching, like the stray cat who sometimes comes over our back fence, but it is a human voice and it is inside the house.

Rugby says, "What the deuce?" and Papa's body stiffens with alertness. A moment later Stanwick enters the room gasping and pale.

"Stanwick?" Papa says, taking her by the wrist. "What is it?"

"In the library. I thought I felt a . . . " She catches her breath. "I'm sorry, Mr Wylie. You must think me a fool."

"What did you feel, woman?"

"A cold hand. On my . . . " She touches the side of her throat, where it meets her shoulder. "Sir, it felt so real. The shock made me scream. I oughtn't alarm you."

My gaze travels from Stanwick to Mama, who has put down her sewing and stares directly at the wall. I can tell she is listening. I want to remind Papa about the door that slammed closed on its own the other night, but Rugby is already laughing.

"You have been reading too many sensational novels, Stanwick!" he says, clapping his hand on her shoulder.

She smiles weakly. "Perhaps you are right."

Papa is kinder. "It is very cold in the library," he said. "I will have the window frames checked for gaps. But here, let me come with you while you finish preparing the room."

"Oh thank you kindly, sir. I know I am such a ninny."

"A loveable ninny," Rugby says, following them out of the parlour.

I stand by the tree a few moments. Mama is sewing again. I approach the hearth, reach my hands out towards the fire as if warming my palms. I give Mama a sideways glance. She senses it and looks up, her eyes sad and empty. In the beginning, I begged her from dawn until dusk to speak to me. My pleading made her cry and Papa said she had cried enough.

Our eyes are locked for a long time. Five seconds. Ten. Then she returns her attention to her sewing, shifting in her seat so she faces the lamp.

I stand there a little longer, then drag my feet out to the hallway. I pause in the threshold to the library. Papa and Stanwick are lighting lamps while Rugby feeds logs to the fire. I see my peg cat, lying on Papa's desk.

Rugby stands and stretches, sees me looking at the cat.

"Is this yours then, Joe Fish?" he says, scooping it off the desk and handing it to me.

I nod. "It's from the Christmas tree."

"Go put it back on then, before Stanwick thinks it's possessed."

I do not know what possessed means, but I take the peg cat and return it to the parlour. Mama has gone, leaving her sewing in a hasty heap on her chair.

⁂

Something is going on, and I feel it under my skin rather than in my brain. I try to remember what I said at the Well, when I made my wish, and I have a vague sense that I chose my words poorly and that is why Stanwick got a fright. She seems fine again when she brings up my supper, though, and I am reassured and go to bed.

I wake in the night because I can hear something with my bad ear. I should not be able to hear anything with it, as Doctor Paterson said that everything inside my ear is broken forever now. And yet, I can hear with it. A muffled voice, like something underwater. I can not make out words. It reminds me of the dream I had. I screw my eyes tightly shut and hope it will go away but it doesn't.

I push back the covers and go to the window. Nothing outside.

Downstairs. Downstairs. The thought appears in my head as though I thought it myself, but it is coming from outside. From whatever is making the noise in my ear. I pull my dressing gown on. All the fires in the house have gone out and the air is frigid. The sour smell of ash hangs in the air. In slippers, I scuff quietly down the stairs towards the parlour. It's the Christmas tree calling me, I decide. It is trying to tell me that the peg cat has fallen off again.

I open the parlour door. It squeaks softly. The dark presses on my skin coldly. I blink rapidly, trying to see. A grey shape in the corner of my vision. I turn to look at it but see nothing now. It slips into the other corner.

"Who is there?" I ask, my voice very loud in the dark.

The muffled voice beats against my deaf ear. I go to the Christmas tree, and I find myself standing in a patch of air that is colder than the rest of the house. It makes me shiver. I stand, eyes fixed on the peg cat, breathing shallowly.

Then it loosens itself and falls on the ground, as though moved by an invisible hand.

I bend to pick it up. As I do, I am aware I am looking at a pair of shoes. They are attached to legs, and a body. The body is not like me: not flesh and blood and pink. It is pale grey, like thin smoke. It is my sister, Teresa.

"Teresa!" I cry.

She moves her mouth rapidly, but I hear no words. Just the muffled beating against my deaf ear. Her expression is urgent. She is trying to tell me something.

"I cannot hear you," I say.

Again she tries to speak to me. I shake my head and she closes her mouth and looks at me sadly. Her hair is wet and bedraggled, her clothes sodden and clinging to her body. She begins to fade.

"No! Don't go! You have to make Mama better!" But before my sentence is even finished, she is gone. The sound in my ear vanishes with her. I realise that I was taller than her. I have grown; she never will. This thought makes me so sad that my ribs ache.

Papa's footsteps on the stairs. He finds me crying next to a small damp patch where Teresa had stood.

"What is it?" he asks, pulling me against his side.

"I miss Teresa," I manage through my sobs.

He says nothing, but I know he misses her too.

❋

Papa has to go to London the next day and so I am home with Stanwick, who is busy in the kitchen, and Mama, who is silent in the library. I bother Stanwick first, before getting under her feet so badly that she drops a panful of potatoes and shouts at me, so I go to sit under the Christmas tree and try to remember what it sounded like when Teresa talked in my bad ear. I decide that I can hear her in my bad ear because it is dead like her, so I press it up against the Christmas tree and I even put the peg cat right up against the side of my face, but I neither hear nor see Teresa.

I go to find Mama.

She sits in the library on the chaise, with her feet up. Her shoes lie beside her on the floor, and her stockinged legs are crossed at the ankles. She has a book open on her lap but she gazes at the mouldings on the ceiling.

"Mama?" I say softly.

Her eyes turn to me. I smile hesitantly but she does not smile in return.

"I saw Teresa last night," I say.

She flinches as though I hit her. I talk quicker to reassure her.

"She has come back. I cannot hear her yet, but I'm sure I will if I keep trying. She wants to tell me something."

Now Mama grows extremely agitated. She jumps to her feet and paces away from me, out of the room. I grasp her hand.

"Mama, wait! I'm not lying. She was right there under the Christmas tree—"

Mama wrenches her hand away from me and strides out of the library. I hear her thunder up the stairs to her bedroom and her door slams.

I sit on the chaise where Mama was just a few moments ago. The leather is still warm. I pick up the book she was reading. It is a book of plays by Shakespeare. On the page she was reading, Mama has scribbled a pen across two lines. I can partially make them out, through her scribbles:

Death . . . on her, . . . untimely frost . . . sweetest flower . . . the field.

I flip further through the book, and find other scribbles over other lines. Some I cannot read because they have been so comprehensively obliterated, but others I read shreds of. They are all about death. My mother is reading the plays of Shakespeare so that she may strike out any mention of death.

Yield my body to the earth. Hideous death. Come away, death. To be imprison'd in the viewless winds.

I wonder how many other books she has done this too. Perhaps that is what she does in the library every day. It makes no difference that Mama removes death from the history of English. Teresa is dead. Teresa is imprisoned in the viewless winds. But she has come back and she wants to tell me something. If I know what it was, maybe I can fix Mama.

Stanwick appears at the door with the mail. "Oh, hello, young sir. Where is your Mama?"

"I upset her."

Stanwick placed the letters on Papa's desk. "Did you now? Well, she is easily upset. Will you come back to the kitchen? I'm making treacle toffee."

"Yes, please!" I stand and close the book. As I slide it onto the desk next to the letters, the name *Humboldt* on one of the envelopes catches my eye.

"Come along, then," Stanwick says. She has turned away and so does not see me seize the letter from Doctor Humboldt and cram it into the pocket of my breeches, then follow Stanwick to the kitchen.

The letter weighs a hot pound in my pocket all morning. Before lunch I run upstairs and shove it in my drawer, under my summer clothes. I will not let Papa see it, for I know what it will be about.

❋

Aunty Ruth comes at the end of that week, for her Christmas visit. Aunty Ruth visits at Easter, on Mama's birthday, and at Christmas every year. She brings her three daughters—my cousins—Ellen, Jane, and Alice. Ellen is the oldest. She is twelve. Jane and Alice are twins and they are eight. We are immediately bundled into mittens and scarves and relegated to the garden as it is such a pretty day. There are two seats in the garden and Ellen takes one and Alice another, leaving Jane to cry about how beastly her sisters are. I find a corner on the grass near the garden beds and sit watching a blackbird with a worm on top of the garden wall. The sun is weak and distant, but it feels soothing on my face nonetheless. The air is very still.

Jane harrumphs over and sits heavily next to me, frightening the blackbird away.

"Oy, steady!" I say.

"Which is your deaf ear?" she asks.

I indicate my right ear with my index finger. She gives me a smile; perhaps it is a cruel one. Then she rejoins her sisters and I hear them whispering among themselves. The blackbird doesn't return.

I wonder what Papa and Aunty Ruth are talking about. I left them in the parlour, with Mama nowhere in sight. Usually Papa fetches Mama immediately when Aunty Ruth comes. We have extra servants on today, and they are baking a Christmas dinner under Stanwick's iron rule so the house is very noisy. Perhaps Papa thinks Mama will be bothered by the noise.

Three shadows fall over me so I look up.

With a trio of terrible smiles, the girls all sit themselves down on the grass on my right side.

Ellen says something to me that I can't quite hear.

"What is it?" I say. "Speak up."

Giggles.

Now they start to have a conversation, in very quiet voices, on my right side, giggling as they go.

I decide the only way to deal with their teasing is to ignore them, and so I do until I indistinctly hear the words "Teresa" and "fish pond". That they would sink to using my dead sister as an occasion to tease me sets a fire in my belly.

"Stop it!" I shout, and I climb to my feet and so do they, but they gather again on my right and continue to chatter quietly. I suspect they are insulting me, I suspect they are saying beastly things. I turn to hear better but they move too. I hate them and all their blonde curls so violently that I pull back my arm and strike Ellen across her chin.

"Ow! You little toad!" she cries. "Uncle Henry! Uncle Henry!"

The door to the house opens but it is not my father who stands there. It is Aunty Ruth. The corner of Ellen's mouth is bleeding and I am sure that I am going to be sent to gaol for this, but Ruth walks over to us, tells the girls to go inside, and gently takes my hand.

"But, Mama!" Alice cries. "Joseph hit Ellen!"

"Go and help her clean herself up, then," Ruth barks. "Enough of your nonsense. Leave the boy be."

Astonished, the girls flounce off. Something about Ruth's partiality makes me frightened. Normally she acts as though her daughters are the most precious things in the world.

"Were they teasing you?" she asks.

I nod. "Yes."

She glances back towards the house, then me, and fixes on a smile. "They do love you, though. We all do."

I shrug. My hand stings from where it collided with Ellen's chin.

"Would you like to come stay with us for a while?"

I was shaking my head before the end of the sentence. "I want to stay here with Papa and Mama."

"Your papa has to go away for business."

"Mama is here."

Ruth's mouth tightened around her smile. "Perhaps just think about it. If you came to stay with us, you could make our spare room your very own. Your papa says you like trains. We can get you a train set."

The train set is very tempting.

"Perhaps just think about it," she says again, ruffling my hair. I see her eyes go to the empty fish pond before returning to me. "You must be lonely here."

"I'm not lonely." I didn't want to go away before, and I definitely didn't now. Not now Teresa had come back.

"For now, let's enjoy our Christmas feast, shall we? If I get Ellen to say sorry to you, will you say sorry to her?"

I shrug again. "I suppose so."

"I want you two to get along. She could be like a big sister to you now that . . . " Aunty Ruth runs out of words, but I don't mind in the least.

⁂

Even though I am very tired, I make myself stay awake that night. I lie on top of my covers so I am cold, and when I start dozing anyway I stand up by the window and watch the outside for a while. A bitter wind has sprung up through the village, and the trees rattle. The gaslight makes my eyes feel gritty. I am so very very tired . . .

Finally, I hear it. The bedroom door below my closing. Papa has gone to bed.

I wait a few minutes, then make my way quiet as a cat to the Christmas tree.

I must speak to Teresa. I am fixated on this idea as the only way to solve all my problems. If she speaks, she will tell me what to do, what to say to Mama, how to keep Doctor Humboldt from taking her away.

I close the parlour door behind me. The fire is still burning low and I feed it another log. I do not know how long it will take for Teresa to come. I sit under the tree and say her name softly. Nothing happens.

All is silent apart from the wind beyond the glass. My eyes are heavy.

When I wake, the log is almost burned down and I am shivering. I climb to my feet to find another log, and nearly run straight into her. Teresa stands there, her hands at her sides, her mouth moving rapidly.

"I can't hear you," I say.

She tries again slower. This time, one of her words blossoms out of muffle. "Mama."

"Mama hasn't spoken since you . . . " I stop, unsure if mentioning death to a ghost is considered impolite.

She speaks; I do not hear. The occasional sound makes it through. I can tell from her lips that she says Mama and Papa many times. Her eyes are sad. She misses them.

"Can you try to talk to Mama?" I say. "A doctor has told Papa she has to go away if she doesn't speak. I have hidden the letter but I know we don't have long."

Her mouth moves again.

"You can hear me, can't you?" I ask.

She nods. I smile and reach out to touch her hair. When I was little, I loved to play with her hair. It was long and straight and felt like silk. Tonight it doesn't feel like silk. My fingers cannot grasp it. Instead, a cold shiver runs up my arm.

Teresa smiles at me weakly. She lifts her hand and points to the peg cat.

"Yes, you made it for me."

She motions putting it in her pocket, then points to me.

"You want me to put it in my pocket?"

She nods, patting her hip.

I remove the peg cat from the Christmas tree and slip it into my pocket. She smiles encouragingly. It is important to her that I have the peg cat with me. I don't know why, but the fact that we're communicating gives me a warm feeling.

"Will you try to appear for Mama?" I ask.

She shrugs.

"You don't know if you can?"

She shrugs again.

"Well, you were a fine sister, Teresa, but you make a very poor ghost."

She smiles broadly, and I laugh, but then I hear footsteps beyond the parlour door. I turn, then back to Teresa. She's gone.

Papa opens the door. "Joseph? Were you talking to someone?"

"No," I lie.

In the dim light of the low embers, I can see his brow furrow. I did not think he could look more tired than he already had. "But I heard you."

I do not answer. I know Papa won't understand if I tell him Teresa's ghost has been here. He runs his hand through his hair. "One of you will not talk, and the other talks to the shadows," he says under his breath. "Come along, boy. Back to bed. No more of this."

As Papa takes me upstairs I see Mama on the landing. She is wearing her thick pink nightgown with the lacy cuffs. Her hair is plaited and her eyes are round and frightened as she watches me. I want to shout out to her that Teresa came again, but Papa's presence stops me.

I fall asleep clutching the peg cat close against my chest.

❄

I am only nine and so I need to tell somebody, and Stanwick is the only somebody I have who might believe me.

After breakfast I seek her out. She is on her knees with her ample bottom in the air, sweeping ash out of the stove.

"Stanwick?" I ask, my voice shaking a little.

She emerges, smudged with soot. "What is it, young sir?"

"Do you believe in ghosts?"

Her eyes go round, her voice urgent. "You have felt it too?"

"I have seen her. It's Teresa." I produce the peg cat from my pocket. "I think she's attached to this cat somehow. She told me to keep it with me."

"She told you . . . ?" Stanwick's face is pale and her hands shake.

"She can't speak, but she is trying to communicate. But it's only Teresa. There's no need to be afraid."

I can tell my words do not persuade Stanwick at all. She is very afraid. "Joseph, it's against nature for somebody to come back from the grave."

"But it's so important that we find out what Teresa is trying to say. It might make Mama happy again."

She stands and wipes her hands on her apron, her expression sad. "Oh you poor lad," she says. "I know somebody who can help. Get dressed for the cold, and meet me at the door in ten minutes."

❈

We head down Long Street past pubs and tea shops and saddlers and milliners. Christmas wreaths and baubles and banners hang in shop windows. The air is very cold and crisp and smells of peat smoke and horse dung. Stanwick leads me around onto Back Lane and up a muddy path to a little wooden house that looks out onto farmland. Whoever owns the house has not swept up their leaves, and I nearly slip. Stanwick steadies me and mutters something under her breath, but takes me resolutely to the front door nonetheless. She knocks twice, then stands back to wait. It doesn't look as though anybody lives here. Empty flower pots line the path.

But then there are footsteps and the door opens, and a woman glowers down at us. "Who are you and what do you want?"

"Is your name Eugenia Candle?"

"Yes."

Eugenia Candle is tall and thin, with hands like claws and hair that seems too dark for her very lined face. I don't like her.

"We have a problem with a ghost. Word is, in the village, that you can help."

Here Eugenia smiles, and I like her even less. "Come in then," she says.

Stanwick follows her in but I have to be prompted. Her house is dark and smells like cats. All the windows are covered and dust gets up my nose.

"I charge five pounds to contact the dead," Eugenia says, leading us through her cluttered kitchen and into a dim windowless room that is down three steps. She lights a lantern, that gives the room an eerie glow.

"I don't have five pounds," Stanwick says. "But I have two weeks off after Christmas and I will come and work for you every day." She glances around. "This place could use an airing."

Between them, they haggle over the price and how it will be paid. I slowly circle the room looking at all the objects. Eugenia Candle has cabinets full of books and potions and preserved animals. A mouse, an owl with glass eyes, a two-headed lamb. I hear a miao, and then a cat winds between my legs. I bend down to stroke it but it spits at me and runs.

"Come on then and sit down, young sir," Stanwick says. She pulls out a chair at the round table in the middle of the room. I sit next to her. The tablecloth is made of velvet and I run my hands over it softly.

Eugenia Candle sits too, and she spreads out in front of her a deck of cards with strange designs on them. She begins to hum tunelessly, then closes her eyes and lets her head fall back.

"What is the name of the spirit you want to reach?" she asks in a whisper.

"Teresa," Stanwick says, gulping over her fear.

I reach for her hand and squeeze it. No need to be afraid of Teresa.

Eugenia's humming turns into a strange moaning noise. Her fingers feel about among the cards, until she seizes upon one and presses it against her forehead. "Teresa, Teresa, come to us," she says. Then she bolts upright and her eyes pop open and fix on the corner of the room behind me and Stanwick.

"Teresa is here," Eugenia breathes.

I turn to look, but I cannot see Teresa.

Stanwick moans with fright. "What does she want?" she manages.

I am fairly sure Eugenia Candle cannot see Teresa. I would be able to see her too. I reach into my pocket and feel the peg cat. From the corner of my eye, I see a shape move. A soft grey wisp that resolves into the shape of my sister then dissolves again. It is not where Eugenia is looking.

"She's not there," I say. "She's over here."

Stanwick turns round eyes on me. As she does so, Teresa resolves again. She smiles at me.

Eugenia is still looking in the wrong place. "Teresa says she wants you to know she is happy and she must go now," she says. "She wants to cross over in peace."

Adults are such liars. "But she's not where you're looking, and she's not saying anything," I say. "Her mouth isn't moving, and there's no tickle on my deaf ear."

Eugenia snaps her head around and glares at me. "Who is this little devil?"

Stanwick pushes back her chair and grasps my hand. "You're a fraud," she says to Eugenia. "The boy sees his dead sister. You do not."

"She's right there," Eugenia says, stabbing a finger towards the dark corner. "She's wearing a blue dress."

"It's red," I say. "It's her favourite dress. It's the one she drowned in." I put my face up to Stanwick. "You oughtn't have to work for Eugenia Candle on your holidays. She's just pretending."

"The boy says his sister is here," Stanwick says to Eugenia. "Can you speak with her? Can you ask her to move on?"

Eugenia, sensing she may yet earn her two weeks of free labour, closes her eyes again and starts to mutter, "Teresa, be gone. Teresa, be gone."

Teresa rolls her eyes and laughs. I laugh too, and this unnerves Stanwick so badly that she shrieks. "We are leaving," she says.

"My payment!" Eugenia cries.

Teresa steps forward and swings her arm out across the cards on the table. Even though I see she has used all her might, only one card flies up and flutters to the floor. Eugenia shrieks.

Stanwick nearly pulls my shoulder out of its socket getting me out of the little room. When I look behind me, Teresa is gone and Eugenia is staring at the fallen card in terror. We nearly trip over a cat, but then we are outside closing the door behind us. Stanwick keeps her pace until we are back on Long Street, then she turns to me and puts her hands on my shoulders. "If you can speak to Teresa, tell her she's frightening me."

"I will," I lie. I don't want Teresa to go away even though Stanwick does. I want Teresa to stay and make Mama better.

❄

Mama is poorly and retreats to her room for the next few days. The house is very quiet and I am bored and lonely. My new governess hasn't arrived. Papa said he wrote to her to tell her not to come because she was not a "good fit", but I suspect Papa kept her away because he intends for me to move to Aunty Ruth's soon. I suppose he sometimes wonders why Doctor Humboldt has not written to him yet. I suppose he sometimes wonders whether he really is going to send Mama away to Mercy House.

On Sunday, it is one week until Christmas. When Papa and I return from church, we can smell that Stanwick has roasted a leg of pork. Mama finally comes out of her room at lunch time. Papa gently helps her into her seat while Stanwick bustles from one end of the table to the other, setting out bowls of peas and apple gravy, and a steaming pan of roasted potatoes. Mama's skin is so pale I can see blue veins at her temples. Her eyes are swollen and red, as though she may have been crying for days. Seeing her so sad and frail makes my heart clench against my ribs.

"Mama, I've seen something, and you mustn't be frightened but—" I begin, but Papa shushes me.

"Leave her be, Joseph. Just be quiet."

"I do not want to be quiet. There is enough quiet in this house."

Papa glares at me. Stanwick, sensing the tension, drops the platter of roasted meat and leaves quietly.

"Your mother has been poorly," Papa says, keeping his voice even. "I do not want you to bother her with nonsense." His eyes are on the plate in front of him, which he heaps with slices of meat and potatoes and peas and sprouts, and slides it in front of me.

"She will want to know what I have seen," I say.

"Joseph." His voice is a warning. He prepares another plate for Mama, and she doesn't even look at it. She stares at the wall behind me.

I concentrate on my food, but I am tired and bored and sick of adults and want to fix Mama, so I am only four mouthfuls of food into my lunch when I say, "Mama, Teresa's ghost has been here."

Mama sharply takes a breath, blinking rapidly. Papa throws down his fork and has me around the ear in two seconds, yanking me to my feet.

— 93 —

"That's it!" he shouts. "No lunch for you. To your room and stay there."

"You can't stop me telling her!" I shout back, feeling my blood fizz with fury. "Mama, Teresa is trying to talk to me but I can't hear her." Papa's hand covers my mouth for most of this, so only the words "Teresa" "talk" and "can't hear" make it out. I clamp my teeth down on Papa's palm, and he yelps and jumps back as I run towards Mama and put my hands on her shoulders. "I think Teresa wants you to talk. I think she will say something to me then."

At that precise moment, I am swept off my feet by Papa, and he slams out of the dining room with me under his arm. I recognize my defeat and go limp. He takes me upstairs and drops me roughly on the floor of my room, where I sob while he bolts the door behind him. I hear his footsteps retreating. Shortly after, I hear Mama's bedroom door close.

❋

For my sins, I am confined to my room for four days. I sob and pound the door until I am hoarse on the first day, then I submit and spend my time reading and playing and staring out the window as dark clouds creep across the wintry sky. I think about the wound on my father's hand where I bit him, and I feel a mix of shame and justice. Sometimes I imagine that Mama will get sent away and I will not be allowed to say goodbye or see her go. The most upsetting thing is that I have left my peg cat in the pocket of my walking coat, and so I do not have it for days and days. And I do not have Teresa.

On the fifth day, I wake up to Stanwick lighting the fire in my grate. The air in the room is frigid.

"Good morning, Stanwick," I say, pulling the blanket around me.

"Good morning, young sir. It snowed in the night."

"Snow!" I am out of bed in an instant, and wrenching the curtains apart to look down on a street blanketed in thick white. Snow. *Snow.* And I am confined to my room.

Stanwick comes to stand beside me, her arm through mine. "I have an idea, young master Joseph. Why don't you write a nice letter to your Papa, saying sorry and promising to stop talking about ghosts? I can give it to him, and then he might let you out to play in the snow. That Camelia Brightwell will be out as soon as breakfast is over and building a snowman. You won't want to miss out."

"Do you think that will work?"

"I'll bring a pen and some ink up with your breakfast, and we will see."

So I write a message to my father, in letters so neat I am certain they will persuade him. When the grandfather clock on the landing chimes ten, he comes to my door.

"Hello, Papa," I say as he looks down on me sternly.

"I need you to be better than that," he says. "Your sister died. Your mother has lost ... your mother ... " He cannot finish, pinches the bridge of his nose, then resumes. "This family is not what it was and never will be again. Whatever happens from now, I need you to endure it obediently."

"I am sorry, Papa," I say, but I am not sorry, and I will not endure being sent away to Aunty Ruth's.

"Stanwick says you want to go outside and play in the snow."

I nod.

"You ought to have some fresh air, I suppose. Make sure you put on your coat and gloves, and I expect you back inside for lunch. I had a telegram this morning. We are expecting a visitor."

I nod again, and then he is gone and I am pulling on my warmest clothes. Snow!

Camelia Brightwell is indeed building a snow man in her front garden, so I go to join her. We laugh and sing carols and throw snowballs and jump from the low fence to the snow and back again, until we are both wheezing with joy and cold and our cheeks are red as bricks.

I hear the carriage before I see it, and Camelia and I stand on the fence to watch it arrive. To my alarm, it stops in front of my house.

I had a telegram this morning. We are expecting a visitor.

Doctor Humboldt has arrived.

I leap down from the fence and hide behind it to watch him. He straightens his hat and gloves, casts a glance up at my window, and strides up to the front door to knock.

"Who is that?" Camelia asks.

"A man my father knows," I say nonchalantly. I do not want her to know how afraid I am.

"Let's build a snow dog to keep the snow man company," Camelia suggests.

"Yes, let's," I say but now my mind is only half on the snow and the fun. The other half is wondering why Doctor Humboldt is here.

I am not sure how much time passes before the door to my house opens and Doctor Humboldt is standing there, staring across the street at me.

"Joseph," he calls. "I need you to come inside and talk to me about something very important."

Talk to him. *Whatever happens from now, I need you to endure it obediently.* The realization is fully crystallised in my mind and horror seeps into my veins. Papa has told Doctor Humboldt that I have seen a ghost, and Doctor Humboldt wants to lock me away in Mercy House just like Mama.

"Come along, boy," Doctor Humboldt says. "It's too cold for me to stand out here all day."

I am not going to Mercy House. Never.

I push Camelia out of the way and I run.

❊

I scurry down Long Street and around the Oak, aware that Doctor Humboldt is close behind me. I turn up Abbey Street past the church and down the side of Mr and Mrs Welford's house. Teresa was great friends with the Welfords' daughter, and we often used this short cut through to Mill Lane and the river. I glance behind me and cannot see my pursuer, so I stop and grasp a tree trunk. Catch my breath.

Footfalls. My half-deafness means I cannot tell which direction they approach from.

I run again, between the trees that line the side of the river. The sky is white and there is a freezing, wet road of leaves beneath my feet. I see Farmer MacMillan's gate up the rise, and I know that he always leaves it unlocked. I land up to my ankle in a puddle of muddy water just outside his fence, and it nearly trips me up. I unlatch the gate, go through, then slam it behind me so that it rings out in the quiet air.

In front of me, up the muddy trail, I see the farmer's shed. I put on a burst of speed, listening with my one good ear for the sound of the latch, the gate. I hear nothing. Perhaps he hasn't found me after all.

I yank open the door to the shed and then I am inside, closing out the daylight. Hiding behind a stack of tidy hay bales. I sit on the ground, shivering, frightened. My good ear thuds with the sound of my own blood rushing past. My bad ear gives me only hollow silence.

The gate creaks.

I wet my breeches and start to cry.

A shaft of light as the shed door opens.

"Joseph," Doctor Humboldt says. "I found my letter in your room. There's no point running from what you've done."

I try to cry silently, but it feels as though the sky is falling towards me. I let out a hiccough of misery and his footsteps draw close. A moment later, he gazes down on me.

"Bad boy," he says.

I say nothing.

"If your Mama is sick, she needs to be treated by the right doctor," he says. "That is me, and Mercy House is the best place for her. You want what's best for her, don't you?"

I cannot speak. Everything has become too awful.

He leans down, reaches those terrible fingers for my shoulder. "Your father says you've made up some nonsense about Teresa's ghost. You will need to stop saying such things."

Don't touch me, I think. I think it hard, but he doesn't respond.

"Now come home with me."

I shake my head.

"Little wretch," he says. "Do as I say."

No.

His hand tightens on me. "Do as I say or I will make sure your Mama only gets cold porridge for every meal at Mercy House."

I shake him off violently with a shout, and he overbalances and falls back. His hand flails out for a hay bale, and that is the only thing that stops him from hitting the ground. His eyes go hard and silver with fury. He reaches for a riding crop that hangs on the wall. I plunge my hand into my pocket, close it around the peg cat.

"You are a wild little boy who has been allowed to get away with too much," he says, raising the crop.

"No!" I scream, cowering from him.

And she is there. My sister. Made of smoke and whispers, standing between me and Doctor Humboldt. She has her hand raised and he can see her. I know he can see her because his mouth opens and a little choking sound comes out, and all the blood drains from his cheeks. He looks as though he is carved from alabaster.

"Leave me alone!" I shout, emboldened by Teresa's presence.

Then Teresa vanishes, as though it took all her effort to appear for a moment and frighten my enemy. I hear a pop against my deaf ear. Doctor Humboldt drops the riding crop. He turns, and then Papa opens the door of the shed.

"What the blazes is going on?" Papa demands.

Doctor Humboldt strides directly past him, wordlessly.

❋

Papa is angry and relieved. Angry because I did not obey him, but relieved that Doctor Humboldt says he won't take Mama to Mercy House.

I expect to be locked in my room again, but Papa simply waves me off and tells me to behave myself until the new year, when my new governess will arrive. Perhaps he is too tired to punish me. I go to my room anyway, and nobody brings me dinner. Late that night, I am so hungry I sneak downstairs to find some bread and cheese. I see Papa sitting in Mama's wingback chair with his elbows on his knees and his head in his hands. His back shakes. He is crying.

I return to my room hungry. I do not want him to know I saw him crying.

❋

Teresa does not come. I call out to her in my head, and I ask the peg cat, but she does not come. I think that maybe she used all her strength to frighten Doctor Humboldt and now she is tired. Resting somewhere. I do not know where.

Rain comes and melts the snow and turns it to muddy slush, and it is Christmas Eve. I sit in my room after lights out and close my eyes tight, and remember everything about last Christmas when Teresa was still alive. The house was brighter, cleaner, noisier. We had more servants and more lights were lit. Papa had friends over and they sang and played carols. I am not sure if the piano has been opened since that night. Teresa and I were sent to bed, but we sat on the stairs looking down through the banisters. The house smelled of roasting chestnuts. I press my brain, but I cannot remember what Mama's voice sounded like. I cannot remember her laugh.

I open my eyes. The sad, dim reality of Christmas Eve this year is all around me.

I fetch the peg cat from my dresser, pull on my robe, and creep down the stairs. All is quiet and dark. In the parlour, the fire burns low. The curtains are open and a half-moon provides just enough light for me to position the peg cat on the Christmas tree.

Then I sit beneath the tree and say to Teresa, "Wherever you are, you were the best sister I could have asked for." I cannot think of what else to tell her so I pause a little while, and embers pop in the fireplace, and I shiver from the cold. "If you know how to make Mama better, please give me a sign."

— 98 —

Am I talking to myself? Perhaps Teresa is never coming back.

I put my head on my knees and cry.

I do not hear the parlour door open, but I feel Mama's hand on the top of my head. I look up and she gazes down on me with such raw sorrow in her eyes that I cry harder. She sits next to me and puts her arm around me and I lean into her. "Teresa is gone," I say.

Her whole body shudders, as though a lightning bolt of horror has passed through her.

"I mean her ghost is gone," I say turning my face up to hers.

Mama stares into the fireplace, her eyes shining and wet.

"She was trying to tell me something," I say. "But I couldn't hear her. I think it was important. I think it might have made you better." I look up at the peg cat. "Please, Teresa. Please come back."

Mama's body starts to shake.

"Mama?"

No words.

"Mama? Maybe if you call her?"

She raises a trembling hand to her brow, brushes away a lock of hair.

"Maybe if you say her name?"

Mama takes a deep breath. Her face is so uncertain. She licks her lips.

"Teresa," she whispers.

And now I remember her voice. I remember it calling me for supper. I remember it telling me she loves me. I remember it chatting patiently to Teresa as Mama taught her to sew.

"You did it!" I say, and put my arms around Mama. I have forgotten about Teresa for the moment. "Mama, you spoke."

"I'm sorry," she says, in a voice like a croak. She clears her throat and says it again. "I'm sorry, I'm sorry, I'm sorry," and she is covering my face in soft kisses and saying, "I'm sorry" a hundred times. A thousand times.

Papa arrives at the door, half-dressed, disheveled, a look of wonder on his face.

"Margaret?" he gasps.

"I'm sorry," Mama says to him, and he leaps forward and pulls her into his arms.

My sister's ghost does not return.

The True Confession of
Obedience-to-God Ashe

November 1645

I, OBEDIENCE-TO-GOD ASHE, DO hereby confess that I have communed with the Devil and done his bidding.

Methinks I must be a witch.

My hand shakes so much as I write these words that it is all I can do not to blot the page with ink. But I must write down what happened. I must make my confession, before I am condemned to eternal damnation in the fires of hell.

I did not mean to do the Devil's will. It was such a small sin, I thought. Yet my father is right when he says Satan lays snares for us all. The snare laid for me was one of vanity.

I just wished to be pretty.

In the small village in which we lived, it had long been the custom for maidens to rise early on May-morn and venture forth to wash their faces in the first dew that fell on the leaves of the hawthorn.

Such foolish superstitions are ungodly, I know. Yet I watched them from behind my shutter as they went laughing up Abbey Street, baskets over their arms, coming back with branches of hawthorn to hang on their doors.

From the day my father came to this wretched place, he has preached against the May-Day revelries. He bade the maypole burnt and the faces of the statues in the church hacked away, but the church wardens obeyed him most unwillingly.

Only the statue of the Virgin with her baby in her arms remained, being too high to reach easily. I gazed up at her every time I went to church, wondering if my mother had held me like that before she had died. I doubted she had had the strength or the desire.

Mine had been a hard birth, my father said.

It happened that the day before May-morn in the Year of Our Lord Sixteen-hundred-and-forty-five was a Sunday. My father preached fire and damnation against the old heathenish ways, and reminded us all that Parliament had banned the maypole and all other such unchristian practices. There was a low mutter in the church, and I saw Alder Brightwell scowl and cross his arms. His daughter Marigold turned and, laughing, whispered something to her great friend, Annis. And I saw that Sir Ralph Beaufort had his eyes fixed on Marigold's glowing face, and I felt such a suffocation in my throat that I could scarcely breathe.

She will wash her face in the May-dew, I thought bitterly, *and she will be more beautiful than ever. And Sir Ralph shall love her and not me.*

On Sundays, my father preached seven times and so much of my day was spent standing in silent contemplation, my feet aching, my father's voice thundering around me. I should have listened. I should have paid attention.

But my thoughts were firm fixed upon Sir Ralph, who was struggling greatly with his conscience and had been coming to my father for spiritual guidance. Ralph's family were Royalists to the bone, and perhaps even secret followers of the Anti-Christ, that man of false exaltation who sought to rule us from Rome. My father had high hopes of winning Ralph to the cause of the righteous, and persuading him to fight for Parliament against the king. It was a good sign, I thought, that he was here worshipping in our church and that he had abandoned his silks and velvets. Secretly I mourned the loss of his long dark curls.

I imagined Ralph being wounded in battle, and brought to our house for me to nurse, and smoothing his fevered brow, and praying by his bed till he was healed, and how grateful he would be.

Then I remembered the way he had looked at Marigold Brightwell, and all my hopes were like ashes in my mouth.

For she had been born in the midsummer, and was as blithe and bonny as a meadow in full bloom. Hair as yellow as ripe corn, eyes as blue as a cloudless sky.

And I had been born in the depths of winter, and was pale as frost. Hair the colour of bare-blasted trees and eyes the colour of thunderclouds.

No wonder no-one ever looked at me when she was near.

That night I did not sleep, so determined was I to be awake in the dawn. As soon as I heard the first twitter of the thrush, I slid out of bed and drew on my gown, combed my limp brown hair and pinned it in place under my coif, and then, in stockinged feet, stole out of my room and down to the kitchen. Forsaken slept on her pallet by the fire. I unbarred the door and, amazed at my temerity, slipped out into the garden.

The air was full of mist, drifting and swirling like ghosts. I groped my way out and sat on the bench to buckle on my shoes. I tiptoed down the passageway towards the street, then hesitated, looking to see if there was anyone stirring next door, in the long, crooked house with its out-jutting first floor and ancient oaken doorway. That was where the Brightwell clan lived, the clack of their looms and the stink of their dyer's vats displeasing my father every day.

All was quiet now. No chink of candlelight showed.

I gave a little smile, and hurried along the laneway towards the old graveyard. There was a hawthorn tree that grew down by the old saint's well. I would wash my face in the dew on its white petals, and be back home before my father began to stir.

It was dark under the avenue of linden trees and I went carefully, not wanting to trip on a loose stone. I could see the white blur of the may-bush in the shadows, and heard the faint tinkle of water running over pebbles. Step by step I went forward, hands held out, and found the tree by tearing my skin open on the thorns. I sucked my wounded hand, then brushed my fingers over the soft petals. The dew was cold, and made the skin of my face and hands tingle.

Just then I heard soft girlish laughter, and the sound of wooden heels clattering on the cobblestones.

"Sssh. We don't want to wake the parson." I recognised Marigold Brightwell's voice.

"Or his sour-faced daughter," her companion giggled. I recognised her voice too. Annis, the daughter of the village brewer.

"You know she watches us all day long through her window?"

"Well, plenty to admire at your place," Annis said. "All those big strong brothers of yours."

Blood scorched my face. It was true Marigold had a great many brothers—six of them—and that they were a handsome family, if one admired such gaudy colouring, which I did not. But I did not watch the Brightwell family from my room because I lusted after any of those tall, brawny boys. It was just that I had always longed to be part of a big family.

Our house was quiet and lonely. The only sound the scratch of my father's quill from his study. I would sit by my narrow window and sew, or pretend to read my little Bible, and look down at the garden next door, planted with hollyhocks, goldenrod, tansy, marigolds, dahlias, woodruff, chamomile and woad. I'd see Marigold and her mother laughing as they cut flowers or harvested leaves, stems and roots, and hung them to dry or put them in big barrels to soak. I'd hear her brothers singing as they worked the looms, and sometimes the sound of piping and the thud of dancing feet on wooden floors.

In the centre of the garden was a pretty white dovecote. In the mornings Marigold went out to feed her birds, and they flew about her head with flashing white wings. She'd hold out her arms and they would settle on her and let her stroke their soft plumage. Sometimes she would play with her kitten, throwing a ball of coloured yarn for it to chase and pounce upon. I would watch. Wishing for doves. Wishing for a kitten.

The two girls clattered down to the holy well. I pressed myself back into the old wall, hiding behind the hawthorn bush, hidden by the darkness and the mist. They must not find me. I could not endure it if they knew I was there, if they knew I had heard what they said.

"As if any of your brothers would even glance in her direction," Annis said. "She's meek as a mouse and as miserable as a wet week."

"Poor thing," Marigold said.

I found her pity harder to endure than Annis's scorn. I turned my face away, closing my eyes.

I heard the hawthorn twigs rustling as the girls dabbled their fingers in the dew, then bent to wash their faces.

"Did I tell you Sir Ralph is coming to watch us dance about the maypole?" Marigold's voice was full of pleasure. "He says he is interested in such old customs, and that it's a shame to ban them."

Annis laughed. "Oh, I don't think it's the maypole he's coming to see, Marigold!"

"Well, not just the maypole, of course. The morris dance too, and the Ooser, and Pa playing the fool. And he was most interested in seeing the Giant's Frypan, thinking it must be very old."

"I think it's you he really wants to see," Annis teased. "Didn't you see the way he was watching you in church?"

"No, was he? Do you really think . . . ? But he is the son of a lord . . . "

"He's a Leveller now, ain't he? No reason why a lord's son can't marry a weaver's daughter these days . . . and anyone with eyes in their head can see he's smitten with you!"

Marigold protested. Annis laughed and said, "And why not? You're the prettiest girl in the valley. Just promise me you'll find me a lord to dance with at your wedding."

Marigold laughed. "I'll find you two!"

The girls hurried back up the avenue of linden trees, and were soon gone from my sight.

Crouched in the shadows, my bleeding hand clutching the hawthorn's sharp twigs, I ill-wished Marigold with all my strength. I hardly knew what I wanted. Her weeping and bereft. Her broken and bruised. Her dead.

That was the beginning of it. That was when I, unwitting, first made my pact with the Devil.

❊

I crept into the dim, fire-lit kitchen, my apron wrapped about my hand. Forsaken was awake. She was a thin, slump-shouldered girl who had been brought up half-wild by her grandmother, the local cunning-woman. When her grandmother died, she had been left destitute. My father had employed her, changing her name from Daisy Brightwell, the heathenish name she had been given, to the far more suitable Forsaken. Her kin next door had offered to take her in, but my father had refused. He had needed someone to spin and toil for us, and I think it gave him pleasure to have one of the Brightwells under his hand.

"Mr Ashe wants you in his study, Miss Obedience," she told me, looking up from the pottage bubbling over the fire.

My heart quailed within me. For a moment, I was motionless as a leveret in a furrow, the shadow of a hawk swinging above. Then I unwound my apron from my hand and splashed out some water to wash my bloody palm clean.

"Gracious, miss, what have you done to your hand?"

"Hawthorn," I answered absently.

"You haven't brought any into the house, have you?" she asked, turning me around and checking my dress and coif for leaves or petals. "'Tis a fairy tree, you know, and terrible bad luck to bring within four walls. Though not as bad as blackthorn. That's the tree the witches use for cursing, you know. Prick their poppets with the thorns so that the person shrieks in pain."

I paid her no mind. Forsaken believed in many old heathenish superstitions, such as always stirring the pot clockwise and tying a twig of rowan to the handle of the butter-churn. I made sure my hair and dress were neat and proper, and then went with leaden steps down the corridor towards my father's study.

He was writing in his black book. I stood in silence before him for some minutes before he put the quill back in its holder and scattered sand over the paper.

"Where have you been, Obedience-to-God?" he asked eventually, not looking up.

"Please forgive me, Father. I . . . I heard Marigold Brightwell and Annis Brewer going past at dawn. The . . . the clatter of their shoes woke me. I looked out my window. To see what the noise was. I heard them say something about maypoles, Father."

He stiffened and looked up. "Why did you not come and rouse me at once, Obedience-to-God? What made you dress and got outside in such an imprudent manner?"

"I . . . I was sure I must be mistaken, sir. I did not wish to bear false witness against them. I got up and ran out, just for a moment, to be certain. I was not wrong, sir. The Brightwells are raising a maypole at a place they call the Giant's Frypan."

My father slammed his hand down on his desk so hard I jumped involuntarily, and had to press my hand against my heart to stop it banging against the bones of my chest.

"Idolatrous nonsense," he said, very quiet and cold. He got up and put on his tall steeple-hat, and picked up his Bible and his whip. I stood quietly, head bowed.

"You should have informed me with greater haste," he told me, as if it was not his will that I had stood there for so long while he wrote in his book. "It is already close to dawn, and I do not know where they have gone."

"I think I may know, Father," I said.

He stared at me for a long moment, and my breath shortened.

"How so?"

"I . . . I followed them a short while, to see which way they went," I lied. My second sin that day. How easily I fell into Satan's snare.

"Then you must show me." He strode out of his study, shouting at Forsaken to fetch the beadle and the constables. I scurried after.

We went through the old abbey graveyard, and onto the hills. I did not know if I was leading my father the right way, particularly as the fog still lay heavy around us. I had heard the steep slope of the downs to the north-west called Frying Pan Hill, however, and had wondered at the odd name. And Marigold and Annis had turned in that direction.

As we climbed up the steep slope, I heard the eerie ring of bells, and a pipe and fiddle, and knew I led my father true. His step quickened, and I laboured alongside him, my skirts heavy with mud. The ground was rough. Every now and again we lurched down into a kind of ditch, and had to clamber out. Still the white vapour swirled about us, though above the sky was faintly starry, rimmed with fire to the east.

Suddenly the Devil loomed out of the mist. I screamed and stumbled back, and my father fell to his knees and cried out to God in his heaven.

Taller than a man, with spreading horns like a bullock, he stood over us, glaring down at us with wild white-rimmed eyes. Then he turned and disappeared once more into the mist.

"They have raised Lucifer himself," my father whispered. Snatching up his Bible and whip from where he had dropped them, he scrambled to his feet and ran with great leaps and strides up the hill, shouting to God to protect him. I picked up my skirts and scrambled after, though my heart was drubbing against my ribs.

At last, hot and panting, we reached the curve of the hill and found there a stretch of flat land that seemed to float above the mist like a platform. The six Brightwell boys danced in lines, large white handkerchiefs in their hands, bells tied beneath their knees, green sprigs in their hats. A small crowd watched them, waving leafy twigs joyously, flowers in their buttonholes and tucked into their hats. Dressed in bright green rags, their father capered about them like a demented fool, waving an inflated pig's bladder. Occasionally he darted forward to strike one of his sons so they leapt higher.

Nearby, a tall maypole had been set up, its green and white and golden ribbons fluttering in the rising breeze. Six older girls stood nearby, dressed in green with crowns of flower and leaves on their heads. I saw Marigold and Annis, and four other of their circle. Galloping about on wooden hobby-horses were some younger children, their heads crowned with flower wreaths, while Tom Brewer stood nearby, dressed in cow hides, some great bundle at his feet.

My eyes searched the crowd feverishly. Then I found him. Ralph, dressed soberly enough, but laughing and talking eagerly with the lord of the manor, Denzil Holles. A small man with dark curling lovelocks and a neat curling moustache, Lord Holles's coat was made of fine port-red velvet slashed to show the fine white lawn beneath, and his collar was trimmed with lace. He was the second son of an earl who had grown up with the king. Although he was a member of Parliament, rumour said that he had been in secret communication with his childhood friend, and had earned Colonel Cromwell's enmity as a result.

It smote me hard to see Ralph here, so comfortable in the company of the unrighteous.

My father strode forward into the centre of the field. "How dare you!"

Everyone turned. The music died away. The jangling of the bells stilled.

"You were warned to abandon your heathenish idolatry. Now you shall suffer the consequences. Your maypole shall become your whipping post!" My father lashed out with his whip, sending the crowd screaming and scattering.

"You have worked with dark forces and raised Lucifer himself out of Hell," my father ranted, laying about him with the whip as he spoke. "I saw him with my own eyes."

Alder Brightwell laughed. "What? You mean the old Ooser? Why, he's nothing but a mask of wood with some horns glued on. Show him, Tom."

Tom Brewer grinned and lifted up the great bundle at his feet, putting it on over his head. It was the terrifying face that we had seen in the mist, with enormous upcurving horns and wild staring eyes. Now, in the brightening morning, it was easy to see that it was a mask carved of wood, with ox-tails for hair and beard. Tom galumphed about, making the wooden jaws gnash, and pretending to nip at the pretty girls.

"Did we frighten you, pastor?" Alder said, grinning.

My father struck him across the face. Alder stared at him in surprise, one hand lifting to his cheek where a red weal showed.

"That's enough!" Lord Holles strode forward, and seized my father's whip. "There is no harm in a little merry-making, particularly when times seem so dark."

"There is great harm," my father said, and wrested his whip free. "Parliament has issued an ordinance against it and other such ungodly pastimes. It is against the law of this land. And I warned the congregation against it just yesterday. This is an act of outright defiance and rebellion, and must be punished."

"Good Queen Bess herself used to dance about the maypole," Alder cried. "It's been the way of our people for centuries. And how can it be the law of the land when our king don't agree with it? He said we could have our May-games and our morris-dances and our maypole, even on a Sunday!"

"Blasphemer!" White with anger, my father struck out once more. Alder ducked back, then gathered himself up, his big calloused hands tensing into fists.

Once again Lord Holles stepped forward, placing himself between Alder and my father. He was not nearly so tall as my father, nor as broad and strong as the weaver, but he had such an indefinable air of authority about him that both men stepped back.

"I am your Member of Parliament, and therefore was present at the making of that law. It was called an Ordinance for the Better Observation of the Lord's Day, was it not? Today is Monday." He smiled sardonically at my father, who burst into angry speech.

Lord Holles held up one hand. Much to my astonishment, my father stopped speaking.

"Perhaps you are right, and the law against maypoles covers all days. Even so, the punishment for raising a maypole was the payment of a fine, not a whipping." Lord Holles put his hand in his pocket and drew out a few coins which he tossed at my father. Taken by surprise, he failed to catch them and had to bend and search among the grass.

Alder gave a snort of amusement to see him so undignified.

My father straightened, two long white dents on either side of his nose as he drew down his mouth in a terrifying frown. "Nonetheless, that man has defied my authority . . . I insist he must have his time in the stocks!"

"I'll happily rest my weary bones in the stocks awhile if it means we can carry on a-dancing and a-maying," Alder said cheerfully. "Now that his lordship has paid the fine, many thanks to thee, sir."

"I think that seems fair," Lord Holles said. "I will deliver the miscreant to the stocks myself this evening. Have a good day, sir."

And he nodded to the fiddler and piper to take up their instruments again, which they did with great verve. Amid much laughter, the dancing began again. Marigold came across the grass towards Ralph, her hair escaping from under her wreath of flowers in bright ringlets. He smiled, and took her hands, and they began to dance together. As I watched, an adder of jealousy uncoiled within me and bit me with venomous fangs.

My father was left looking like a fool, which he hated above all things. He gripped my arm and towed me away down the hill so fast it was all I could do not to stumble and fall. And as we went down the hill he castigated me for not having told him that Lord Holles was present at the maying and for not knowing about the bull-mask. We passed the parish constables and the beadle, panting up the hill, and he snapped at them and told them the fine was paid. Then he took me into his study and beat me hard.

Each stroke of his whip made me hate Marigold more. I know it was unjust. But then so was my punishment.

That night Alder was locked in the stocks by the church door. The people of the village brought him tankards of ale to drink and twists of tobacco to smoke, and there was much toasting of him and laughter against my father.

But once twilight fell, it grew chilly. The people of the village drifted back to their own hearths. I could feel the cold of the window pane against my forehead. Then I saw Marigold cross the road, a heavy wool blanket in her arms. She wrapped it around her father's shoulders. I saw him smile, and lift a corner of the blanket. She sat beside him, and he drew her close under the shelter of the warm covering and kissed the top of her head.

I could not watch any longer. I went to lie on my stomach, biting my lip at the pain in my back and shoulders. I wept slow bitter tears into my pillow.

❀

A week or so later, I heard a great banging on our front door. I had to shove at Forsaken and urge her to open it, for my father was at the parish meeting and so we were alone. Trembling with fear, she unbolted the door and opened it just a crack.

A Roundhead stood outside, dressed in a long buff coat and heavy thigh-high boots, an iron helmet under his arm. He wore a sword at his side, and carried a long-barrelled flintlock musket in his hand. He used this to slam the door open, almost striking Forsaken in the face.

"We're requisitioning supplies," he said, without any preamble. "Bring out whatever food you've got. We've an army to feed."

"I am sorry, sir, I'm afraid we don't have very much," Forsaken said, with a bob of a curtsey.

"Bring out what you've got. Sacks of flour, barley, dried meats. Got any chickens?"

"Yes, sir, but . . . "

"Kill them and bring them out."

"But what shall we do for eggs?"

"Not my concern. Bring them out, else I'll send my men in." He jerked his gloved hand over his shoulder, and I saw the street was full of armed men. Some were banging on the doors of my neighbours, some were dragging sacks or carrying legs of ham, and throwing them into their cart. Quite a few were drinking and carousing down at the inn on the corner, while others rolled out barrels of beer and casks of wine to load up.

The soldier at my door said, "Be quick about it, else we'll take what we want ourselves. We've got the king's army hot on our heels."

I rushed to obey him, dragging Forsaken along and ordering her to help me. It was true we did not have much—my father was both frugal and abstemious—but we gave the soldier enough to keep him satisfied. While Forsaken struggled out with sacks of flour and

— 113 —

barley, I went out to the coop and quickly wrung the necks of two of our chickens. It cost me dear. I had raised those hens from chicks. But I had heard enough of the danger of refusing the depredations of soldiers on either side of the war to risk arousing their ire. Better the hens that us, I thought.

I carried out the two dead hens and was stowing them in the cart when I heard screaming and shouting from the Brightwells' back garden. The Roundheads rushed down the covered passageway to investigate, and I slipped after them, keeping close to the wall.

A soldier had set about slaughtering Marigold's doves. They lay in a bloodied heap of white feathers in a basket. Marigold had evidently tried to stop him, and he had struck her hard. Her mouth was bleeding, and she was weeping as he turned her roughly and shoved her up against a wall. His other hand was swiftly undoing his breeches.

Marigold's father and brothers came running, roaring with rage, and the soldier turned and pulled out his sword. The Brightwells were not daunted. They seized the soldier and disarmed him, tackling him to the ground.

The sergeant fired his flintlock into the air. Marigold screamed, and the Brightwell boys slowly stood up, hands held high.

The soldier spat a bloody gob on the ground, then buckled himself up again, insolently adjusting himself within his breeches. He jerked one thumb at Marigold, who had run, weeping, to her mother's arms. "You have to admit she's a bonny lass, sir, ripe for the plucking."

"No time for that," barked the sergeant. "We need to ride on to Dorchester just as fast as we can. You can come back later."

"I will," the soldier said and winked at Marigold.

"If you lay one finger on my daughter, I'll cut your balls off myself," Alder said, his huge fists raised.

"You could try," the soldier replied, picking up his sword and holding it menacingly.

At once the six Brightwell boys bristled up, grabbing whatever tools laid to hand. A rake. A pitchfork. A spade.

"But here's a fine troop of hotheads," the sergeant said, regarding the six angry lads. "We could use men like you in our company. Round them up, lads, we'll take them with us. You fear God, don't you? You'd like to strike a blow against the despot? No? Well, we'll take you anyway."

The Brightwell boys were quickly and efficiently disarmed by the other soldiers, hustled down the passageway and tied roughly to the back of the cart. I had to press my back hard against the wall to avoid being jostled, but no-one paid me any mind.

Alder stormed after them, shaking the pitchfork, but was struck hard and fell to the cobblestones. Marigold flung herself beside him, trying to shield him, while her mother dropped to her knees, hands raised, begging the soldiers to release her sons. She was ignored. Bleeding, raging, but helpless, the Brightwell boys were forced to stagger behind the laden cart as it trundled away down the road. The soldiers all followed, laughing and swaggering and waving to the sullen crowd. Marigold wept piteously.

I could not settle to anything. It was like a wasps' nest had been slashed open inside me, and a plague of them whirred their metallic wings within my body. I had seen Marigold bloodied. I had seen Marigold weeping. She had lost her brothers whom she adored. It was because of me. I had ill-wished her. See what I had wrought? Such a dreadful thrill it gave me, to know I had such power.

Father was most displeased with me for giving the soldiers so much of our food, and ordered me to fast for a few days as punishment. I went to bed hungry, and lay on my stomach, unsleeping, my back and shoulders twinging with pain at every breath. The men of the village all went to the inn to drown their sorrows. I could hear the angry roar of their talk. Eventually the night quietened, but I could not rest. I kept seeing Marigold's face, made ugly with tears and blood.

The king's men arrived soon after dawn. They took everything that was left in our pantry, and found and killed the last of the chickens. Then on they marched, leaving us with nothing.

"What are we to do?" I said, so hungry and dizzy I had to hold on to the dresser to keep from falling.

"We could go to the forest, see if we can find any chicken-of-the-woods," Forsaken suggested.

I gaped at her in surprise. "Any chickens we find in the woods will belong to one of the villagers."

"Not that kind of chicken," Forsaken said.

"What other kind of chickens are there?"

She gave her rare gap-toothed grin, took up a basket and led me to the copse of trees higher up the valley. There she found an old oak that had sulphur-yellow fungi growing in wide platters from a fissure in its trunk. I looked at it in horror. "Tastes good," Forsaken said. "Tastes like chicken."

She amused herself then by showing me all the weeds of the woods that could be eaten. New hawthorn leaves, which she called "bread-and-cheese". Dandelion leaves, which she called "swine's snout." Wild strawberries which I ate ravenously. (Two more sins to my account. The sin of greed and the sin of disobedience.) Nettles. A ring of fairy cap mushrooms that Forsaken would not pick till she had bobbed a little curtsey and thanked the good people.

As we came home in the dusk, our baskets laden, we took the shortcut through the graveyard, with its path that led down through the linden trees to the old well. Through the arched gateway, I saw Alder Brightwell stumping up the road towards Abbey House, where Lord Holles lived. The mansion had been built from stones taken from the ruined abbey, parts of which still stood in the grounds. Lord Holles had invested a great deal of money in extending and restoring the house, which had been inherited by his wife Jane from her first husband. It was a fine place now, with great mullioned windows which glittered in the last rays of light.

I wondered why the weaver would be visiting the lord of the manor, and took Forsaken by the arm and made her stand silently beside me, hidden from view behind the ancient lichened walls.

I heard Alder bang the knocker, then ask for Lord Holles. Sometime later, he came to the door.

"Shall we walk in the garden, Brightwell?" he said courteously enough, though I could tell by his voice that he was surprised by the visit.

I heard them walk round the side of the house and into the garden at the rear. Pinching Forsaken's arm hard, I told her to go home and start making supper. She began to whine in protest, but I told her to do as she was told else I'd tell Father I'd seen her stealing butter to sell at market. She gazed at me in hurt surprise, but did as she was told, leaving me alone in the twilit graveyard.

Then I crept over the low wall, and found a tree to climb. It was not something I was used to, and I'd grazed my cheek and torn my sleeve before at last I was high enough to see over the wall and into the garden.

The two men were leaning nearby, smoking their pipes and talking. Alder was begging for help in releasing his sons, and Lord

Holles was looking troubled. "I'm afraid there is nothing I can do. It's not uncommon for young men to be pressed into service."

"It ain't right," Alder said. "We're just ordinary folk, trying to make a living. I can't work the looms all on me own. Come winter, we're likely to starve. And I'm not the only one."

"I will do what I can for you," Lord Holles replied. "But I'm afraid there is no early end to this war in sight. We went to the king in February, with a proposal for peace, but no settlement could be reached." He lowered his voice. "I fear that there are hot-tempered men among the parliamentary forces who now seek to do more than simply force the king to bow to Parliament."

Alder stared at him in consternation, his long white pipe burning unheeded in his hand. "Do you mean . . . ?"

"I mean nothing," Lord Holles said hastily. "I am just troubled in my heart. We never meant for things to go this far, and I dread what may come. That is all."

"There's a group of us who've decided we'll stand for no more of it, from either side," Alder said bluntly. "We're taking up arms against any who'd try and rob us, Roundhead or Cavalier. We may not have muskets or swords, but we can cut ourselves clubs from the forest, or take up our scythes and our pitchforks, and we'll defend our land and our families the best way we can."

"I admire your courage," Lord Holles said after a long moment. "But your clubs will do little good against cannon."

"We must do something," Alder said.

He hesitated, then, gesturing with his pipe, said, "you may not know this, sir, not being born in these parts, but up on yonder hill there's a great white carving of a giant with a club in his hand. A club in the shape of an oak leaf. The old abbots thought it pagan and would not pay to keep it free of grass and weeds, and so slowly it was overgrown and lost. But my grandfer remembers when they cut it again, after the abbey fell into ruins. It's a symbol of the old ways, sir, and of wisdom and strength and fruitfulness, all of which we want to honour."

"And is that why you dance up there on May-Day, rather than down here in the village? Because that is where the giant is?" Lord Holles asked with keen interest.

"Yes, sir, that's so. The thing is, we want to cut the giant again. As a warning to all who come here with robbery and murder in their hearts. We're taking up clubs in defense of our homes, and plan to wear white armbands to show that we stand for not one side or another, but for peace. So the white giant on the hill is like our mascot, sir, and we want everyone to see it."

Lord Holles smoked thoughtfully for a while, clouds of smoke obscuring his face.

"If you would pay us for cutting it, we'd be able to make enough to get us through the winter," Alder said. "We'd rather work than be given charity, and there'd be pride in the labour, even for those of us used to being our own man."

"Yes, I can understand that," Lord Holles said. "But a pagan symbol? It would be dangerous. What would your pastor say?"

Alder said something then that I cannot put down on paper, no matter that I have sworn to tell everything and leave nothing out. Up in my tree I blushed scarlet and hid my face against my arm.

Lord Holles chuckled. "Indeed, he is a sanctimonious prig. And I mislike the way his little daughter cringes away from him."

"So what say you, sir? Will you pay us to cut the Giant again?"

"I will think on it. That is all I can promise for now. I still have hopes that . . . " Lord Holles hesitated, then said, "that we shall soon see peace again."

But we heard there had been fierce and bloody fighting at Taunton, less than forty miles away from our little village. At first the Cavaliers prevailed, and the Roundheads were forced to retreat into the castle where they had a lean and hungry time of it. But the Roundhead commander Sir Thomas Fairfax marched in from London, and the Cavaliers fled in the face of his New Model Army. Then Fairfax marched against the king's stronghold at Oxford, and once again all the pantries and gardens were stripped bare as the army took whatever it needed, less gently than before.

✿

One day in late May I was sitting as usual in my window that looked down over the Brightwells' garden. Marigold and her mother were perched on stools in the sunshine, their drop spindles spinning in the air. I saw Alder come out, dressed in stout shoes and wide-brimmed felt hat, a stout stick in one hand. Around his arm he had wound a broad white riband. His wife and daughter leapt up, and threw their arms about him and kissed his bearded cheeks. His wife checked his pockets to make sure he had bread and cheese, and Marigold ran to fill his leather bottle at the well. He smiled and kissed them farewell, and then went down the covered passageway and was lost to my view. I went at once to my other window, which looked down at the street and across to the church.

At least two dozen men were milling about there, all with white ribands on their arms or hats, and most carrying some kind of tool as a weapon. Tom Brewer carried a crudely stitched banner that read, "If you offer to plunder or take our cattle, be assured we will bid you battle."

They marched off together, and were gone for several days. I wondered where they had gone. The men of our village rarely went anywhere, unless it was a fair day.

It was Forsaken who told me. She heard all the gossip as she cleaned the church with the other women, or went to market to bargain for flour or mutton. Four thousand Clubmen had gathered together at Wimborne St Giles—some thirty miles away across the hills—to organise a force of watchmen to guard against marauding soldiers.

Then, on the 15th June, the news came.

The king had been defeated at the Battle of Naseby. Six thousand Royalists had been slaughtered out of an army of seven and a half thousand. The king's private correspondence was captured. It proved he had sought help from the Anti-Christ in Rome. It was said that Cromwell—now promoted to Lieutenant-General—laughed before the battle and said that God would bring to the king to naught.

And so it was.

Two days after Naseby, a troop came riding up Abbey Street. At their head was a man in a mud-stained buff coat and a scratched and battered breastplate. His face was blunt and square, and marked with warts at temple and chin.

Some children were playing in the middle of the road, and stood and stared at the soldiers. "Make way for General Cromwell," one of the soldiers cried.

I let my sewing drop on to my lap and leaned forward to see better. I thought the general most ugly, except for his eyes which were piercingly clear and blue. He sat impatiently, drumming his fingers on his sword-hilt, while the children were chased off the road, then asked one, "Is that fine place yonder Abbey House? Where Denzil, Lord Holles resides?"

With his finger in his mouth, the boy nodded and the troop spurred their horses on.

I ran downstairs and knocked breathlessly at my father's study. "Why do you disturb me?" he snapped.

"Father! General Cromwell is here!"

In moments he had opened the door and was gazing down at me. "Are your wits addled, Obedience-to-God?"

"No, sir. He is here, in Cerne Abbas. Knocking on Lord Holles's door as I speak."

My father hastened out to the street. I ran after him, as did Forsaken, and indeed, half the street. We gathered in a crowd at the gate of the Abbey House, and watched as Lord Holles was led out of the house, a burly soldier on every side.

"What is the charge?" Lord Holles shouted.

"For conspiring with the tyrant and his malignants against Parliament," Cromwell answered tersely. "And if I have my way you'll lose your head for it."

As Lord Holles was hustled down the steps he reached into his pocket and pulled out a heavy purse. He flung it at Alder Brightwell.

"Here's work for you while I am gone, my lads," he shouted. "Cut the Giant free!"

❄

Every man in the village rose before dawn the next day and marched up the hill, tools over their shoulders. Even my father. His tools, though, were his Bible and his tongue. He harangued the men as they worked, till Alder Brightwell respectfully took his Bible away and told him to return to his pulpit. By that time my father was weary of being mocked, and so he warned them all of the everlasting torment of the fires of hell, then went home, white-lipped with fury.

I was not there to be beaten. Forsaken and I had gone out foraging in the woods again, ostensibly to find mushrooms, but really so I could watch the giant slowly being freed from his prison of brambles and weeds.

"Heave ho, lads! He must be finished by midsummer," Alder shouted.

Four dozen men or more worked from sunrise to sunset every day. They began by clearing the grass, cutting away the turf and excavating the remnants of ditches that still dissected the hillside. The ones down the bottom of the hill had been filled by mudslides, and so needed to be dug out again. The ones up the top were cleared out more easily, but then had to have fresh white powdered chalk poured into them to make the outlines of the figure clearer. It was hard work, and the women of the village were kept busy bringing up pitchers of ale and baskets of bread and cheese for the workers. The atmosphere was festive, and many ribald jokes and gestures filled the air.

By Midsummer's Eve, the giant strode northwards across the slope of the hill, his oak-leaf club brandished high. His other hand was flung high, as if in warning. Most shockingly, though, he had between his legs an upstanding virile member such as you may see on a stallion when it scents a mare in heat.

Hot with embarrassment, I scarcely knew where to look.

"My father will be most angry," I whispered to Forsaken from our hiding-place in a copse of trees on the hill opposite.

"I'd say that's why they done it," she answered wryly.

"But why give him such animal parts? Is it akin to the horns on their wooden mask? I do not understand."

She gave me an amazed look. "But all men have pricks like that, Miss Obedience. Even your father."

"They do not! You lie."

She gave a little grimace. "I ain't lying, Miss Obedience. Men have pricks, just like any male creature. They put them inside the women and that's how babies are made."

I shook my head. "You should not say such things, Forsaken. I shall not listen."

"I'd bet you a ha'penny that there'll be plenty of it going on tonight, it being Midsummer's Eve and all, and the Giant's prick there putting ideas into all their heads."

I stood up, agitated beyond reason. I looked across the valley at the gigantic white figure, and panic flared deep down inside me. I ran down the hill, lifting my skirts so I did not trip. My thoughts were all helter-skelter. I remembered the soldier who had held Marigold against the wall, unbuckling his pants. I had not fully understood what he had intended. But now I knew.

My breath came short. I slowed to a walk, my hand pressing against a stitch in my side. It was ridiculous that I was jealous that a rude soldier had thought her ripe for the plucking, but had not even noticed me. I did not want to be so noticed, I told myself.

Then—as if thinking about Marigold had conjured her—I heard her laugh. Quietly I crept through the trees and came to a little sunlit dell where Marigold sat on a cloak, her vivid blue dress spread about her. It made her eyes the colour of cornflowers. Sir Ralph Beaufort lay beside her, his steeple hat discarded on the ground. A swarm of butterflies flitted above the meadow flowers.

"But I do not understand why you think colours are sinful," Marigold said. "Did God not make all the colours? He made these green meadows and the yellow of those dandelions and the pink of the foxgloves. All I had to do to make a dye this blue was soak some woad leaves in water, and add some ashes. Did God not make the woad plant too?"

"Well, yes . . . but the pastor preaches that vanity is a sin . . . "

"He also preaches that singing is a sin, but if that is so, why did God give us tongues? Or feet for dancing and hands for clapping? It seems to me the pastor thinks anything natural and joyful is a sin!" Marigold was flushed and indignant.

She pointed to the butterflies. "Look at the colour of their wings. They are as blue as the sky. God made them that colour. And look how he dances for the lady butterfly. He wants her to love him and agree to be his mate. See how beautiful she is, with her brown velvet wings and orange spots. God gave her those pretty wings . . . "

"Just like God gave you your pretty eyes," Ralph murmured, kneeling so he could grasp her hands. "So that I may love you."

He kissed her and Marigold gave a little gasp, then drew him closer so they could kiss again. Ralph drew her on to his lap, and then—some time later—lay her down beneath him. I watched it all from my hiding-place. I saw that Forsaken had spoken true.

Dusk was falling by the time they lay, spent, in each other's arms. Marigold sat up, tying her bodice together again. "Will you come to the Midsummer fire with me?" she asked. "We could be handfast in the old way, by jumping the flames together." Her eyes were bright with laughter.

"I will," he said. "But tomorrow I shall call formally on your father and ask his permission to marry you."

She kissed him in her joy.

"What of your father? Will he be angry you plan to marry a weaver's daughter?" she asked a little anxiously, coiling her hair up and pinning it under her coif.

"I think he'll be pleased to know I'm not riding off to join the Roundheads or marrying some long-faced Puritan's daughter!"

She laughed. "Like poor little Obedience-to-God Ashe."

"Heaven forbid," Ralph said with a shudder. Then, fingers entwined, her head resting on his shoulder, they wandered up the hill towards the midsummer fire, which had already been lit on the Giant's Frypan.

I crouched in my hidey-hole like a hunted animal. My breath was coming fast and uneven, and my fingers bled a little where they had clutched at sharp grasses. At last I got to my feet and stumbled back towards the village. The fire on the hill roared. Dark figures danced about the leaping flames. Sparks spun towards the stars like burning bees.

As I came in the door, Forsaken looked up with a cry of relief. "Oh Miss Obedience, I didn't mean to upset you. Forgive me if I was too forward. I . . . "

"I'm not well." I pushed past her. "I'm going to my room. Please . . . tell Father . . . "

"He is in his study, praying, and says he must not be disturbed. He says the Devil walks among us tonight."

I nodded, and went towards the door. I had to pause on the far side, and try and catch my breath and stop the sobs trying to burst free. I heard Forsaken put on her clogs and slip out the kitchen door. She was going to the Giant, I realised.

I did not light a candle, but undressed in the twilight dim and crept into my cold hard bed. I drew my knees to my chin. I could not stop my mind from replaying all that I had seen and heard. I felt as if all those butterflies were deep inside me, brushing me with their feathery wings.

I could hear laughter and singing and music from the Giant's Hill. Everyone from the village was there. Except my father and me. Except poor little Obedience-to-God Ashe.

The butterflies inside me were needling me now, as if they had tiny barbs along the edges of their wings. I put my hands on my groin, pushing down, trying to stop them. But they only fluttered more frantically. Inside me. I had to try and crush them. I slipped a finger within me. I jerked it, trying to smash the tiny winged things. They burst up around my finger. Wasps, not butterflies. That dangerous thrill. My whole body writhed in the moment of recognition. I jabbed my fingers in and out, feeling the buzz of their angry wings. Burning bees. Swirling sparks. Must snuff them out. Must pinch them to ashes.

But instead they became a shower of white petals, a gush of released waters. My body arched, as if I was a bird taking flight. For a moment I was lost to myself entirely.

When I came back to myself, I knew at once that I had sinned. Perhaps even more grievously than Marigold and her lover on the hillside. I could not be sorry. See how far I had travelled down the road to Hell?

I lay awake, thinking and making plans, but at last slipped into darkness. I slept more sweetly than I had for a long time.

❈

I woke some time before dawn, disturbed by the drunken song and laughter of those wending their way home. It was pitch-black in my room but I knew exactly where my dress lay, neatly folded, my shoes laid side by side as I had been taught. I went downstairs. I could hear my father, muttering at his prayers. He had not slept. Forsaken's pallet by the kitchen fire was empty. I took a knife and slipped out into the garden. A bird was singing. The air smelled of smoke. I drew my shawl up around my head, and went down the road and into the graveyard. I could see quite clearly, for the eastern sky was lit with scarlet and crimson. One star still burned.

Down I went into the dark mouth of the avenue of linden trees. Leaves shaped like hearts. Fluttering like green wings. There was the hawthorn bush, its barbed branches fluttering with ribbons and twists of torn material. All its petals had fallen. Hard nubs of forming fruit.

The sun was rising above the Giant's Hill. A beam of light shone straight down the valley and into the hidden hollow where I crouched by the ancient well. Sun-scald on the water, dark-dazzle in my eyes.

I cut thirteen long thorns. They stabbed me cruelly. Thirteen was the number of the Devil. My hand bled. I blotted away the blood with the old cloth I had brought, then tied the stained rag to the hawthorn.

"Make her die," I said in a clear, loud voice.

❈

Forsaken had lived with us since my father and I had come to Cerne Abbas. At seventeen, she was only two years older than me. We should have been friends. Yet I spurned her. Many days I pinched or slapped her. And I was pleased when my father beat her, because it meant he would not beat me.

— 124 —

I cannot truly explain why I was so unkind to her. Except that she was the only creature lower than me.

That summer, we had spent a great deal more time together than ever before. Gathering chicken-in-the-woods. Escaping my father's rage. Forsaken was much happier out on the hills. She had told me many things. How to make nettle soup. How to cast a curse.

Take an animal heart and stick it through with thorns.

Chant a word for each barb:

"Thorns in her heart go.

She who hurts me so.

Make her die."

Plucking the thorns was easy enough. Plucking a heart much harder. I had worried about this half the night. But I knew it had to be done.

With the thorns hidden in my apron pocket, I went back to the long stone archway that divided the house in which I lived from the home of Marigold Brightwell. I slipped down it, fumbling in my pocket for some smoked herring.

"Puss, puss," I called. Laid the herring on the cobblestones. Marigold's kitten came prancing and pouncing. Tabby-rippled, bright-eyed. I picked her up. Little heart beating against my palm. I took a deep breath. Wrung its neck. It only took a second. Then I cut out its wet red heart. Wrapped it and put it in my apron pocket. Laid the dead kitten on the doorstep for Marigold to find.

I was feeling that thrill again. My hands were bloody. I wiped them clean, and crept home. Forsaken was washing her hands and face in the water barrel. She went scarlet when she saw me.

"Miss Obedience . . . you're awake . . . "

"Yes. But I'll not tell Father you've been out all night, dancing and fornicating. He would be so angry. He'd beat you till your back ran with blood. He'd cast you out. You'd have to wander from town to town, begging. He'd have you branded on the cheek so all knew what a slut you were."

I could not control the foam of words on my lips. Forsaken was weeping and begging me not to betray her.

I smiled at her. "Your secret is safe with me."

Her eyes dropped to my lap. I looked down and saw my apron pocket was angrily splotched with red. I turned and hurried up to my room. I took the tiny heart and pierced it through with thorns, chanting the curse low and heartfelt.

I had to hide the mutilated heart in the Brightwells' chimney now. I did not know how I was to do that. Seven years I had lived next door to Marigold and her family, and not once had we been invited inside.

I went to my father. "I am sorry to disturb you, sir," I whispered, eyes downcast. "All night I have struggled with my conscience . . . but I feel I must confide in you. Yesterday I saw Marigold Brightwell seduce Sir Ralph Beaufort. She offered him her body if he swore to join the Brightwells in their pagan rites about the midsummer fire. He took her most eagerly, sir, and then went with her to that ungodly carving on the hill."

My father frowned at me, the quill motionless in his hand.

"They mocked you, sir. Laughed at you. Called you a blind fool."

He snapped the quill between his fingers. I saw the white dents driven down from nose to mouth. I stood back, quaking. He did not strike me, though. He snatched up Bible and whip. Strode from the room. I followed him, smiling demurely.

The sun had risen, and the day was warm and bright. My father went and roused the constables and the church wardens. He would not make the same mistake of facing the Brightwells alone again. They were reluctant, as always. But my father drove them on with the lash of his tongue and the sting of his whip.

I heard Marigold weeping even before the constables hammered on the front door.

She has found her kitten, I thought.

Something shook me. Remorse, perhaps. Or dread.

But the constables had shouldered in the door and I followed, quick on my father's heels.

Ralph held Marigold in his arms. White-faced and horror-stricken, she held the cat's limp body in her hands. Her parents were doing their best to comfort her.

Accusations flew thick and fast through the air, like enraged wasps. No-one paid me any heed. It was like I was invisible. I crept close to the hearth, where the fire was but newly kindled. I drew out the awful thing in my apron pocket and I quickly shoved it up the chimney.

"What is she doing?" Marigold asked.

I turned. My hand was red-stained. I clenched my fingers closed. Marigold stared at me. I met her eyes. "Father, something reeks most dreadfully here. And look! A red dribble. Like blood. What could it be?"

My father came, and looked up the chimney. He found the blood-stained bundle of rags. Unwrapped it and found the cat's heart pierced with thorns. He lifted his head and looked at Marigold. "Witchcraft," he breathed.

They dragged her away, the constables having to strike Ralph to the ground. I saw him wounded, blood running down his face, and went to him, wanting to help. But he shoved me away, with a look of such revulsion on his face. "It was her! She hid it there! She is the witch! Not Marigold!"

Of course no-one believed him.

Witch-prickers were sent from Essex, along with instructions from the Witch-Finder General, the one named Matthew Hopkins. I do not know what they did to Marigold. Next I saw her, her feet were bare and bloodied, her skull shorn of its bright corn-gold hair. Her face cut and bruised, her cornflower-blue eyes blackened and bruised. She wept in a pitiful, defeated way. She was ugly.

They bound her right thumb to her left toe, tied a rope to her waist, and ducked her in the mill-race. It had been raining hard since the day I had cursed her. The millpond was black and foamy. Down into the depths she went, sobbing and gasping.

"God has bade it be . . . a supernatural sign of the monstrous impiety of the witch is that the water shall refuse to receive them . . . they shall throw off the sacred water of baptism . . . " My father read from the pages the Witch-Finder General had sent him.

Her butterfly-blue skirts billowed out at first, buoying her up. "See! The proof! She is a witch!" my father cried.

The people of the village could hardly bear to watch. Some wept, but were shushed with frightened looks at my father and me.

Forsaken did not look at Marigold, but at me. Her eyes were black with horror.

Up Marigold was dragged, then flung again into the river. This time she sank. I saw her face swallowed, one hand desperately grasping at the air.

When they dragged her up again, she was boneless. Lifeless. Water poured from her dress. Pond-weeds tangled in her bedraggled hair.

They buried her at a crossroads, a rowan stake through her heart, a misshapen boulder dragged to mark the spot. Her father died a few months later, shot in the only battle between the Dorset Clubmen and the Roundheads, at a place called Hambledon Hill. Her mother was turned out of the long crooked house, and had to take to the streets, begging. I do not know what became of her.

Ralph went to fight for the king, but was killed at the Battle of Langport. Less than thirty miles from the Giant on the Hill. My father said the defeat was the king's death knell.

It is growing colder now. I feel winter in my bones. I cannot forget Marigold's face. Her blue lips, her limp hand. I cannot forget Ralph's revulsion. *She is the witch!* he had cried. And he was right.

I cannot bear it anymore. So I have come here to the old well, hidden deep in its stone-bound hollow. This is where it all began. And this is where it should end.

I have eaten a handful of foxglove berries and filled my pockets with stone. I feel sick and light-headed and dizzy. Once I have written my last words, I shall roll this paper into a scroll and tie it to the hawthorn tree. Then I shall let myself sink into the water.

This is the true confession of I, Obedience-to-God Ashe. I have communed with the Devil and done his bidding.

The Bible says thou shalt not suffer a witch to live.

So I must die.

The Cunning Woman's Daughter

July 1540

 WAS CONCEIVED UNDER THE GIANT, in the old way, with a man my mother never knew.

She wanted a child of her own, she said, after having brought so many other babies into the world.

She was a midwife, my mother, and a hedge-witch. People came to her for hurts to the body and the soul. She made wine from dandelions, and love spells from daisy-chains, and could break a bewitchment by corking up your piss and fingernail cuttings in a bottle with pins. She raised me alone, in our tiny thatched cottage by the village pond, and taught me everything she knew.

Sometimes the other children taunted me for being a bastard. I would only laugh and make the sign of the Devil's horns at them, and they would run away, screaming with excitement. I had no need of them as playmates. I had Ambrose. He was a bastard-child too. We grew up together, running wild through the meadows and the forests. His black hair was matted as a bird's nest, his clothes little more than rags, but he sang and laughed all the day long.

Like me, he had no father.

Unlike me, he had no mother either.

She poisoned herself the day he was born. They buried her at the crossroads with a stake through her heart.

Now, seventeen years later, they hung Ambrose above her grave, in an iron cage they had bolted around his body. He could not crouch or sit or lie down. He could not shake his fist at the ravens that came pecking at his eyes. He could not protect himself from the stones flung at him by the villagers. He could only wait to die.

"I have to rescue him," I told my mother, pacing up and down, my skirts swishing apart the sweet-scented rushes.

She looked up from her sewing. "You'll be in sore trouble if they catch you."

"I know. But I cannot bear it!"

"Where shall you hide him? There'll be a hue and cry for him."

"In the ruins of the abbey. There are many old nooks and crannies there, and everyone thinks it is haunted."

My mother nodded. "Be careful, my sweet girl. And take Thunderdell with you."

At the sound of his name, the huge dog lying by the door raised his head and looked at me, tail thumping.

"Of course," I said impatiently. I never went anywhere without my dog.

I packed my basket carefully. Some food and ale. A leather flask of feverfew tea. Some tools to help me crack open the iron cage. Flint and tinder. Ointment made of comfrey, yarrow, rosemary, and my namesake, sweet cicely.

"Come on, boy," I said.

Thunderdell rose ponderously to his feet. He was so big, his head was level with my waist. I caught up my staff, then eased open the door. The sun had set long ago, but light lingered in the sky. I went quietly through the garden to the edge of the pond. A stream flowed into it from the old saint's well, hidden on the other side of the wall. I crept under the willow tree and dipped my handkerchief into the water. Then I slapped it hard on a stone by the water's edge, chanting:

"I knock this rag upon this stone,
to raise a storm in the devil's name.
It shall not rest until I please again."

The willow fronds stirred, and the rushes bent. A cat's paw of wind disturbed the dark water.

With the great dog at my side, I went out on to the hills, climbing towards the giant whose vast form glimmered white in the twilight.

My mother had told me that once, a long time ago, the giant had come roaring down the valley, laying about him with his club. The men of the village had chased him up the hill, and killed him with their bows and arrows. Down he had crashed, dead. To celebrate, the men of the village had carved deeply about his shape, so that he was emblazoned upon the hillside as a warning to all those who dared threaten Cerne Abbas. For thousands of years, the giant's shape had been kept sharp and clear.

Then the monks had come and called the great white figure an abomination. They had ordered the ditches to be filled in with stones. Brambles and wild flowers and grasses grew over him. Five hundred years passed. But he was not forgotten. Every child that grew up in Cerne Abbas went searching, at one stage or another, for the giant's enormous balls. Women who wished for a baby led their lovers there by the hand, and lay on the soft turf under the stars, and felt the giant's life force surging under their buttocks. As my mother had done, seventeen years earlier, when she had wanted me.

Then, a few years ago, a young monk called William Christchurch had dug the giant out again. His tools no more than a pick and shovel and, at times, his bare hands. He had carried bucket-loads of chalk upon his shoulder, struggling up and down that steep slope. He had given the giant a most impressive bodkin.

Brother William hated the abbot, Thomas Corton. He said Father Thomas was a lecher and a heretic, who besmirched the abbey and all who lived nearby. Brother William had had been banished for his pains. He had come back, and dug out the giant, and preached against the monks in the village green, and been run out of town by the church wardens. So he had written to Sir Thomas Cromwell, the king's chief minister and chief enemy of the monasteries. Cromwell took heed of his complaints. The abbey of Cerne Abbas had been dissolved, the great buildings knocked down or burned, the few remaining monks paid off.

Father Thomas had been given a pension of a hundred pounds a year for going quietly. The prior ten pounds. The lowliest student-monk a measly forty shillings.

Brother William received nothing.

Cromwell did not like traitors, it was said.

The wind was blustering strongly now. My skirts billowed. Thunderdell's ears were blown inside out. I stood on the top of Giant Hill and held out my handkerchief. It fluttered so hard I almost lost it to the wind. I tied one knot in it, whispering "rain". At once it began to spit. I tied a second knot. "Thunder," I muttered. My dog growled deep in his throat. The sky answered. I tied a third knot. "Lightning," I cried.

The sky was split apart with the white forked tongue of the devil's fire.

I ran down the hill, in a deluge of rain. I felt that strange rush of terror and excitement I always felt when summoning a storm. Below me, Cerne Abbas lay veiled in white mists. I could scarcely see where to put my feet. To the west, the sky glared crimson through the thunderclouds.

I went the long way around, through the muddy fields. Thunderdell whined. He could not understand why we were not at home, lying by the fire.

I heard the gibbet before I saw it. Chains clanking in the wind. An eerie rhythmic creaking. I went slowly, listening with all my might, one hand on the dog's head to keep him quiet. The road ran down like a green tunnel through high banks overgrown with thorns and brambles. Above, the sycamore trees shook their hand-shaped leaves.

Then I saw the iron cage, illuminated by a flash of lighting. I saw Ambrose, each limb encased. I saw the guard huddled nearby. I pulled out my handkerchief and, with stiff fumbling fingers, unfastened one knot.

The wind howled. The rain cascaded.

I unfastened another knot.

Thunder roared. A tree branch fell.

I unfastened the third knot.

Lightning struck again and again, on every horizon. White. Dazzling. Stinking of hell.

The guard ran for home.

I struggled forward, mud sucking at my boots. Thunderdell was a picture of misery, ears and tail drooping, heavy jowls swaying. I came to the gibbet. It swung back and forth in the wind. It had been hung from a tree branch. I had to climb up the bank, tearing my clothes and skin on the briars. I caught hold of the iron bars. The chains jangled.

I tried to peer within. All I could see was a body slumped against the bars of the cage. "Ambrose?" I whispered.

Please don't let him be dead, please don't let him be dead . . .

A hoarse groan. The cropped head lifted. "Cicely?"'

I sagged with relief, and almost slipped. The iron cage swung as I grasped it to save myself. "Yes. It's me. I'm here. I'll get you out."

It was a task almost beyond my strength. I struck again and again with my hammer. Each blow clanged like the toll of a funeral bell. Ambrose tried to help me, but he was could scarcely lift a finger within the narrow confines of the cage. At last I managed to knock out enough bolts to lift the top part of the cage over his head. Then he struggled to climb out. Blinded by rain and darkness, he could not support his weight on his enfeebled arms. He tumbled down into the lane. Struck his head. I scrambled down and fell to my knees beside him, lifting his head into my lap. He stirred, moaning. Thunderdell licked him awake.

"Sweet Cicely," Ambrose said in a dazed voice. "Is it really you?"

"Yes," I whispered.

He lifted one hand and slid it behind my neck, drawing my face down so he could kiss me on the mouth. I drew away, startled and blushing.

"I can happily die now," he said.

His lips had been scorching-hot against mine. He was delirious, I realised. No wonder after so many months locked in the gaol at Dorchester. I uncorked the leather bottle of feverfew tea and held it to his lips. He gulped it down greedily.

"So thirsty," he whispered.

My heart smote me. Two days he had been in that cage, without food or water. But I had not dared come earlier. "I know," I whispered. "But you can drink more later. Now we must go."

Through the storm we crept, buffeted by the rain-laden wind. He was barefoot, and barely able to limp along. I gave him my staff to lean on, and supported him with my arm about his back.

He stank.

Somehow I got him to the little chapel built over the old saint's well. It was hidden down in a hollow beside the abbey graveyard, much overgrown with brambles and wild rose. I could hear the rushing of the water under the stones.

I could not help feeling afraid as we crept down the long avenue of linden trees.

It was down here that the murder had been done.

"Brother Jerome," I whispered, stepping in through the doorway. "Are you here?"

A dark shape moved in the shadows. My heart jerked. But it was the old monk, shuffling forward in his black robe, the hood drawn up over his head against the dank chill that struck up from the paving.

Thunderdell growled, his massive hackles rising. I put one hand on his head to calm him.

"I am here, my child," the old monk whispered. "Do you have the laddie?"

"Yes." I helped Ambrose over to the wall, where I had laid a mattress stuffed with fresh lady's bedstraw and woodruff. He slumped down upon it gratefully. I then crouched beside him, fumbling with shaking hands to light the lantern I had set beside it earlier in the day. At last a flame caught, and the tiny chapel was filled with golden light, chasing shadows into corners.

Brother Jerome watched me, his hands tucked within the sleeves of his rough black habit. He was an old man with scanty white hair, naturally tonsured, the bare top of his head age-spotted and black-scabbed. His face was all bone and hollows, the skin of his brow deeply graven with lines. He had lived in the abbey since he was a boy and knew no other life. The abbey's closure had been a calamity for him. The few pounds he had been paid was not enough to support him, and so he took refuge in the abbey ruins, eating what he could scavenge. I had discovered him after seeing him drink the milk we put out each night for the Good People. I had told no-one but Mam. If the constable knew, he'd have driven the poor old man away, for the abbey ruins belonged to a foreign fellow now, the king's favourite lutenist.

"Do not fear," he told Ambrose. "I did not see your death in the pool past Easter morn."

"I'm glad," Ambrose said with a crooked smile. "I confess, I thought the end of my days had come."

"I saw the faces of others. The traitor, the infidel, the martyr, the whore, the sodomite, they shall all die as the lecher died."

The poor old thing was half-cracked, I thought, and no wonder.

I went and knelt by the well, filling my leather bucket with water, and then my drinking flask. The water of the well had healing magic, my mother had taught me. For a moment I knelt there, looking down into the glimmering water. Nearby lay the old wishing-stone, carved with the shape of a wheel. I laid my hand on it. "Let me keep him safe," I whispered. Then, with my body growing warm, I whispered, "let us be together."

Ambrose's ragged clothes were caked with filth. I drew them off and threw them in a corner. His naked body was slender and well-muscled, though showing the effects of too little food in recent weeks. I rubbed him vigorously with a soapy cloth, and he curled away from me, covering himself with his hands. "Cicely, you should not," he whispered.

"I must get you clean," I said.

"I'll do it. Don't watch."

So I turned and faced the wall, my face hot, listening as he feebly washed himself with water from the bucket. The old monk had sat down on an old stool, and was clinking prayers with his wooden rosary. Thunderdell had flopped down on the ground, his head resting on his paws. I heard Ambrose sigh, and then the sound of him pulling on the old woollen robe I had stolen from a washing-line earlier that evening.

I turned and kneeled beside him, drawing out the ointment and a cloth.

He reached out and cupped my face with one hand. "Cicely," he whispered. "You should not have come. They will find me, and punish you."

"No, they won't," I said stoutly. "I'll hide you so well they'll never find you."

He sighed, and moved his head restlessly. I could see the sheen of sweat on his skin, despite the chill of the old damp stones. I gave him the bread and cheese, but he could not eat. He was shivering. I gave him the half-empty flask of feverfew tea, and he managed to gulp a few mouthfuls while I tended his cuts and bruises.

"Cicely . . . they think I killed him. They think I killed my father. But I didn't. I swear I didn't."

"I know that," I said scornfully. "Why would you bother?"

"They'll find me," he whispered. "There's no escape. Wherever I run, they'll hunt me down."

I sat back on my heels. "We need to clear your name. We need to prove you are innocent."

He laughed, high and wild. "You think I did not try?"

I caught hold of Ambrose's restless hand. "We shall have to find the true murderer. Then you'll be safe."

"I will never be safe," he whispered. "They want me dead."

❋

When I left the chapel, it was an hour short of midnight.

I felt so weary I could barely drag my feet along, but my work for the night was not yet done. I had tied Ambrose's stinking clothes to my staff, and now I trudged along, the bundle over my shoulder, heading away from the village. Thunderdell loped along at my side, whining every now and again in complaint. The rain still fell in drifting sheets, and I was wet through and shivering with cold before I reached the river. I flung the clothes into the water, letting them be washed away downstream. I hoped the constable would think that Ambrose had run to the river, rather than to the ruined abbey.

I then hurried home. My mother was awake. The fire danced merrily, the kettle was boiling, and the wooden tub stood ready, rosemary twigs floating on the surface of the steaming water. She looked up as I came in and raised her eyebrows, and I smiled at her.

Quickly she helped me strip off and climb into the bath, and then she went to rinse out my mud-streaked clothes in the wash-tub outside the back door. Then she came and washed my hair for me. When I was clean and warm again, I climbed out, dressed in a clean chemise and combed my wet hair. My mother made me some hot lemon balm tea, and I drank it gratefully as she wrung out my dress and hung it to dry.

We were both safe in bed before the church bells finished ringing out the midnight hour.

I did not sleep well that night. The rain lashed against the thatch, for I had not reknotted my handkerchief. I wanted the storm to wash away our footsteps. I was most anxious about the hue-and-cry that would inevitably arise once it was realised Ambrose had escaped from the gibbet.

Had it been clever to hide him in the very place in which his father had been murdered? Or stupid?

I could not tell.

It was, however, the only abbey building left with a roof. All the others had been torn down by the king's men. And I had known the

— 140 —

storm would be wild. I had wanted Ambrose to sleep warm and dry, out of the rain.

One thing comforted me. Ambrose had shown no sign of a guilty conscience when he had seen the shadowy pool where his father had been found lying three months earlier, on Easter morning, his head stoved in with a boulder.

Surely he could not be the only suspect?

Surely many people had wanted Thomas Corton, the former abbot, dead.

❋

The whole village knew that the abbot was Ambrose's father.

Certainly, Ambrose looked like him, with his thick dark hair, bright blue eyes, and long straight nose. Yet Father Thomas had never acknowledged Ambrose, even though he had been generous with his other by-blows. Perhaps Ambrose's mother had angered him by resisting. Perhaps the abbot had been shocked by the scandal she caused, killing herself on the day her baby was born.

Yet the abbot had made sure that Ambrose was given work in the abbey. Turning the spits in the kitchen, feeding the pigs, hoeing the herb garden. Perhaps he had cared, a little.

Ambrose had never been either dutiful or grateful. He would wait until the monk in charge had turned his back, then slip away. I'd hear him whistle like a robin and I'd untie my apron and run out the door to meet him. We'd come home in the dusk, flushed and grubby, with our sacks full of burdock leaves and sloes and sweet chestnuts, and anything else we could find that would please my mother. The three of us would sit by the fire, eating our pottage, telling stories, singing rounds. Ambrose would linger as long as he could. Eventually, though, he had to return to the abbey. Next time I saw him there would be new bruises on his face but Ambrose would be as light-hearted and merry as ever.

I could not believe that he had killed his father.

Restless, I rose at last in the dawn. My mother smiled at me, and set me to grinding herbs, knowing I needed some kind of exertion to exhaust the nervous energy thrumming through my body. I was hard at work when I heard shouting. I lifted my head, my heart speeding up. So Ambrose's escape had been discovered.

I wondered where Brother Jerome had taken him. Last night the monk had seemed half-crazy. Perhaps I should not have trusted him. I should have hidden Ambrose myself.

"Don't be afraid," my mother said. "Now he is free, Ambrose will take great care not to be caught again. No-one knows the hidden places of the abbey as well as he does."

"But he was sick . . . feverish . . . "

My mother frowned. "Did he eat anything?"

I shook my head.

"Was he delirious?"

I remembered how he had kissed me, then said that now he could die happy. Blood rushed up my face. "I . . . I think so."

"You do not know? Was he hot? Confused?"

"Yes."

"A rash of red spots?"

I remembered his smooth naked body, turning away from me. My whole body was afire, as if it was me who had the fever. "No."

"That's good. We must hope it is not gaol fever."

"I should go to him." I paced back and forth, twisting my hands together. "Brother Jerome is not fit to care for him. I should be there, looking after him."

"Peace, my child." My mother swung the kettle over the fire. "Come, sit down, busy yourself with some work." She put fresh lemon balm leaves in a pot, and shook in a measure of dried chamomile flowers. A calming tea for over-strained nerves.

She lifted down three wooden cups from their hooks.

"For the constable?" I asked, my voice not quite steady.

"He will be here soon."

I nodded in understanding. I knew that many people found it uncanny, the way my mother always seemed to know what would happen, but, really, it was not so hard.

The sound of shouting came closer. I began to feel sick.

Then Thunderdell leapt up, growling deep in his throat. My mother poured the boiling water into the kettle. "Here he is, perfect timing. Show him in, Cicely."

I went to the door and opened it, just as the constable raised his hand to rap smartly upon it. Caught by surprise, he almost struck me in the face. Flushing red, he dropped his hand.

"Good morning, Mr Ward," I said, bobbing a curtsey and standing back. He had to duck his head low to enter. Thunderdell began to bark, and I put my hand on his head.

"Tie up your dog," the constable said sharply.

I opened my mouth to protest, but my mother said, "Of course. Come, sit down. May I offer you a mug of lemon balm tea? It's uncommonly chilly today."

"No, thank you," he answered curtly, and did not sit down at the stool she offered. This was a bad sign, I thought. I glanced anxiously at my mother, but she smiled at me and bade me tie up Thunderdell.

I did as I was told, then sat on a stool beside the dog, my arm about his neck, drawing courage from his great bulk.

"How can I help you, Mr Ward?" my mother asked, pouring a cup of tea and passing it to me. "Is your back acting up again? Would you like some more of my calendula ointment? Or is it baby Grace who needs me? She must be teething by now."

"No, no," he said. "At least, yes, she is teething, and my poor Marjory is beside herself trying to get her to sleep. But that's not why I'm here."

"No? Then why are you here?" she asked, pouring herself a cup. The sweet scent of the steam swirled about the room. I knew it would be working on the constable without him tasting a sip.

"Young Ambrose has been freed from the gibbet," Mr Ward answered. I was conscious of his eyes steady on my face.

I bent to stoke up the fire, hoping the sudden blaze of warmth from the furze would explain the colour in my cheeks. I did not know how to act. Too much disinterest and he would instantly be suspicious. Everyone in the village knew what great friends Ambrose and I had been, before he had run away to become a travelling minstrel. But too warm an interest would surely arouse his suspicion too.

"Freed? From the gibbet?" my mother asked, pausing with her cup half-raised to her mouth. "But who would do such a thing?"

"That is my question also," he answered, still watching me.

"Well, for my part, I have to say that I'm pleased. It's a cruel punishment, caging up a young man like that till he slowly starves to death." My mother spoke with real emotion in her voice. The constable looked at her with narrowed eyes.

I was relieved to be free of his gaze.

"You felt pity for the lad?"

"But of course. Didn't we all?"

"He was found guilty of murdering his father. The judges could have been much harsher." As he spoke, the constable's eyes roamed the room.

There was little for him to see.

A small dark room, lit by the sullenly glowing fire in the centre of the room. An earthen floor softened with fresh-cut rushes. Rafters hung with dried herbs and smoked meats and skeins of wool. A rickety table where my mother worked. Pantry shelves lined with small sacks and glass bottles and ceramic jars. The constable climbed a few rungs of the ladder and looked up at our sleeping shelf. Our beds were neat, the eiderdowns smoothed over the mattresses, our clothes hanging from hooks.

There was nowhere for anyone to hide.

He stepped down into the room, frowning in thought.

"But why would Ambrose kill his father?" I asked, unable to keep quiet a moment longer.

"Revenge," the constable said, after a moment. "For his mother's death, and for failing to support him. When we found Ambrose, he was begging for a crust."

"It was Lent," I said hotly. "A hard time for any street entertainer."

He stared at me. "So how do you know this? You saw him? You spoke to him?"

"It's common sense," I said.

A moment later, I regretted my hasty words. His heavy eyebrows beetled.

"We did not see Ambrose," my mother said quickly. "We only heard that he had returned when you arrested him."

"He was on his way to see us," I added. Somehow it was important that everyone understood that.

The constable looked from one face to another.

"Mr Ward, you know that I do not lie," my mother said. "I am willing to swear on the Bible that I have not seen Ambrose since the day he ran away from the abbey. That's more than a year ago."

He nodded, and stroked his beard. Suddenly he turned to me. "And what of you, Cicely? Have you seen him?"

Slowly I raised my eyes to his. "Yes, sir. I have."

He nodded his head sharply, a gleam of satisfaction in his eyes. "Is that so? Where did you see him?"

"I went to the gaol in Dorchester, as soon as I heard he had been arrested," I admitted. "The gaolers would not let me see him, but they let me give him some food. Or at least, they let me give it to *them*. I do not know if he ever got it. Then I went back, to see the assizes. I was there when the judges convicted him."

"I did not see you," he said slowly.

"I sat up the back, and then . . . when I heard what they meant to do . . . I was so upset I ran out." I met his sharp gaze. "I could not bear it," I said simply.

He was about to ask another question, when I interrupted him. "Please, sir, what made you think it was Ambrose who murdered the abbot? Surely there were other people who wanted him dead? What about the monk that accused him? William Christchurch?"

"Brother William is . . . was a holy brother," the constable said reprovingly. "And no-one saw him on the day. While that young man is a rogue and a vagabond, and was seen skulking about the old well on the morning of the murder."

"He's not a vagabond," I protested hotly. "He's a travelling minstrel."

"Without a license," the constable retorted. "That makes him a sturdy beggar and a vagabond in the eyes of the law."

"And he wasn't skulking about. He was on his way to see me. He said so in his trial. It was just bad luck that he should be passing by . . . "

" . . . at the very moment that his father was murdered only a few hundred feet away?" the constable said dryly. "Very bad luck indeed. No, I'm sorry, my dear. I'm afraid Ambrose is the culprit."

I was ready to argue further, but my mother put down her cup with a snap. "Mr Ward, I don't know what more we can tell you. Neither Cicely or myself have left the house today. We both will swear to the truth of that on the Bible if you should so choose."

"Is that true?" he asked me, eyeing me closely.

"Yes, it's true," I said indignantly, the hot blood still coursing through my body. "We've been here together all morning." I waved at the bread kneaded and set in pans to rise, and the bowls of ground herbs. He stared at me and I met his gaze defiantly. "Check my boots if you doubt me," I said. "They'll be quite dry."

He went across to where my battered boots were turned upside down on rods to dry, and squatted to examine them thoughtfully. After half the night roasting by the fire, they were indeed bone-dry.

He rose to his feet, frowning and looking displeased. "I was sure it must've been you," he said, as if to himself.

"Just as you were sure that Ambrose was a murderer," I said scornfully.

His face reddened. "We will catch him," he said, "and when we do, we'll hang him from the nearest tree."

I had to put out a hand and grip the table to steady myself.

Just then, a deep bloodcurdling howl rose in the distance, and then another. Thunderdell leapt to his feet, barking furiously.

"What . . . what is that?" I stammered.

"It's Sir Philip's hunting dogs. They can track anything, I've been told, in any weather. That baying means they have caught young Ambrose's scent. They'll lead us straight to him." Smiling, he caught up his hat and cloak and headed towards the door. He turned on the threshold. "When we have him, we'll question him. See who broke him out of the cage. And if we find it was you who let him loose, Mistress Brightell, or you, Cicely . . . well, then you shall hang with him."

❊

As soon as he was gone, I changed into my boots. "What are you going to do?" my mother asked.

"I have to find the true murderer," I said. "I am going to find that crazy monk that denounced the abbey, and I am going to ask him to tell me the truth."

My mother sighed. "I suppose you want me to cast a spell of truthfulness on him?"

"Can you do it?"

"It'd be easier if I had a lock of his hair or some fingernail clippings, or even dirt from his footsteps. But I will do my best."

My mother went to the pantry and carefully cut a small square of parchment from her precious hoard. She knelt by the fire and carefully drew out a burning furze twig, blowing on it till the flame was snuffed out. Then, with the blackened stick, she swiftly drew a man's face on the parchment. A thin austere face within a dark hood. Eyes that seemed to burn with fervour. We had all seen William Christchurch many times in the years when he had lived at the abbey, and then during his long battle to denounce the abbot. Still I marvelled at my mother's skill in capturing his likeness with just a few strokes. She held the parchment above the flames. It caught fire.

"Flames so red, let the truth be said," she chanted. "Flames so bright, let what's hidden come to light."

The parchment flared up, then crumbled to dust. My mother threw a handful of salt into the flames, crying, "Let it be so!"

She sank back on to her heels. "He will speak truth to you," she said wearily. "If he is the murderer, he will confess to you."

I trudged wearily into Dorchester, Thunderdell panting along at my side. It had been a long, damp walk, though we had been lucky enough to hitch a ride with a farmer and his wife part of the way. They had been most curious about my dog, and wondered whether I brought him to town for the bull-baiting later that day.

"No," I said shortly. I did not tell them that Ambrose and I had rescued Thunderdell from such a hideous fate, when he was little more than a puppy.

It was market-day, and the streets bustled with people. I saw a man leading a bear on a chain, and another man with his ear nailed to the pillory. Women laid out their homespun cloth and their cheeses in the marketplace, and I laid out my mother's herbal potions alongside them. All the talk was of the king and his new wife. He had set her aside, after only six months of being wed. He planned to marry another, it was whispered. A young girl, not yet seventeen years old. The whore Anne Boleyn's own cousin.

I could not believe what I heard. Already the king had had four wives. One divorced. One beheaded. One dead in childbirth. And now the fourth, to be put aside like an unwanted toy.

Thomas Cromwell, the king's thug, was blamed for arranging the marriage. He had been arrested and thrown in the Tower. Surely the king will pardon him, some said. No, he'll lose his head, for sure, others declared. And so he should, the heretic, a few whispered, looking about them.

I had come to the marketplace hoping to gather news of William Christchurch, whom I had heard had come to Dorchester to work as a scribe. But it was hard to redirect the conversation the way I wanted, with everyone all of a–flutter about the news from London. At last someone told me I could find him in the churchyard with the other scribes, willing to write me a letter for a ha'penny. I recognised him at once. The bony face and thin lips, just as my mother had drawn him. I went and sat down before him.

"What can I write for you, miss?" he asked, not even looking up at me. "A love letter to your sweetheart, I suppose." His voice was full of contempt.

At once my temper rose. "No. Write me a confession."

He looked up at me in surprise. "A confession?"

"Yes. Write the truth. You are the one who killed Father Thomas, not Ambrose. You are the one who should be hanged in a gibbet, not him!"

William laid down his quill. "I did not kill Thomas Corton. I wish that I had. Many a time I've imagined it. He was the Devil Incarnate. But I dared not."

There was such a ring of truth in his voice I was dumbfounded.

"I know who you are," he said, after a moment. "You are the cunning woman's daughter. And the boy's sweetheart. I'm sorry. I know they charged him with the abbot's murder. Indeed, it must be awful for him to know that he sprang from such filthy loins. I do not blame him for killing his father."

"Ambrose did not kill the abbot," I said in a shaking voice.

"Neither did I," the scribe answered. "I swear to you on the Holy Bible, I had nothing to do with that foul lecher's death. Did he not die early in the morning on Easter Sunday? I was here at the church all night, celebrating the Easter Vigil. A hundred people would have seen me."

I dropped my head into my hands. "Then who? Who?"

"I was not the only one who hated him," William said after a long moment. "He did great harm. But . . . one thing that puzzled me when I heard he had been murdered. Why wait so long to kill him? The abbey was dissolved more than a year ago. Thomas Corton had been lording it over the village all that time. Why kill him on Easter Friday? And why at the saint's well? If you can answer those questions, then you will know your killer."

The rain was still pelting down on Cerne Abbas when I returned that evening. The river was rising, and the road was flooded. I had to wade through water up to my knees. Children were out, racing little boats made of leaves and twigs down the flow. Men were building walls from sandbags to keep the water from rushing through their cottages.

"It must be time to knot your handkerchief," my mother said as I stood on the doorstep, dripping water everywhere.

I looked at her with painful anxiety. She smiled and shook her head. "It seems Sir Philip's hunting dogs cannot track in weather like this. All the scent has been washed away."

I heaved a great sigh, and took the sodden handkerchief out of my pocket, tying it in three thick knots. As I sat down on my stool and bent to unlace my boots, I could hear the rain begin to ease.

Mam brought me a steaming cup of lemon balm tea. "So William Christchurch was not the murderer?"

I shook my head.

"I did not think so. What shall you do now?"

"I don't know. But I'm not giving up."

"The way forward will become clear to you," Mam said in her serene way, and went back to stirring the pottage.

That night I put out a dish of milk for the Good People as usual, and then doused the lantern and banked up the fire with turf as if getting ready for bed. But then I sat on a stool by the back door, wrapped in my cloak, waiting.

It was close on midnight when Thunderdell lifted his head and growled. I heard the furtive sound of footsteps, and then the scrape as the bowl was lifted. I eased open the door.

"Brother Jerome," I whispered. "Is that you?"

He gave a startled cry, and I calmed him with one hand on his arm. It was shockingly thin under the weight of his woollen sleeve. "I have some food here," I whispered, showing him my basket. "Take me to Ambrose and I will give it to you."

The abbey was an eerie place at night, the broken walls and great arched windows silhouetted against the sky. I had been within its cloisters many times, for my mother had tended the sick and elderly that had sought shelter within its walls. In its final years, there had been little more than a dozen monks at the abbey, and so there had been no need for an infirmarian.

I did not know the rest of the monastery well, though, for my mother's business had been confined to the kitchen, the herb garden and the sickroom. Brother Jerome, however, had lived there most of his life. He led me swiftly and without hesitation through the ruins. Concealed beneath a broken wall was a narrow crevice.

"We need to creep through there?" I stared at it in disfavour.

He nodded.

"Thunderdell will never fit." I turned to my dog and bade him lie down and stay. "On guard, boy," I ordered. Unhappily the great dog lay down, his eyes fixed on my face. "Good boy. Stay."

Brother Jerome squeezed through the crack. I followed him, scraping one shoulder on the rock. It was a tight fit, even though I was only thin. I found myself standing on the top step of a steep flight of stairs that led down into darkness. I fumbled to light my lantern, holding it within the curve of my cloak to keep away the cold draughts that blew from below. I followed him down the steps, then through one vaulted cellar after another. Once, I imagined, the monks had kept their barrels of wine down here. Now it all was bare and empty and cobwebbed, the ground damp and slippery underfoot.

A tunnel led us to a series of smaller cellars, without the grand vaulting. I thought we might be under what had once been the kitchen. Here there were broken barrels, tumbled boxes, a few empty sacks. Brother Jerome rolled away an old barrel and revealed a tiny wooden door. He unlocked it, and dragged it open. Its rusty hinges squealed.

I lifted high my lantern. Hidden beyond was another dank cellar, its walls green with slime. It was scantily furnished with a rickety old bed frame, piled high with wild grasses and lady's bedstraw and old sacks. That must be where the old monk slept.

Relics from the abbey had been arranged in a makeshift altar against one wall. Broken gargoyles, shards of stained glass, a tarnished abbot's crook, fragments of old bone, part of a stone cross. Otherwise there was only a stool, a broken jug, and a battered pewter plate engraved with the abbey's arms, a cross engrailed between four lilies.

Ambrose lay on his mattress. His clothes and blankets were all tangled, his black curls lank with sweat. He moaned and twitched and occasionally cried out. I ran and fell to my knees beside him.

"He's burning up!" Hurriedly I drew out a flask of feverfew tea, and tried to help him drink. Ambrose shook his head wildly, though, and knocked the flask out of my hand. He was muttering incoherently.

I looked up at Brother Jerome. "It's so cold and damp in here. Was there nowhere else to take him?"

The old monk had crouched on the floor beside me, rummaging through the basket, cramming food into his mouth. He looked up at my words. "Not if you don't want him to be found. This cellar was always kept hidden. It's where the abbot used to keep his concubine. No-one knows about this place but me and her and him, and he's dead, and she won't tell a soul, in fear of being whipped through the town in her nightgown again."

I looked around at the puddled floor, the green-slimed wall. "The abbot kept someone here? Locked in?"

"Joan Postell, her name was. An orphan girl, thrown on the parish's charity. He had her brought here when she was just a lass, and kept her for his pleasure."

I hugged myself close. It was bitterly cold down here, even in midsummer. I could imagine how freezing it must have been in winter.

"How . . . how long was she kept here?"

"Must have been close on seven years," Brother Jerome answered.

I stared at him in horror. "But . . . did no-one help her . . . rescue her . . . "

"Brother William tried, once he knew about her. But the abbot had him thrown out for his pains."

"But . . . what about you? Could you not have freed her?"

"She used to beg me to let her go, on her knees, but I didn't dare. The abbot did not like his will to be crossed. And where could I have gone, if he had thrown me out? Look what happened to Brother William."

I could not believe what I was hearing. I sank down to my knees beside Ambrose, my arms wrapped tight around me. I had thought the accusations brought against the abbot by William Christchurch must have been exaggerated. But it seemed they had been all too true.

Ambrose cried out. He was shivering. I laid my hand against his damp forehead and bit my lip. "He cannot stay here. He'll die!"

"He will not die. I did not see his face. Many others will die, but not him."

I pressed my fingers to my temples. I was so tired, nothing seemed to make sense. "I need to go home. I'll make Ambrose some more medicine. Keep him as warm as you can, and give him the feverfew tea to drink every few hours. Try and get him to eat some of that pottage. Don't you eat it all!"

The monk did not respond, his hands folded into his sleeves, his head bent.

"Come and fetch me if you need me," I said.

I trudged back through the cellars, my thoughts in turmoil. I could not help thinking of the young woman kept here against her will for so many years. What kind of monster had the abbot been? And how could Brother Jerome not have set her free? He must have been very frightened of Thomas Corton, I thought.

As I climbed up the steps, I could hear Thunderdell whining above me. As soon as I had crept out of the little hole, he flung himself upon me, his tail wagging. I hugged him, and petted him, and told him what a good boy he was. The warmth of his body was welcome after the dankness of the underground cell.

We slipped through the graveyard and down to the chapel. What had the abbot been doing here, on Easter morning? I wondered. Why had he not been at the church, enduring the long Easter vigil like the rest of us?

My mother believed in old gods and goddesses that had long been forgotten, but she felt no unease in going to church each week. "The gods can be praised anywhere there is beauty," she told me. "Whether we are walking in the woods, or sitting by the silver well, or watching the glory of the sunset, or singing as we work, it doesn't matter. As long as you are filled with joy and reverence, you are thanking the gods."

"Then why must we go to church? Can't we just walk in the woods or sing in the garden?"

"It does us no harm to join our friends each week, and sit in silence a while, thinking and praying."

"If only we could sit in silence! But that old priest does nothing but talk the whole time."

She laughed. "Oh, I know. But it does you no harm to learn to listen and hold your peace. You are always quick to argue and put forward your own view, Cicely. I love that you are so sharp-witted and bold. But it is not always wise. Spending a few hours listening in peace and patience will help you bridle your tongue."

"Then why can't the priest bridle his? He is the one trying to force us to believe what he believes."

"He has not lived enough lives to be wise," my mother said serenely. "He will learn in time."

So we went to church, and sat quietly, hands folded, and said Amen when we should. But I preferred to praise the gods and goddesses in the woods and the meadows, and by singing and laughing and working with a good will.

How had the abbot preferred to worship? I wondered. Had it been hard for him to lose his great church with its glorious rose windows? Did he find it hard to sit still and listen to the parish priest drone on, when once he had been called Father and had led the prayers himself?

Was that why he did not come to church that day? Had he preferred to come to this tiny chapel and worship on his own?

I had paused in the shadow of the chapel for some time, thinking these thoughts, enjoying the sweet scent of the linden blossoms on the breeze. The moon had come out, and silvered the softly running water. Thunderdell sat quietly beside me, leaning his weight against my leg. Then he lifted his head and growled softly. I put my hand on his head, and he quietened, though his body quivered with tension. I gazed out into the night anxiously.

A dark hulking shape stood half-concealed in the shadows under the trees. If it had not been for the bright moonlight, I would not have seen it.

Someone was watching our house.

But who?

Or what?

Silently I chanted, *Blind from sight, try as they might. Blind from sight, try as they might.*

Slowly a cloud drifted across the moon. Imagining myself and my dog wrapped in a protective cloak of darkness, I crept as quietly as I could through the little back gate and into our garden. By the time the moon shone once more, I was safe inside with Thunderdell, the door barred behind us.

But it was a long time before I slept.

✳

"Mam, did you know a girl was kept captive in the abbey? Locked in a cellar?" I asked the next morning, perched on a stool in my nightgown, eating my porridge.

My mother's hands stilled. "I know that such an accusation was made. And I know the king's commissioners whipped a woman from the premises when they first came down to investigate, close on two years ago now. It was said she was the abbot's whore. I tended her afterwards, and wondered about her then. She had been badly mistreated. I asked her who had done such things to her, but she shook her head and would not speak."

"Do you know what happened to her?"

My mother nodded. "Yes, indeed. I delivered a baby for her just a few weeks ago. She is living just a mile or so north of here, in Up Cerne. Married to the village baker, I believe. She was still strangely silent, I thought. But she seemed very glad of her new daughter."

I ate a few mouthfuls thoughtfully.

"You think she may be the one who killed the abbot?" my mother asked, laying down her knife.

"If she had been kept locked up in a cell for years, beaten and raped and whipped through the town as a whore, do you not think she might have cause?" I cried.

My mother came and sat down on her stool, her hands folded in her lap, regarding me thoughtfully. I looked back at her, chin tilted defiantly.

"The wheel turns," my mother said slowly. "We are born, we die, we are reborn. To kill another human is to break this natural turning. The murdered soul may not be able to find its way forward. It may wander this earth, its pathway lost to it."

"You mean . . . it may become a ghost?" I thought of the dark shape I had seen lurking in the shadows last night. Goosebumps shivered my skin.

My mother nodded. "Death out of time can tie the murdered soul to that of the murderer, or to the place where it happened. If you have eyes to see it."

"Did you see . . . " I did not know how to express my thoughts.

My mother nodded. "There was a great shadow in her, Cicely. I thought it was fear, or perhaps grief. But it may have been guilt. It may have been a haunt. But if she was the one . . . well, she must have been very close to giving birth. And she is not strong. Her bones are weak and crooked, unlike anything I have seen before. I do not think she would have had the strength to bash in a man's head with a stone."

"I must see her for myself," I said at last. "I must be sure."

My mother nodded and rose to her feet. "I will give you a gift to take to her. A tincture of blessed thistle and goat's rue, to enrich her milk. And, Cicely . . . "

"Yes?"

"Be careful. Wounded beasts will lash out if they feel threatened."

❈

It was a pleasant and easy walk to Up Cerne along the country lanes. Thunderdell should have been trotting along, sniffing at the verges, lifting his leg at every tree. Instead he turned often, growling. I turned too, but saw no-one. But the back of my neck prickled, and I quickened my pace.

Up Cerne was a tiny hamlet built about a stone church in a green hollow surrounded by rolling chalk downs. I only had to follow my nose to find the baker's home. He frowned at the sight of me, but when I explained who I was he reluctantly showed me into the inner room. It was dark and stuffy in there. All the windows were shuttered, and no lamp or candle had been lit.

"Joan. A visitor for you." His voice was all tenderness.

"Who is it?" a frightened voice lisped.

"The cunning-woman's daughter. She has brought you a gift." He shot me a suspicious look, and went back to his ovens.

It took my eyes some time to adjust from the brightness of the day.

Joan sat in a rocking chair, wrapped in a heavy shawl. Her beauty was strange, almost elfin. She was delicate as a sickly child, with wrists like twigs. Her hair was pale golden but very thin. Her eyes were pale blue, but set a little too far apart under a bulbous forehead and fringed by eyelashes so pale they were invisible. Her baby was only tiny, tightly swaddled, and yet it seemed Joan hardly had the strength to hold her.

I held out the tincture for her, but she only stared at me with wide, anxious eyes. "Why are you here, witch-girl?" she asked.

She had only a few teeth left in her mouth, like an ancient crone. Yet she was scarcely older than me. As she raised one hand to hide her mouth, I saw her fingers were all bent and crooked. As if they had been broken and not set properly.

I did not know how to question her. In the end, I said simply, "You were at the abbey?"

She looked stricken. Her eyes fell, and she clutched the child closer.

"Yes?" I asked.

She nodded, not meeting my eyes.

"You must have been glad to get away? Did . . . did you hate him? The abbot?"

"Yes. I hated him with all my heart. I was glad when he died. I wanted to dance on his grave, but Owen said I must not."

"Owen is your husband?"

She nodded again.

I did not think Joan had the strength to raise a rock and bring it down on to the abbot's head. Unless he had been on his knees praying. Unless she had been maddened with hate.

Her husband, though, he was a burly young man. He could have killed the abbot.

"Did you sit the Easter Vigil?" I asked. "You and your husband?"

She raised her eyes to mine for the first time since we had met. "Yes," she said, in that hissing lisp that was both strangely childish and horribly old. "For God is good and forgives me my sins. That is why Jesus died on the cross. So I might be clean again."

"You went to the church here? In Up Cerne?"

She gazed at me, puzzled. "Yes. Of course. I cannot walk far, you see." And she laid the sleeping child down in the cradle beside her, then lifted her skirts so I could see her legs.

Bent, twisted, bowed like a Gothic arch.

I saw only a glimpse before Joan lowered her skirts. "So, you see, I could not have killed the abbot. Much as I wanted to. And I know you think Owen might have done it, for love of me. And he would've, I know. But we did not. We were here, in the church, till dawn."

✽

I felt sick and shaken as I walked home. What had caused her limbs to be so misshapen? Lack of food, lack of sunlight, lack of room to run and dance and scramble? Or had she been deliberately broken?

I was frightened. The abbot seemed to stride next to me, his shadow encroaching on mine. I thought about what my mother had said. How a murdered soul could tie itself to a person or a place. The abbot did not seem like a man who would surrender his essence to the air. He would hold on grimly. Was he holding on to me?

Thunderdell was growling again. I looked over my shoulder. A dark shape. Watching from the woods. My steps quickened till I was almost running. The figure began to hurry too. A slant of sunshine fell upon him.

It was Mr Ward. The constable.

My first reaction was limb-weakening relief. Then I felt a flash of rage. I left the road and began to wander through fields and forests, up hills and down dales, leading the constable a merry dance. As I walked, Thunderdell at my heels, I thought.

I knew Ambrose was innocent. Knew it as my mother knew where to dig for water. But William Christchurch had not been the murderer, and neither had Joan Baker or her husband. So who was it? Who had killed the abbot?

I picked and gathered the hedgerow harvest as I walked, filling my basket with sweet-scented herbs, blackberries and early hazelnuts. When my basket was brimming, I hid in the bracken till Mr Ward had hurried out of sight, and then I went to visit Ambrose. He was no better; indeed, he seemed worse. His eyes were sunken, and he was thinner than ever, as if the fever was burning away his flesh.

Tears welled up in my eyes. I could not bear to see Ambrose so ill. I had a flask of cool spring water with me. I lifted him and brought the flask to his lips. He gulped thirstily, and I saw that his lips were parched. He drank it all, then I laid him down again. He smiled at me, and croaked my name. I tucked him in tenderly. "You must stay warm," I whispered. "Else you'll not get better. I am hunting for the true murderer, Ambrose. I'll find him any day now. Then your name will be cleared and you'll be set free."

I smoothed back his sweat-tangled hair with one hand, then looked about me for some more water so I could dampen a cloth and lay it on his forehead. But the jug was empty. I glanced up at Brother Jerome, who stood staring down at me, his face in shadow within the curve of his hood. "You must make sure he has enough water to drink, Brother Jerome. Bring him water from the old saint's well, it will help him heal. I will come back tonight, with some powdered willow bark. I must get his fever down!"

The monk did not answer me. I sighed in exasperation and got to my feet.

"I will see you tonight," I promised Ambrose and then picked up my basket and staff, and hurried away. I was still feeling ill-at-ease and jittery. Every looming shadow seemed malevolent. I looked back over my shoulder and saw the silhouette of Brother Jerome crouched in the low doorway. I raised a hand in farewell, but he did not respond.

Thunderdell was waiting for me out in the sunny garth, his tail wagging so hard his whole body twisted from side to side. I wandered about the abbey, picking useful weeds, in case anyone was watching, then slowly made my way home, my thoughts preoccupied.

As I walked past the old gatehouse, I saw the king's lutenist ride up the street, dressed in a crimson velvet doublet, his sleeves puffed, slashed, and folded back to show the golden embroidered sleeve within. His wife rode with him, in a rose–coloured gown with blue sleeves. Despite their finery, both were grim-faced and the lady's eyes were red and swollen with weeping. I gazed after them, wondering what could be wrong.

Sir Philip von Wilder, the lutenist's name was. He came from the Low Countries, and had risen high in the king's esteem. He had been given the abbey lands, at a peppercorn rent. When? I wondered.

If I remembered rightly, he and his retinue had arrived around Easter. He had hired carpenters, stone masons, bricklayers. They had been busy ever since, building him a fine manor house out of the remnants of the south gatehouse.

What if the king's lutenist had come by the abbey lands illegally? What if the abbot had threatened him? Asked for more money for his silence? What if the lutenist and his wife were racked with guilt, knowing a young man was to die for a crime they had committed?

I was clutching at straws, I knew. Yet I had nothing else. Ambrose was ill. He might die. I needed to bring him home.

I followed the lutenist and his wife up the road to the old gatehouse. I watched them dismount, and give their horses to grooms, and sweep inside, arm-in-arm. I stood outside, sorting my herbs into pretty bunches, ready to offer an excuse for my intrusion. Then I timidly knocked on the door.

It was flung open by a fat, cheerful woman in an apron. "Hallelujah! At last!" she cried. "He's been at his wit's end. Come in, come in. They're waiting for you in the drawing-room." She hustled me down the corridor and into a big room hung with tapestries. Light streamed in through huge mullioned windows. "She's here!"

"Excellent!" Sir Philip cried in a thick foreign accent. "We have not much time. Come, come. What shall you sing for us?"

"Sing?" I said stupidly.

"Yes, sing! Is that not why you are here? What can you sing?"

I looked from one face to another, all tense with anticipation, then took a deep breath and began to sing. I had been born singing, my mother always said.

When I had finished, Sir Philip sighed and clasped his hands together. "She sings like the angel! The king shall adore her."

"I'm sorry," I said. "I don't quite know what you mean . . . the king?"

"Yes, the king. He marries this week, quite in secret, you understand. To the little Howard girl."

"So sad," his wife murmured. "Surely it is not a good omen?"

"To marry the same day his chief minister is executed? I would say he does it on purpose. The death bells shall ring and then the wedding bells."

"I cannot quite believe it," his wife said, shaking her head. "Thomas Cromwell, his right-hand man, to lose his head. So suddenly. Who can feel safe?"

Sir Philip's round kindly face was troubled. "None of it makes sense. Why does the king plan to kill his most faithful man, calling him a traitor? He plans to put him to death on the same scaffold as a sodomite. Then, two days later, he plans to hang, draw and quarter his first wife's priest and make of him a martyr. On the very same day, the Lutheran Robert Barnes is to be burned to death as an infidel. It's as if the king is mad with bloodlust."

"No-one is safe, no-one," his wife whispered. Her eyes brimmed over. "And poor Bessie Blount, his mistress for so many years, dead this week of an ague, and yet still he persists in marrying in haste, as if he feels not the slightest pang at her death." She wiped her eyes with her handkerchief. "Indeed we live in terrible times."

My head was reeling. The king, to marry in secret this week! And Thomas Cromwell was to be executed as a traitor. Along with a sodomite, a Catholic martyr and a Protestant infidel. And the king's mistress, who had been called for so long the king's whore, was dead.

Brother Jerome had foretold all their deaths. He must have the Sight.

I had a weird sensation. As if the world receded around me. Their voices faded, then became strangely loud.

"But I have found one singer at least," Sir Philip was saying. "That is a start. I need one more at least. A boy with a glorious voice."

"I'm afraid," his wife whispered. "All these deaths. Can we not just stay here, away from court? At least till all the killing is over?"

"I cannot," her husband said. "The king's will must be obeyed."

He turned to me. "We will ride for London tomorrow. Be ready to go."

I stared at him in utter stupefaction.

"To sing," he said. "At the king's wedding."

"I know a boy," I said. "With a glorious voice. I . . . I could bring him."

Sir Philip's face lit up. "It's a miracle. I am saved!"

"He's . . . he's sick."

"Not the plague?"

"No. No! Just . . . a fever."

The lutenist's face puckered. "Is he well enough to travel?"

"I will make sure of it."

He laughed and caught his wife close, kissing her cheek loudly. "If he is well enough to travel, he'll be well enough to sing. Our bacon is saved!"

I felt giddy with relief and joy. "When? When do you want us?"

"At dawn," he said decisively. "We can practise on our way. Let us get ready." He turned to me, smiling. "I have not even asked your name?"

"I'm Cicely Brightwell, sir. I live just a few houses down the street, in the thatched cottage by the duck pond."

"Just think, wife. I've been riding all over the country looking for a girl who can sing like an angel, and I find her just across the road! Well, Mistress Brightwell, we shall see you tomorrow at dawn."

He made a gesture of dismissal. I stood my ground. "I am sorry, sir, I have just one question."

"Of course, of course. Your fee. Do not worry, you shall be amply rewarded. Here is a down payment." And he tossed me a bag of coins.

"Thank you, sir. But that's not it . . . "

"You wish to know if you can bring your dog? But of course! My wife and I love dogs. We have eight of our own. Another one will be no matter."

Again I tried to ask my question, and again he forged on ahead with great cheerfulness. "You are worried about your clothes? We shall provide you with costumes. Something blue, I think, to bring out the colour of your eyes."

"Thank you, but . . . "

"You worry for your virtue, in the oh-so-wicked court? Reassure your good mother that my wife shall look after you as if you were her own."

"No, sir . . . I mean, thank you sir, it's just . . . what I want to ask . . . " I found myself suddenly and uncharacteristically tongue-tied.

"Let her speak, Philip," his wife said, laying her hand on his arm.

He smiled at me encouragingly. "What is it, my dear?"

"Where were you on Easter morn?" I blurted.

Sir Philip gazed at me in surprise. "Why, in London, of course. I wish we had not been. The king was in the worst rage I have ever seen. Hating his new wife, blaming poor Cromwell. Monks marrying, the Lenten fast being broken, false recantations on every side. We rode for the peace of the country as soon as we could make an excuse, I promise you."

"So you were not here in Cerne Abbas on Easter morn?"

He shook his head, looking puzzled.

"I will see you at dawn," I said in an unsteady voice. "With the boy . . . "

"The boy with the glorious voice," he agreed.

I walked down the muddy road in a daze. I could not believe that I had found a means of getting Ambrose away. And a job with the king's own lutenist. To sing at the king's wedding. It seemed impossible.

As I hurried away down the street, I saw a girl picking her way through the rubble. She carried a lute in a polished case. "I'm sorry," I said to her. "The singing job has been taken."

When Ambrose had run away from the abbey, he had asked me to go with him. He had imagined a glorious life for us, wandering the country, singing like birds, sleeping in haystacks.

"But what about Mam?" I had asked. "I cannot leave her."

My mother had wanted me so badly she had taken a stranger by the hand and led him to Giant's Hill, and lain with him under the stars, clenching his seed inside her. If I went off wandering with Ambrose, she would be left all alone, with no-one to teach her Craft.

"Stay here with me," I had begged, clutching Ambrose's hand. "Mam would love to have you. You could help us . . . "

He had shaken his head. "I don't want to be a charity case anymore, Cicely. I want to make my own way in the world. And . . . I don't mean to be rude . . . but I don't want to stay in this tiny village forever, tending pigs and hoeing vegetables. I want to sing!"

"Can't you sing here? At feasts and fair days?"

He shook his head. "I want to see the world, Cicely. Don't you?"

"Yes," I had answered uncertainly. "But . . . "

"But not yet." He finished my sentence for me. "I understand. You're only sixteen. And you love your Mam. I tell you what . . . I'll come back for you in a year. See if you are ready then."

For a moment, I had thought Ambrose meant to kiss me and my heart had leapt in my breast like a bird. But he just squeezed my hand, picked up his bundle, and went whistling away down the lane, leaving me forlorn and lonesome.

As the months had passed, I had regretted not going with him so many times. My mother had seen me moping and had, in her quiet way, told me that I must follow my heart. And so I had resolved to tell Ambrose, when he returned, that I would go with him.

But he had never made it back to my door. He had been arrested only five minutes away.

I was determined that we should never be parted again.

So I told my mother what I planned as soon as I whirled in through the door. She did not seem surprised. Indeed, she went to the pantry and drew out a satchel that she had packed for me. I looked inside and saw food, a flask of cool lemon balm tea, a spare chemise, clean stockings, and a thick homespun shawl.

I laughed and hugged her fiercely. "You do not mind? Me leaving you?"

She shook her head and kissed me tenderly. "I shall miss you every day, my sweet girl, but it's time for your own life to begin now. You'll come back one day, when you're ready."

"I will, I promise." I clutched the satchel close, thinking of Ambrose. Wondering what he would say when I told him the news. Imagining him swinging me up in his arms and kissing me.

Then I bit my lip. "Mam, I may not be able to come back. I haven't been able to prove his innocence. Surely they will arrest him if we ever return? Won't the constable keep searching for him?"

She frowned. "I hope not. But it's a shame we could not clear his name, or find out who the true murderer was. I do not like to think he or she may still be here, in the village, living amongst us."

"No," I agreed, shivering at the thought.

She ladled me some pottage and brought me the bowl. "What are your plans, dear heart?"

I ate hungrily. "Mam, I want to bring Ambrose here, so he can have a sweet night's sleep and I can tend him properly. He cannot recover in that horrible little cell. The only problem is . . . "

"Mr Ward the constable," my mother interjected. "Well, that's no problem. I shall creep out in the dark, with my shawl over my head, and my basket over my arm, and make a great show of looking about me to make sure I am not watched, and then I shall lead him in quite the opposite direction. I had best take Thunderdell with me, though, else he'll never believe it's you."

I laughed and nodded eagerly. "You'll need to lead him on a rope. You know he'll never leave me willingly."

*

Our ruse worked perfectly.

Mr Ward crept down the road after my mother and Thunderdell, dragging against the rope. I waited till they were out of sight, then tiptoed the other way, towards the ruined abbey. The sky was swarming with stars, the east beginning to glow. My heart was singing as joyously as the blackbird. Today Ambrose and I would escape. I remembered the way he had kissed me, and my whole body tingled.

I found it hard crawling through the hole and down into the dank-smelling cellars. I told myself it was for the last time. My small lantern did not shed much light, and wavered wildly in the cold draughts.

The barrel had been rolled over the little wooden door. I managed to roll it aside, only to find the door was locked. I was taken aback, not liking to think of Ambrose locked up inside that filthy little cell. I knocked on the door. "Ambrose, it's me. Cicely. Are you there?"

"Yes, I'm here."

I was so glad to hear his voice. He sounded a little stronger.

"Where is Brother Jerome?"

"I don't know. He went away and took the light. It's as black as the pits of hell in here. Can you let me out?"

"The door is locked, and Brother Jerome has the key."

He sighed. I heard him sit down against the door. "I'm glad you are here. I woke up and was afraid that I'd been forgotten and would moulder to death down here. It was almost as bad as being in the gibbet."

"I'd not forget you." I pressed my hands against the door and leaned my forehead against it.

"I was coming to get you. Do you know that, Cicely?"

"Yes. If only your father had not been murdered."

He croaked a laugh. "If only I'd not stopped at the river to wash my face and hands, trying to make myself presentable for you. Then I'd have been safe at your house."

"Safe in my arms," I whispered.

I heard his sharp intake of breath and knew that he had heard me. "What are we going to do, Cicely?" he asked after a moment, in tones of despair.

"I have news. Such news! As soon as Brother Jerome comes back and unlocks the door, we can go home. You can have a bath, eat some hot pottage, sleep in fresh sheets. And then tomorrow . . . . Tomorrow!" My voice thrilled with triumph. "We ride for London. You and me and Thunderdell. We go to sing at the king's wedding!"

He sighed. "What a lovely dream. I wish it were true."

"It is true! Listen." And I told him all about Sir Philip.

"But . . . the constable . . . the murder charge . . . "

"I've been trying to find out who did it, Ambrose, really I have. I'm so sorry I've failed you."

"Sweet Cicely," he whispered. "You could never fail me."

How I wished he lay in my arms, so that I could bend and press my lips to his. My longing choked me so that I could not speak.

"When you are well . . . when you are safe . . . then we shall solve the mystery," I said at last. "Together we will find the truth." A thought occurred to me. "Did you see anything, Ambrose? On the day of the murder? Someone running or hiding? Or anything strange or out-of-place?"

There was a long pause. "It was misty that morning, I remember. As I passed through the abbey ruins I saw a dark shape flitting away. It startled me at the time. It looked like a monk in a long black robe. I remember laughing at myself, telling myself that the monks had all gone. Later, as I lay in that stinking gaol, having learned that the abbot was dead, I could not help my flesh creeping. Thinking I must have seen his ghost, you know. But then you took me to the chapel . . . and I saw Brother Jerome . . . I realised it must have been him I saw that day, hiding in the ruins."

"Yes . . . " I sat quietly for a moment, thinking. The cold of the stone floor struck up through the wool of my dress. "Ambrose, why do you think the abbot was at the silver well on Easter morning?"

"I doubt he was there to pray," he answered with a snort. "Probably he was drawing up some of the healing water for whatever pox he had caught from his whores." His voice was bitter, but he caught himself up and added with a laugh, "Or he simply wanted to see which of his enemies would die that year."

"What?" I pressed closer to the door. "What did you say?"

"It's an old superstition. Brother Jerome told me about it, years ago. If you want to know who will die in the coming year, then you look into the well on Easter morning."

For a moment I was motionless. Then I scrambled to my feet.

"Ambrose, I know who killed the abbot. Oh, what a fool I am!"

"What? Who?"

"Brother Jerome," I jerked out. "He knew . . . he knew you would not die in the gibbet . . . he said he had seen in the pool who would. A traitor and an infidel and a martyr and a whore and a sodomite . . . he said they would all die like the lecher had. He meant like Father Thomas!"

"Stop! Slow down. I don't understand."

"Brother Jerome killed the abbot. Oh, Ambrose I need to get you out of there!"

I looked about me for some kind of tool to break down the door, and only then realised that another pool of light had reached out to touch mine. Slowly I raised my eyes. Brother Jerome stood not ten paces away.

He stood hunched, his hood up over his head. His eyes reflected the flames of his lantern. He lifted his other hand. He held a hunk of rock, carved with a winged imp. With a few swift strides he stood over me, swinging the rock at my head.

Instinctively I lifted my staff and struck his hand away. He dropped the rock which crashed against the wall and then to the ground.

"Cicely!" Ambrose screamed through the door.

Brother Jerome scrambled to pick the rock up again. I hit him hard over the head with my staff. He dropped to the floor, dazed. I flew to his side and searched him feverishly. He tried to seize me and I kicked him hard in the side. He doubled over, moaning. I found the key and ran to the door. My hands shook so much I could not fit the key in the lock.

A flash of movement in the corner of my eye. I ducked. The rock hit me a glancing blow on the temple. I cried aloud in pain, and fell to my knees. Ambrose shouted my name.

"Coming," I panted, and put the key in the lock and turned it. As I fell back, the door burst open. Ambrose charged out, wielding the broken abbot's crook like a club. He managed to strike Brother Jerome down just as he raised the rock over my fallen form. Ambrose caught my hand and pulled me to my feet. We stumbled away into the darkness.

Behind us, we heard the old monk begin to mutter prayers and the clink of his rosary. He raised high his lantern, searching for us. Trying to calm our breathing, we crept along the wall.

Without any light, we were soon lost, feeling our way forward with our hands. I felt the curve of an archway, and pulled Ambrose through so we could crouch on the far side. Moments later, the old monk's light fell where we had been standing. I held my breath, my head ducked down, afraid the light might glint on the white of my eyes and give us away. After an agonisingly long moment, we heard the monk limp away.

Ambrose stood up and helped me to my feet. "There is only one thing I shall regret if we die tonight," he whispered.

"What?" I whispered back.

One hand slid around my waist. The other tilted up my face. His warm mouth found mine. The kiss was unbearably sweet.

"I have wanted to do that a very long time," he whispered, when at last he let me go.

"You kissed me the night I rescued you from the gibbet," I told him, my voice uneven.

"I had thought that a dream." There was laughter in his voice.

"I'd best make sure you know this one was for real," I answered, and rose up on tiptoe to kiss him again.

Then, hand-in-hand, we crept away through the darkness.

The vaults seemed to stretch on forever. Blind, both of us weak and dizzy, we could do nothing but stumble along and hope to find the way out. Then Ambrose kicked his foot against a broken barrel. The sound reverberated through the cellars. The light swung our way, and we heard the monk begin to run.

"Which way?" Ambrose cried.

"I don't know!" I sobbed.

Then I heard a far distant howling. "Thunderdell!"

I ran in the direction of the howling. Ambrose ran with me and, closing the gap behind us, the monk with his swinging lantern and bloodied rock.

I saw a dim crack of light above us, and the stairs going up. We scrambled up the steps like squirrels, me holding up my skirts so I did not trip. I managed to squeeze out the crack, and then Ambrose wriggled out behind me. Thunderdell flung himself upon me, whining and wagging his tail.

"Good boy! Good boy!"

He leaped up, almost knocking me over. Then suddenly he swung around, snarling.

The monk stood behind us, mist swirling about him, the sky

above the palest of blues. He stepped forward, the rock in his hand dripping rivulets of red down his hand and wrist. My blood. I put my hand to my temple, and only then realised the side of my face was wet with blood.

Ambrose put me behind him. "Don't you come any closer," he panted. I put my hand on Thunderdell's head, keeping him still.

The monk stood silently, a strange intent expression on his face.

"Did you really kill the abbot?" Ambrose asked. "But . . . why?"

"He was an evil man," Brother Jerome replied. "He made me do evil things. He besmirched this holy place. He brought it tumbling down."

"But . . . why wait a whole year?" I cried. "Why kill him at the holy well?"

Again a long pause, as if the monk was thinking how best to answer. "I saw his death in the pool," he answered at last. "I saw him lying on the stones, blood on his head. And then I turned and there he was, the lecher, coming down to the well. At the very moment in which I had seen his coming death. I saw that I was to be the instrument of fate. So I picked up the wishing stone and I smote him hard."

"Why did you not come forward and confess when Ambrose was accused in your place? He was condemned to death for a crime he did not commit."

Brother Jerome gazed at me with old cloudy eyes. "I did not see his death in the pool. I saw many others. The traitor, the sodomite, the infidel, the martyr, the whore. I knew he would not die."

For a moment his hand faltered, and the bloodied rock was lowered. "I should have seen his death and yours too. But I did not."

"No," I said. "Because we shall not die today."

Then I shouted, "Thunderdell! Strike!"

My dog leapt forward, knocking the monk backwards. He stood with his heavy paws on the monk's chest, pinning him down. The monk struggled to be free, then raised his arm as if to strike with the rock. Thunderdell closed his jaws upon the monk's wrist.

I heaved a great sigh, then looked up as my mother ran towards us, the constable at her heels.

"Did you hear all that?" I said accusingly.

The constable nodded. "I did. You saw us? You asked those questions so he would confess?"

I smiled wearily. "I knew Mam would be near."

She came to me, clucking her tongue over the wound on my head.

Mr Ward bowed his head to Ambrose. "I am sorry for your ordeal. I will take Brother Jerome into custody and inform the assizes of your innocence."

"Thank you," Ambrose said unsteadily. He squeezed my hand.

"He's quite mad, the poor old thing," I said, pulling Thunderdell away from the monk. "You will not put him in a gibbet, will you? It'd be so cruel."

"I think he'll be sent to Bedlam," the constable answered. "Nearly as cruel a fate, I'm afraid."

I sighed.

The mist was swirling away. I looked at Ambrose, filthy and exhausted, and down at myself, my skirts stained with blood and dirt. I began to laugh.

Ambrose smiled at me.

"It's dawn," I explained. "We are meant to be riding to London to sing at the king's wedding."

"The king is to be married again?" the constable asked in surprise. "Is he not already married?"

"He has set Anne of Cleves aside. He plans to make a queen of Catherine Howard, Anne Boleyn's cousin. She is only just seventeen."

"I hope they will be happy," the constable said politely.

"I know we shall be," Ambrose said, suddenly catching me by the waist and swinging me around jubilantly. Then he set me down and kissed me.

"I think perhaps we'll be hearing wedding bells ourselves," Mr Ward said to my mother.

She smiled. "Oh yes. I've already made the wedding dress. I think the king must wait to hear my two love-birds sing."

I laughed. Ambrose smiled and drew me closer, bending his head to kiss me again.

The End of Everything

May 999 AD

 AM TOO OLD FOR THIS AND SURELY too wise.

Dusk has lately fled and the soft mantle of night falls around the chestnut trees and unkempt blackberry hedges. The evensong of birds fades from the sky and I am alone as I hurry on quiet feet—secret feet—to the Well.

Down the gently sloping path I go, past the new-planted rows of linden trees that, in some distant future, will stand like God's warriors guarding the Well; for the Well is a holy place. So say the monks at the nearby Abbey. So I should say, for I am one of them. Not a monk, but an Abbess, albeit one without an Abbey to live in.

I may have travelled far from Hundley Vale but I have travelled no distance at all from God.

And yet, I do not come to the Well for holy reasons.

Forty-four summers I have seen, and forty-three long winters that have turned streaks of my hair to snow. Never before have I thought to turn to the Old Ways.

I pause near the edge of the water, taking a moment to glance around me. Nobody is here, nobody sees me.

God sees me. I cast my eyes heavenwards. *Forgive me.*

From my sleeve, I pull out a length of yellow ribbon and reach inside the hedge, scratching my hands. With blind fingers, I tie the ribbon to a sturdy twig, then kneel over the water to make my wish. Godric's face is clear in my mind.

"I wish," I say, "that I were not in love."

❄

On the day that Godric came for me, I had lived for four months in Wynnie's dim little house. The house was surrounded on all sides by thick woods and I fell asleep every night to the sound of the stream running beyond the shutters and woke to the riot of birdsong. Wynnie was not the first old, ill woman the Lord had led me to, and I did not believe she would be the last. The afternoon had turned cold, after five days of mild May weather, and the fall in temperature caused a fall in Wynnie's spirits. A rough wind from the north, heavy and grey with moisture, rattled the beams and plucked at the thatching.

I stood by the hearth, trying to thicken up a parsnip stew with flour, grateful for the warmth of the fire, when her querulous voice rang out from the adjoining bower.

"Eadwyn! Do come!"

I tapped the spoon and laid it on the stone edge of the hearth, and made my way between the candle wheels and hanging posies of dried herbs. I am tall, and the low ceiling made me stoop. Wynnie lay on a straw mattress, elevated on a box bed, in a windowless bower adjoining the house. All she had ever owned in her seventy years, it seemed, was piled on either side of her. Boxes and clothes and bags full of sewing and thread, her dead husband's hunting gear, her long-flown children's wooden playthings. She could not be persuaded to part with any of it.

I came to her side and she reached out her thin hand.

"What is wrong?" I asked, stroking her worn fingers.

"It feels like winter," she said.

"But it is spring, God's favourite month."

"It feels like winter in my bones," she replied, and I could see she quaked for fear. "Am I dying?"

The fear of death. I had seen it many times. One would think such a close perspective on the end of life would make me peaceful with it. I never was. I never would be. And yet, they came to me. Back at Hundley Abbey, I was known for the special talent God had given me: the ability to make people calm in the most agitating of circumstances. In four months in Cerneli, my reputation had already spread, and I spent my days talking softly to uncontrollable children and giving comfort to widows, as well as easing Wynnie towards her approaching death. My talent was the result of no great philosophy, no gilded mastery of words. My presence and no more calmed people, and for that I thanked my Lord; and I did not question why He gave me this talent but no inner sense of calm with which to comfort myself.

"The sky is blowing cold and that is all. Come and sit by the fire and you'll be in good spirits soon enough. Tomorrow it will be blue and warm again, you will see."

"I am in too much pain to sit by the fire," Wynnie said, for she was stubborn. Her illness was in her back and chest, and I knew she would feel better if she moved from time to time, rather than lying here looking at the dark, cobwebbed ceiling.

"Then I will fetch you some hot stew shortly and that will warm you, and you will see it was only the weather that caused your dread. Look you. Your cheeks are quite pink. Dying? What nonsense. Why, one of the nuns in Hundley Abbey was as pink-cheeked as you, and she lived to seven-and-ninety."

"Really?" Wynnie asked cautiously, the first hint of a smile tugging the corner of her lips. "Seven-and-ninety? Well, I am almost a chicken by comparison! How did she die?"

"God took her gently one warm morning, when—"

I stopped at the sound of a knock on the door, and a man's voice calling out, "Hello within!"

I gently released Wynnie's hand. A look of concern crossed her frail brow.

"Are you expecting a visitor?" I asked.

"Perhaps my brother and his wife?"

"I will go and see," I said, smoothing her wispy grey hair off her face. "Be at cheer. The Lord is still with us."

I opened the door and it was most certainly not Wynnie's boorish and corpulent brother. Rather, it was a man of my height, dressed in the black robes of the local Benedictine order. His black hair was streaked with silver and neatly tonsured, and he had a severe face; hawklike and watchful.

"May I help you, brother?" I asked.

"Eadwyn of Hundley Vale?"

"Yes."

"I am Godric, one of the Deans at Cerneli Abbey. May I speak with you about a matter of some . . . controversy?"

Rain was beginning to spit from the sky, so I stood aside and brought him in, gesturing to a stool by the fire.

"Who is it?" came Wynnie's nervous call.

"Someone from the Abbey. All is well," I called in response. I noticed Dean Godric had not sat down, and so I remained standing too. I picked up the spoon and began to stir the pot again, waiting for him to speak.

"One of our brothers," he began, "a young fellow promised to us by a noble family in the north, has grown ill. Or not."

I smiled, puzzled. "Or not?"

"He rambles. The things he says . . . let me simply say that some of the older brothers think he may be speaking the words of angels. Some of us, including me, think that he has a fever on his brain. The Abbot cannot decide and so has instructed us to keep him calm and see if it passes, while keeping a record of everything he says."

"I see."

"Your work at Hundley Vale and here in Cerneli is known to us. You have tended such a patient before? One with . . . disturbed thoughts?"

"Many a time, Dean Godric."

"Will you come, then?"

"To the Abbey?"

"Yes. I would be grateful for your opinion, as would the Abbot I'm sure."

It had been three years since I had set foot in such a place. I longed for the long silent spaces, the firm press of the hours and offices. "I cannot come now. Wynnie needs to eat."

"After Vespers?"

"After Vespers." I smiled.

He smiled in return, and it transformed his face. I could imagine how he must have looked as a boy, full of wonder and hope. I was reminded of something I couldn't quite grasp, a sunny, careless time; and for a moment I was happy, unexpectedly so.

"The northern gate to the Abbey is always open," he said, moving towards the door. "God be with you."

"And you."

He closed the door behind him, and Wynnie called for me immediately. I tasted the stew and spooned some into a wooden bowl for her.

"Here, Wynnie," I said, at the door of her bower.

I helped her to sit up and handed her the bowl, then sat on a box next to the bed.

"What did he want?"

"I must go to the Abbey tonight after supper. I won't be long."

Wynnie's illness hadn't spoiled her appetite. She spooned the soup into her mouth with enthusiasm. "This is very good, Eadie," she said.

I do not like being called Eadie. "Are you still cold in your bones?"

"Not quite as much. You did not finish telling me about the very old nun. How she died."

"Ah, Sister Saxburg. She passed one warm morning surrounded by her sisters, who sang her into God's arms."

Wynnie smiled over her stew. "A pleasant way to die."

"Yes." A pleasant way to die for an unpleasant person. Sister Saxburg was a tyrant in good health and in illness.

"The Lord be with me, and ensure that when I die, it is pleasantly," Wynnie said, crossing herself with her spoon.

I did not tell her that most do not. That most die in panic and pain. I did not tell her that the most innocent sometimes suffer the worst.

❄

In the long afternoon shadows, I followed the stream down towards the Abbey, under sycamore and oak and ash. At the northern gatehouse, I lifted the heavy brass ring and pushed open the carved wooden door. A moment later, a croaking voice called out, "Thanks be to God" and I heard the shuffling of feet. The porter emerged from his cell. He was shorter than me, with fluffy silver hair and a hunched shoulder.

"I am Eadwyn of Hundley Vale," I said.

"Brother Godric expects you. Please follow me."

He closed the gate behind us and started his slow shuffle past the mill and the brewhouse, past a fishpond bright green with water lilies, and around the Abbey hall. Then I saw the Abbey proper, with its stone cloisters and tower, and its wooden upper storey. The porter led me through a vaulted stone arch and we passed into the cloister garth, whose thick grass was crossed by a stone walkway. On either side, the wooden dormitories rose, with their narrow shuttered windows. But it appeared the porter was taking me towards the refectory.

"I am sorry that I am so slow," the porter said. "I am old."

"A slow journey is always a more pleasant one," I replied. "Do not hurry."

At last he opened the wooden door into the refectory. I found myself in a wooden and plaster hallway, surrounded by familiar smells: wax and lemon and sweet steam and timber. Godric must have heard the door open because he was with us a few moments later.

"Warmest welcome, Sister Eadwyn," he said, dismissing the elderly porter with a nod and a kind smile. "It must be some time since you last entered an Abbey."

As the door closed, the hallway grew gloomy. Grey daylight from under the door and Godric's candle were the only illumination.

"I have missed it," I said, running my fingers along the fresco painted on the lime-plastered walls. A bishop, a procession of black-robed monks, an arch of intricate knotwork.

He began to walk and I followed two steps behind him. "Why did you leave, then?" he asked.

"We had a fire. As there were so few of us and our endowment so small, the Archbishop decided not to repair the building and commanded we be absorbed into Barking Abbey."

"That is a long way from Hundley Vale."

"Indeed it is, Brother Godric."

"You did not want to travel?"

"I did not want to . . . be absorbed. Barking had its own abbess."

He gave no indication he thought my motives vain or arrogant.

"So you see," I continued. "I did not leave the Abbey, so much as the Abbey left me."

We had come to the end of the hallway and now stood in front
of an unadorned wooden door. He turned to face me in the dim
candlelight. "Your eyes are grey as storm clouds. Is your heart
heavy?"

Heat flushed my face under his close consideration of me. I felt
both exposed and thrilled. "All of us have heaviness in our hearts,"
I managed.

"God has not abandoned you, Sister."

"I know."

He turned once again to the door. "The refectory is through
here," he said. "Alfgar does not know I have brought you. He is
difficult to reason with. I must warn you his behaviour may alarm
you."

"I am well used to the alarming behaviour of the troubled," I
said.

He opened the door on a huge refectory, with a vaulted wooden
ceiling and eight long tables laid out in rows with narrow sitting
benches. A large cross, carved out of stone, hung over the threshold
to the kitchen, a muscular and alert Christ spread upon it. Partially
finished frescoes lined the white walls. The air hung with the smell
of their last meal here: fish, ale, parsley. And huddled in the corner,
his black cowl pulled all the way over his face, his hands tucked
inside his sleeves, was Alfgar.

"Brother Alfgar," Godric called.

Alfgar muttered something inaudible.

Godric gave me an apologetic smile and moved towards the
stricken brother. "I have brought somebody to see you."

Alfgar lifted his head then, and pushed back his cowl. He was an
uncommonly handsome young man, with thick fair hair and eyes
almost as blue as cornflowers. But those eyes were distant, glazed.
He looked through me. Or inside me. I could not tell which.

"We sin greatly against God," he said in a strong, deep voice.
"Warfare and famine, burning and bloodshed, theft and murder,
malice and hate. The Anti-Christ is at the gate. God must purify the
earth through destruction and fire."

A cold tendril of fear unfurled inside me at his words. It was true
that the times we lived in seemed dark and heavy with troubles. Yet
I had seen men and women before, caught in the trap of the brain
shivers, who repeated words imagined monsters had whispered to
them. Alfgar may very well have the same affliction.

"You shall know," he said. "You shall know by the lamb in the sky that becomes a lion. By the fiery storm that follows."

"Hello," I said, crouching beside him. "My name is Eadwyn."

Alfgar blinked and focussed when he heard my voice. His gaze fixed on my face, but he said nothing.

"Would you be more comfortable in your bed, Alfgar?" I asked. Again, no answer.

Godric stood over us. "He has been here in the refectory since it started, six days ago. It was his turn to read sermons while we ate, but he began to preach freely instead. Soon it had descended into these prophecies."

"For I am a prophet!" Alfgar boomed, startling me.

"Does he eat?" I asked.

Godric shook his head. "He drinks a little water in his quiet moods. He sleeps here in the corner. We brought him a piss-pot after the first time he relieved himself on the floor."

"Why must you stay here in the refectory?" I asked Alfgar, adopting the slow, soothing voice God had granted me to comfort the sick.

As so many before had, Alfgar responded to my tone. "This is where I first knew."

"First knew? What did you know?"

"Time is ending. The Anti-Christ is coming. God will crush us all in his mighty wave of fire. There will be no millennium."

I studied his gaze while he said all this. I was struck again by the flatness of it, as though his irises were mirrors rather than windows. I reached for his forehead to feel if he was feverish, but he flinched away.

"I will not hurt you," I said.

"You shall burn," he said softly.

"I need to see if you are sick."

"The world is sick!" he shouted, and spittle flew from his lips and landed in my hair. "You are sick! You have offended the Lord."

Now he climbed to his feet and began raining abuse down on me. "You shall not have the Lord's love. You shall not pass into the holy land of Heaven's king. For you have sinned so fiendishly that you shall spend eternity mourning in the burning welter of Hell!"

"Brother Alfgar, calm yourself," Godric said, grasping me under the elbow and pulling me away and up, and standing between me and my abuser. "This is Sister Eadwyn lately of Hundley Abbey. She is no sinner."

"That is for God to decide," Alfgar said gruffly, dropping once more to the ground. He pulled his cowl over his face again.

My heart was ticking fast and my breath felt thick in my throat.

Godric turned and grasped my elbow again, moving me wordlessly away from Algfar, out of the refectory and into the cloister. Rain had started in earnest.

"I am so sorry for alarming you," Godric said as the door to the refectory closed behind us.

I nodded and tried a smile. "I understand. And you did warn me."

"He won't remember what he has said to you. You aren't to think these accusations have any truth in them."

"All of us sin," I said lightly. "I trust in my salvation." The world seemed a little too bright at the edges. I took a deep breath.

"Do you know, now you have seen him, if he is sick or if he speaks God's warnings?"

My eyes went back towards the refectory door. "Common good sense would tell us he is sick. In my twenty-five years as a nun, I have never once met a true prophet. I have met several dozen people who speak imagined horrors."

"Can he be cured?"

"If he is sick, perhaps. If he is a prophet, it seems the end of time will make all these problems insignificant."

Godric smiled, and again I was reminded of something pleasant and long past. "I suppose you are right. Let us proceed, then, as if his affliction is illness. What would you ordinarily do in this situation."

"Sit with the person, somewhere with trees and calm nature noises, and listen to them until their mind slows."

"Would you sit with him on the floor of a refectory?"

"I could at a pinch," I answered with a laugh. "Would you like me to come back?"

"I would appreciate that very much, Sister Eadwyn. Though he may threaten you with damnation again."

A little tighten in my chest. I breathed through it. "I will be back tomorrow," I said. "I am not afraid."

❊

The sun had finally struggled through the clouds when Godric met me at the gate the next day. As he turned to lead the way, I caught the odor of meadowsweet clinging to his robes: sweet and astringent at once. He must have spent the morning in the brewhouse. I found myself wishing I could be closer to him, to inhale it from his clothes. These were such unusual thoughts for me that I shocked myself. Of course I had found men attractive before, but my abiding feeling with other men was that they were not for me. They existed in a parallel world to mine, where women married and bore babies and grew old and watched their husbands die, or were watched by them. I was married to God. Like all marriages, there were times it seemed less than satisfactory, but I acknowledged the lack of satisfaction was probably felt by Him the most: I had let Him down terribly after all.

I still hoped He would forgive me.

"Alfgar seemed calmer last night," Godric was saying. "I am hopeful it was your presence. I must say, I find it rather calming being around you too."

I blushed at his smile. "I want him to be calm enough that I may see if he is physically well," I replied. "If he has a high fever, we could treat him with sticklewort leaves steeped in boiling water."

"I'll have one of the brothers go to the woods to gather some." We crossed the garth and down past the mural and once again into the long refectory. I crossed myself in front of Christ, then looked around for the shivering hump of black cloth that was Brother Alfgar.

"Leave us be," I said to Godric. "He is likely to be calmer with fewer people nearby."

"Are you certain?"

His concern warmed me. "I am certain. I will call if I need you."

Godric nodded and left, closing the door behind him. I turned my attention to Alfgar, huddled in the corner, his face deep under his cowl.

I moved to the closest bench and sat, without speaking, and waited. The refectory was hollow and cool, with a faintly yeasty smell. The quiet pressed upon my ears. I could hear distant sounds of the wind in the leaves.

Minutes passed. Then more.

Finally, he looked up. "Who are you?"

"Sister Eadwyn." He didn't seem to remember his outburst of the day before.

"Evil has been heaped upon evil!" he cried. "The Lord will purify this world and all will burn away before Him."

I said nothing.

"We have earned our miseries, with our false gods. The stains of sin spread across the land." He climbed to his feet, his voice booming against my ears, his face growing red. "Murderers and slayers of kin and killers of priests and persecutors of monasteries, and perjurers and contrivers of slaughter, harlots and child killers and foul adulterous whoremongers, and wizards and witches and plunderers and robbers and thieves and—" Then he stopped suddenly, catching me in his gaze. "Who are you?"

"Sister Eadwyn," I said again.

This time he nodded. "You have seen it coming, have you not? The plague and pestilence, the murraine and disease, blight and bad harvest? They are the start of God's plan to destroy all."

I said nothing, but I wanted to tell him that all of those ills were part of life. That there had never been a time when the farmer didn't fear the blight, or the mother didn't fear the creeping cold of sickness.

Greeted with my silence, Alfgar sat again, pulling his knees up to his chest. "Why are you here?"

"To keep you company. I could take you outside if you like. Under the trees. Under the sky."

He shook his head.

"Have you been unwell?" I asked.

"No."

"May I come closer and look in your eyes and mouth, and test if you are feverish?"

This time he nodded. I slipped off the bench and knelt on the cold stone floor next to him. I pushed my face close to his, and looked deeply into his eyes. They were not as flat as yesterday. He blinked, and they shone wetly. "Open your mouth," I said, still not touching him. I wanted to move slowly and not alarm him.

He opened his mouth. I saw no lumps nor pustules.

"May I touch your brow?" I asked. "I will do so very gently."

He smiled, and it was a mischievous smile that gave me a chill. "Yes," he said. "Go on."

I almost called for Godric. I do not know what I feared: perhaps I thought he may bite me, or break my wrist. But then I told myself I was doing God's work and I reached out my hand for his forehead.

It was cold as ice.

I snatched my hand back, as though he had bitten me.

He began to laugh. "Try again!" he cried. "Try again!"

I scrambled to my feet but so did he, and he grasped my wrist and forced my hand to his brow. This time, it burned like fire.

"Brother Godric!" I cried.

Alfgar drew down his eyebrows, as though he was concentrating very hard. My hand was still pinned to his brow so I felt as his temperature plummeted again, down and down into frosty depths.

He released my hand and I stumbled back, just as Godric opened the door. Alfgar began to shout and rant again. "The lamb in the sky will turn into a lion!" he shouted. "The woods will burn!"

Godric asked me over the din what had happened, but I motioned we should talk in the hallway.

The door closed behind us, but I could still hear Alfgar's shouts.

"He was calm at first, but then he seized my arm roughly," I said. "I ought not be alone with him again."

"I am deeply sorry—"

"He is ill," I said quickly. "I am certain of it."

"He has a fever?"

"He has—" I struggled for words. "He pitches between hot as the sun and cold as the grave," I said. "Almost as though he wills it."

✳

Godric tried to urge me not to return, but by now I had grown curious. About Alfgar, about his illness, and also about Godric. So after promising to come by the next day to persuade Alfgar outside under the trees, I made my way back to Wynnie's house. The stream bulged from the previous night's rain, and at first I didn't hear the voices near Wynnie's door. But as I approached, I saw the familiar figures of Beorthwiel and Inga, Wynnie's brother and sister-in-law, on the path.

"Hello, there!" I called, hurrying to the gate to open it for them. "Wynnie didn't say you were coming by today."

Inga, a cherub-faced woman of five-and-sixty with wild steel-grey hair, took my hand. "Sister Eadwyn, Wynnie says you have been at the Abbey. Have you heard anything?"

"Heard anything?"

Beorthwiel interjected. "They say a prophet in the Abbey tells of the end times."

"Who says that?"

"In the village. *Everyone* is saying it," Inga answered. "They say the prophet has predicted dragons that fly across the sky and fiery whirlwinds."

I did not want to let Godric down by confirming or denying such an account, though I was amused that Alfgar's lion had been transformed by gossip into a dragon.

"Unless it comes from the Abbot himself, we ought not give such stories credence," I said. "If there is something for us to worry about, the Abbot will let us know."

Inga and Beorthwiel exchanged glances. The sun through the leaves made patterns on the long grass. I was struck by it suddenly, by how beautiful the world was even in its ordinary moments. How sad it would be if God did decide to reduce it all to ash.

"Do not trouble yourselves," I said, in my soothing voice. "Wait and see if the Abbot has anything to say. In the meantime, do not be caught in speculation and the spread of fear. Trust in the Lord's will for nothing evil may come of it."

They went on their way, and I could hear them muttering to each other as they did.

Wynnie was, of course, in an agitated state. I untied my head scarf and folded it on the long bench by the hearth that I slept on, and she was already calling to me through the door.

"Eadie! Eadie! Have you heard?"

I paused at the threshold, with my calm voice at the ready. "I have heard a silly rumour and no more."

"Come and sit by me, for I am icy with fear," she said.

I sat on the bed next to her, and she grasped my hand in her own and held it so hard I could feel the bones in her fingers.

"I'm certain that the Abbot would tell us if there was anything to worry about," I said.

"You have been there. Is that why? Have you spoken to the prophet?"

My loyalty to Godric was tested by my loyalty to this old, frightened woman. "He is not a prophet," I said softly. "He's unwell. A fever on the brain." A fever that sometimes plunged into frost, but telling Wynnie that would only frighten her more. "Put it out of your mind."

She fell quiet a moment, her gaze locked on mine imploringly.

"I fear suffering," she said finally.

"It is only natural to fear suffering."

"When I thought of my own death, I was not as afraid. I imagined you would be here, and perhaps Beorthwiel and Inga if there was time to fetch them, and I would drift off as into a cold sleep, only to wake in the halls of Heaven. Now . . . there is talk of fire and savage creatures in the sky. Of all of time folding up and crushing us to dust and ash."

"Hush now. Even if that were to happen, it would last but a moment compared with eternity in the Lord's company."

"The Lord is so silent, Eadie. How would I know if I have been sinless enough to earn entry to Heaven. How do any of us know?"

And although my voice was calm and sure, and although I saw Wynnie's trembling limbs grow still and her eyes grow serene and her words grow slow, inside me spun a cold whirlpool. Wynnie named the very things I was most afraid of. Suffering. Hell. Eternal torment.

But most of all the uncertainty about God's forgiveness. For He was the only one who knew what I had done.

❃

On the third day, a day of stifling moist heat, Godric and I arrived at the refectory to find Alfgar in an altogether different mood. Rather than hunched and muttering to himself in the corner, he strode between the tables singing. I became aware for the first time of the height and breadth of him, and was grateful he hadn't hurt me much worse the previous day.

"This is new," Godric said softly to me, and he had an expression of admiration in his eyes. He thought I had worked this magic.

"We shall see," I said, not wanting him to raise his hopes too high. "Brother Alfgar?" I called.

Alfgar stopped and turned. When he saw me, that mischievous smile came over his face again, and I was glad for Godric's reassuring form beside me.

"Under the trees," Alfgar said. "Under the sky."

"You want to go outside?"

He strode towards the door with purpose and Godric and I parted and let him through, then followed him out of the refectory and cloister, and down towards the south gate.

"Where are we going, Brother?" Godric called, hurrying his feet to keep pace.

"Under the sky," Alfgar said again, and began to run.

Godric took off after him, past the burial ground and the chapel, past the well and across pasture, then up and up and up the hill they called Helis Hill, which rose over the village. They were well ahead of me now, two figures in black robes trudging upwards one behind the other. I walked after them, already panting and sweating. My pleated underdress and wool pinafore felt heavy against my body. Long grass and straggling buttercups brushed against my hem. I could see that Alfgar had stopped and sat, his face turned to the sky. Godric approached him slowly. I pushed myself along harder, calves cramping. Wynnie had told me that an old pagan figure was carved on the hill, all overgrown with grass, but I could not see it. When I finally caught up to them, Godric sat three feet from Alfgar, while Alfgar lay on his back on the ground, eyes closed.

I sat heavily next to Godric, gulped for breath.

"He seems calm," Godric said. Then his eyes went out over the view and he added, "Unsurprisingly."

I followed his gaze and was greeted with a glorious panorama of countryside. The wildflower-choked hill, the green pasturelands hemmed with hedges, shady clusters of trees, the village huddled along the stream, all lime plaster and thatch, and the great oval of the abbey grounds, its cloister garth a perfect deep green square between buildings, made small by distance.

And a breeze to cool the moisture on my skin.

"It's beautiful," I said, my thundering pulse starting to slow. Bumblebees buzzed nearby. Lambs bleated in a field; the sound carried to me on the breeze.

Godric nodded towards Alfgar. "You were right. Being outside is calming him."

"In nature we are close to God's love," I said. "God's love soothes every soul."

"God works through you to soothe others," Godric said, and that admiring smile came back to his face. "Thank you."

"You are welcome."

We sat in silence for a little while. But for Godric's black tunic and tonsure, we might have passed for any two friends sitting companionably on the hillside on a bright spring day under skimming white clouds. The sun was hot on my scarf. Alfgar did not speak. I suspected he had fallen asleep, with sunshine on his face and quiet in his heart.

Finally, Godric said to me, "If he is . . . if it were the end . . . "

That little chill returned to my heart. "Yes?"

"What would you regret the most?"

"Regrets are for those who don't believe in salvation," I said, then realised I sounded priggish and cold. "But there are things I wonder about," I added. "How life might have been different."

"What things?"

"Marriage. Children, of course. How my life might have looked had I left the abbey sooner. It is too late for anything now. I am in my middle age. I only hope to be useful to my brothers and sisters, with the gifts God had given me." I smiled up at him. "And you?"

He returned his eyes to the view, pressed his lips together thoughtfully for a moment, then said, "The same. Exactly the same."

Something soft shifted inside me, and I was gripped by a deep yearning I had never known before. I ached. I was instantly so embarrassed by these feelings that I turned away and pretended interest in something else entirely. "Doesn't the abbey look small from up here?" I said, recognising how thin and hollow my observation was.

"There!" This was Alfgar's voice, and I admit I had forgotten he was with us.

"There! There!" He was on his feet, shouting at the sky, finger elevated aloft accusingly. "The lamb! The lamb!"

I looked up at the same moment as Godric gasped.

One of the clouds appeared to have formed itself into the shape of a lamb, its front legs raised as though jumping. I blinked hard, shook my head, and looked again. A cloud picture. That was all it was.

But as I watched, my eyes aching from the brightness of the sky, the front legs grew longer, sharper, more like clawed feet; and something that resembled a mane feathered out slowly from around the lamb's neck.

"The lion!" Alfgar cried, and he fell to the ground and began to sob.

"God be with us," said Godric.

❁

After Godric gathered the sobbing Alfgar and took him urgently to see the Abbot, I was left to walk home in the sweltering heat. It was as though Alfgar's prophecies were already coming true and a door to hell had been left open. Perspiration soaked my back when I arrived back at Wynnie's house. Despite the shade, the heat was trapped inside. I took a breath of stuffy air and called out, "Wynnie?"

Then I heard the strange breathing. I raced to her bower, to find that she was curled on her side crying.

"What's wrong?" I asked, kneeling by the bed and reaching for her soft, thin hair.

"I think it will be soon," she said. "And I am sad for the loss of the world."

I touched her forehead. She was clammy with perspiration. "It is just the weather, Wynnie," I said, but there was a cloudiness in her eyes that told me her death was drawing closer. "The heat has made you—"

"The dragon in the sky," she said.

"How did you know?"

"Inga came by."

Clearly I needed to visit Inga and remind her not to upset Wynnie. "It was a cloud," I said. "It looked a little like a lion. Inga oughtn't have worried you." It was a cloud. That was all. Clouds often resolved themselves into pictures, and their misty edges may very well turn a lamb to a lion, if one was looking for it. I knew all of this with my brain, but my belly still lurched as I remembered Alfgar's fervent cries.

The lamb in the sky will turn into a lion! The woods will burn!

Wynnie shifted onto her back, a little sigh of air escaping from her lips involuntarily. "I am so warm," she said.

"I can fetch a sponge and some water."

"No, no. Stay here. You calm me with your presence. I don't want to be alone." Again the involuntary gasp, almost as though her lungs were rattling against her ribs. The first spike of alarm hit my blood. I had never heard her make that noise before. A memory came back to me of another of the deaths I had attended: the patient fighting through pain for breath, frantic and desperate. Whatever sense of calm I brought obliterated by the horror of death, real and cold, pressing against the membrane of life.

Please, my Lord, don't make her suffer like that.

I crossed myself and Wynnie saw it, and her face drew white. She fell silent. Together we formed a tableau throughout the long, hot afternoon. The old woman, still and frightened in her bed, eyes on the ceiling beams. Me in my plain blue gown on the stool beside her, watching her and counting the increasing frequency of those rasping breaths. The room was dim and the heat oppressive.

Suddenly, as the light began to die, she said, "I want to go outside."

I leaned over to catch the edge of her blanket as she tried to fling it off. "Stay still and be calm, Wynnie."

"It is too hot in here. I can hardly breathe." Every word was shallow and thin, stretched over too little breath.

"It would be better for you to rest."

"For what purpose?" she asked defiantly, her eyes sharper than they had been for weeks. "I will be dead soon. I know it from the way you look at me. I want to see the trees and the grass and the sky."

I realised I was holding her blanket down, pinning her to the bed, and she was straining against it. I softened, released her, and she sat up and said, in a very small voice, "Would you help me?"

I helped her out of bed and onto her feet, which could barely flatten out to grip the floor. I took her weight against my shoulder. I could feel her ribs through her back, and she was so light I imagined they were as hollow as a bird's. With my arm crooked around her, I half-guided, half-carried her out of the bower, across the house, and out into the warm dusk.

I lowered her to the grass, under the shade of a chestnut tree. She crumpled forward, arms hanging over her knees and, with effort, looked up to the sky. Then caught her breath in shock and started coughing.

I crouched next to her, arm around her frail and shaking shoulders, and fearfully followed the direction of her gaze. I expected more cloud pictures, perhaps. But what I saw instead was a towering bank of storm cloud, moving in steadily from the north. I have seen storm clouds before, and always on hot and sticky days, but this storm front was enormous, a roiling grey-black swirl eating the sky.

Wynnie brought her coughing under control and sucked in a breath. "Is it coming?"

"The storm? Yes."

"The end?"

"No, it's only a storm."

"I shall be glad to die today rather than in the great conflagration at the end times."

"Wynnie," I said, gently tilting her chin so she was gazing directly at my eyes. "It's only a storm."

"How do you know?" she asked thinly.

"Because I have seen storm clouds before."

Her breath was thready now, barely supporting her words. "Tell me that you have seen storm clouds as black and monstrous as that. In truth, before God."

In truth, before God. No, I hadn't.

I never answered Wynnie, for those were her last words. I would like to tell you that she then passed quietly and swiftly in my arms, but death is rarely like that. She rattled and she gasped, her lips grew blue and her eyes grew frantic as a fox in a trap. She clutched at me heedlessly, her fingernails cutting deep crevices into my wrist as she tried to hang on to life, even though her life was now made of pain and fear.

Then her body fell bonelessly against mine, as God took her spirit. I laid her gently on her back on the grass, and prayed for her, but quickly. I needed to get her inside again. The storm was coming, and I couldn't leave her poor remains outside in the rain.

She was light but awkward to carry, and I asked her to forgive me as I grasped her under the arms and hauled her back inside with her heels dragging along the ground, turning up clods of grass. I kept my gaze averted from the storm cloud, for fear my imagination would make some devilish face from its contours. I laid Wynnie by the hearth and closed the door just as the first rumble of thunder rolled across the world. I yelped involuntarily. No matter how I reasoned that it was only a storm, my heart feared judgement, doom, death. I left Wynnie's body by the fire and went to her room, to her bed, which still retained the oily musk of her hair, and I lay down and closed my eyes and began to pray.

From behind closed lids, I could sense the light in the room change. I could feel the cold waft of the storm displacing the hot air. I could hear the cracking rumbles echoing between the hills. I prayed and I prayed, until the words stopped making sense. There was no rain; only thunder and what I perceived through reflected glimmers to be the occasional flash of lightning.

Then the two came together: a deafening crack and a flash of light so bright that it turned my eyelids red. My eyes flew open and I cried out. My mind whirled with words: parts of prayers, reassurances to myself, and I was so afraid of being alone.

The fiery storm. The woods will burn.

I leapt to my feet and went to the door, flung it open and looked out. The wind had sucked up leaves, and they were yellow-green against the black clouds. Flames and smoke from the woods. The lightning had struck a tree.

A cold drop of rain blew into my face, landing square on my cheek. Then another on the hand that held the door open. I closed it, and the rain turned into a torrent. It would extinguish the fire, but I had seen it. I knew.

Alfgar's second prophecy had come to pass.

❄

The rain stayed long after the storm. It sheeted down on the cottage, finding its way through the thatch and trickling down the corner beams. I slept in Wynnie's bed that night and hoped for it to ease by the morning, but when I opened the door in the morning I saw the ground had been churned to mud, and puddles gathered all up the rutted path.

I needed to go to the village and find Wynnie's brother. I waited until noon and then decided the rain was not going to retreat, so I pulled on an oilskin cape and headed out.

Within a few hundred yards, my shoes were drenched and squelching, my hem spattered with mud, and the breeze in the sodden branches sent a second curtain of rain down on me, penetrating between the corners of my oilskin and soaking the lap of my dress. I rounded the wall of the abbey, past farmsteads and the mill, and across the bridge and down Abbey Street into the village. A dozen or so wattle-and-daub roundhouses unevenly lined each side of the wide road. I wasn't sure where Beorthwiel and Inga lived, so I made my way past the smithy—cold and silent today—and went to ask at the alehouse on the corner of Piddle Lane.

I shut the damp day out behind me, and entered the warm smoky room. It smelled of honeyed steam and the wet dogs at the hearth, and the smoke caught in my throat and made me cough. I did not need to ask the alehouse keeper for Beorthwiel's location, because Beorthwiel was there, at a rickety table with another red-faced man, drinking.

Beorthwiel looked up and saw me, and a puzzled squint came to his eye.

He rose while his friend was in mid-sentence, and approached me.

"Wynnie?" he asked.

I nodded. "She died last night."

His companion had stood and now lurched towards me. He was clearly very drunk despite the hour of the day. "You're the old sister, aren't you?" he asked, jabbing his finger towards me aggressively. "The one that's been up at the Abbey with the Black Monks?"

I glanced nervously at Beorthwiel, expecting him to intervene before his friend poked me in the eye, but he stood back and nodded. "This is her," he said. "She won't tell you a thing."

His friend continued peppering me with questions nonetheless. "The storm last night? They say he predicted it. Is that true? The woods caught fire. My daughter hid under a table for four hours, so sure was she that the Antichrist was coming."

Now the attention of the alehouse keeper and his wife had been caught, and a small circle gathered around me, demanding to know which Black Monk made the prophecies and when the Abbot would help the village. The alehouse wife trembled and shook as she peppered me with questions, and their voices lapped over one another until I cast up my hands and shouted for them to stop.

"I know nothing!" I lied, hoping God would forgive me. "You must go to the Abbey yourselves and ask."

"They have locked the north gate," the alehouse wife said shrilly. "For the first time in two hundred years, they have locked the north gate. We cannot get in."

"Why have they locked us out of the Abbey?" the drunk man demanded.

"I am the wrong person to ask," I said, a stain of sadness spreading over me. If the Abbey was locked, I may not see Godric again. "I visited once to see a sick patient, and nothing more."

"They have locked us out of the Abbey because they know the prophecies are true!" the alehouse keeper exclaimed. "We face the end of times."

More shouting and crying, and the door opened and another couple came in with a large wet dog and they joined in too.

Beorthwiel sidled up next to me. "I will come for her body," he said, his voice sharp. "Take your things and leave her house. If you will not help us, why should I help you?"

I thought about the rain. I thought about Godric. I thought about the locked Abbey and the end of times.

And I turned and walked away from the alehouse. The time had come for me to leave Cerneli.

That afternoon, I moved poor Wynnie's body back to her bed, cleaned the grass from her hair and the mud from her heels, and laid her there as though she were peacefully sleeping.

I closed the door to her bower for the last time, and found my old leather satchel under the long bench, between a basket full of mending that Wynnie had never finished, a battered empty chest, and an old pair of shoes. I thought about tidying the house a little for Beorthwiel: Wynnie had accumulated so much detritus. But then I remembered Beorthwiel was turning me out in the middle of a downpour, and would likely not appreciate it anyway.

I folded my spare dress into the satchel with my blanket and my last few coins, and hitched it all over my shoulder. I closed my eyes and clasped my hands to pray, when I heard the door open behind me. I assumed it was Beorthwiel, and turned to assure him I was leaving immediately.

But it was Godric, huddled under a dripping moleskin.

"Oh," I said, for it was all I could think of to say. I had assumed I'd never see him again, and something about that assumption was a relief. An end to a struggle.

"Forgive me, Eadwyn," he said. "I should have come by earlier."

"Why?"

"To see if you are well after the storm. After . . . yesterday's events."

I spread my arms. "As you see. Wynnie has died and her brother insists I am to leave today."

Godric gazed at me across the room, twin puddles forming on the floor under the front points of his moleskin cape. He seemed lost for words now. "You are leaving?" he asked finally.

"I'm afraid I must."

"It is raining."

"As I have observed, but I have no place in Cerneli now that my charge is dead, and I dare not seek comfort in the village. I am suspected of covering up an awful truth about Alfgar and the Abbey."

"Then we at the Abbey have caused you strife, and we must fix it. You will come with me and I will arrange for you to lodge at the Abbey guest house."

At first I did not answer, because I had a strong sense that it would be dangerous to say yes. Not because of Alfgar or the hostile villagers or the end of the world, but because I would continue to see Godric and I knew that I was falling in love with him. But it seemed, also, I was unable to say no. Because I would continue to see Godric. And I knew that I was falling in love with him.

"What a generous offer," I said at last. "I will kindly accept, but only if you allow me to do some good work to earn my keep."

"We will need you to help with Alfgar. Now that he has left the refectory, he roams freely around the Abbey grounds and shouts his prophecies as he goes. He has not slept."

"Is this why you have locked the Abbey? To keep Alfgar from wandering into the village?"

Godric's hawk-like gaze flickered a moment, and then he said, "It is one of the reasons. The other I am not at liberty to divulge. But should you come with me, perhaps the Abbot will include you in our plans."

"Plans?"

"Come with me. You will be comfortable and safe, I promise."

I glanced around Wynnie's house, which had been my home for months. But home was an illusion: since I'd left Hundley Abbey I had been homeless and I felt it all the way into the foundations of my spirit. In the guest house at Cerneli Abbey, perhaps I would feel I belonged somewhere at least for a little while.

✳

There is a quiet that one only hears in holy places. It is more than the absence of sound; it is the presence of God. His love fills the cracks through which wind whistles, softens rasping edges, and turns the rhythms of the rain to a chanted psalm. Even though I was only in the guest house, a building so new it still smelled of fresh timber, I felt very much part of the Abbey. The guest house was down by the southern gate, looking over the wall to the burial ground, but the bells for None, then Vespers, then Compline were close and familiar, rather than distant and estranged as they had been these last four months, when I had heard them from Wynnie's house.

After Compline, I slept very easily and very well in that little room, on a cot barely long enough for my legs. I would have slept sound and deep until Prime, I am certain, but a visitor came to me in the night.

At first, as I roused, I was aware only of the beating of the rain. But then a false beat alerted me that there were footsteps in my room. I sat, opened my mouth to shout, only to have a hand clamped over my jaw, forcing my head back to strike the wall. I could taste his stale, oily skin, feel the callouses on his palms against my lips. In the dark, the scene around me slowly resolved. The little table and stool under the shuttered window, the fair hair and crazed eyes of my assailant. It was Alfgar.

"The flood comes," he said.

I tried to make my eyes soft, to appeal to his better nature.

"The flood will wash out the sinners. The devil will come in its wake. The devil will come in a whirlwind. The devil will knock down the Abbey!" With each statement he grew more passionately aroused, louder.

I tried to nod, but he had my head pressed hard against the wall. He glared into my eyes, and I saw a hard chill in them that made my bones turn to water. Then the expression faded from his gaze and he looked momentarily puzzled before releasing me and sitting back on his haunches.

I wanted to call for help, but did not want to awaken that icy flint in his eyes again.

"The rain will stay," he said, quieter now but no less passionate. "Day upon day and the river will burst and then on the last day of living, the sky will clear and the wind will come and all the towers will fall."

"Can I take you back to the dormitory, Brother Alfgar?"

The use of his name made him blink. "The devil comes," he said. "For me."

"For you? You only?"

He gave a sly smile, the cold returning to his eyes. "The devil knows what you have done."

My skin prickled. "As does God, who forgives me."

"You hope." Then he descended into peals of laughter, cruel laughter.

More footsteps, and a moment later the door to my room had opened and in a flickering lamp light two of the brothers stood there. Not Godric.

"Sister Eadwyn, our deepest apologies," one of them said, as the other—a large man with a head like a block of wood—rounded on Alfgar and roughly pulled him to his feet. Alfgar began to shout about the devil and the whirlwind and the sinners and the rain, but he was soon marched out into the hallway while the remaining brother said to me, "There is a latch on your door. Here." He showed me a small metal locking device on the door jamb. "You will sleep more comfortably if you hook it closed."

I nodded, too mortified to do anything other than sit wordlessly in my bed with my blanket drawn up to my shoulders. I wore nothing but my shift, and it was threadbare enough in places to see through.

The light withdrew, the door closed, and I was alone and quiet again. I stood, hooked the latch as the brother had instructed me, then went back to my bed. The rain deepened outside, hammering on the roof and the shutters. Sheeting rain. Bucketing rain. Doomsday rain.

I did not sleep again until grey dawn.

For three days, I did not see Godric or anyone else but the brother who brought my meals and emptied my pot. The quiet seeped inside my bones and settled there, comfortingly. I was back in the Abbey enclave again, and God was close. The rain continued to fall. I sat by the window for hours every day, looking down on the graveyard as the ground became sodden and boggy. From time to time, the sky would turn white instead of grey, and the rain would stop long enough for me to believe it was over. On one such occasion I ventured from the guesthouse to walk up to the north gate, but the stream had swollen and the rushing water had swept away the wooden footbridge. The abbey grounds were now bisected by the water. I quickly returned to my guesthouse, as the rain squeezed out of the clouds again. None of the brothers were out in it. We were all shut inside by the grey sky, the cold rain, the creeping dread.

The flood will wash out the sinners.

I prayed. I never stopped.

Then, on the fourth morning, Godric came, along with the Abbot.

Elfric was at least an inch shorter than me, with tiny pale hands; but his size and stature did not prevent him from having a regal, almost godly demeanour. He took my hand and smiled at me and I felt blessed.

"Sister," he said. "I am sorry it has taken me so long to welcome you. I trust you have been comfortable?"

I glanced over his head at Godric, whose eyes met mine with a slow blink. I read so much into that blink: an acknowledgement of the time we had been apart, a protective instinct towards me, a smile born of love. All imagined of course.

"I have been most comfortable, Abbot," I said. "Thank you."

"Apart from Alfgar's visit," Godric said in a grumble.

"Which has not been repeated," I said smoothly. "I blame nobody but myself. I should have latched the door."

A look passed between Elfric and Godric, and I sensed there had been disagreement between them about Alfgar's visit.

"Alfgar sought you out. He trusts you," Elfric said.

"He could have killed her," Godric interjected, and my blood warmed at the idea he felt protective towards me.

"Not Brother Alfgar. He may be many things, but not a murderer. His roughness is born of passion, not of malice."

"Sister Eadwyn is not—"

"How is Brother Alfgar?" I asked, to defuse the tension between them.

"He is no better."

Elfric held out his palms. "The rain continues. The river overflows."

"You believe he is a prophet?"

"I do not seek to know God's will," Elfric said. "I am of this world, though I pray I shall one day sit by His side. But if the end times are coming, we must be prepared."

"You are one of us," Godric said then. "You are the Abbess of Hundley Vale, you are much loved by God, you are our guest and you helped us in time of need. We need to explain to you what you must do if Alfgar's prophesised whirlwind comes."

My stomach turned to water, and I think it was the first time I allowed myself to believe that Alfgar might be right, that the devil was coming in a whirlwind and the world's end shadowed the horizon.

"Follow," the Abbot said, and I fell into step behind him, Godric behind me. We left the guesthouse and, in the rain, crossed waterlogged ground to the Abbey Church. Elfric held open the door and ushered Godric and me in. The door closed behind us on a lime-washed interior that smelled of wood and incense, grey light at its narrow windows. Elfric was rattling a key at his waist, and he led us towards the chancel, behind the altar, and to a set of stairs descending towards a closed door of heavy oak.

Elfric took a candle in a brass ring from the altar. At the bottom of the stairs we stopped and he turned to me with serious eyes.

"We serve the community but we serve God best if we are safe and whole. Godric tells me the villagers are hostile towards you; you can only imagine how they will be when . . . times grow dark. That is why we have locked the gates. That is why we have prepared the crypt."

"Prepared the crypt?"

"You will see," he said, turning away and unlocking the box padlock on the door.

At that moment, a voice behind us called out. "Abbot! Alfgar has climbed the tower!"

Godric flexed, ready to run off, but Elfric held him by the shoulder. "No, Dean Godric, I will go. Show Sister Eadwyn the crypt, and make sure she understands the difficulties."

Godric nodded. He took the Abbot's candle and held the door open for me. Elfric hurried off and Godric and I moved into the cold dark with our little light. The door thudded closed behind us and I caught my breath. The room was dank and chill. On one side, the candlelight illuminated a row of stone coffins, and the faint mouldering smell of death hung under the low ceiling. On the other side were barrels and sacks and blankets heaped up high.

"If . . . Alfgar's warning comes to pass," Godric said, "come straight here. We have food enough to last us and the door is unbreakable."

I turned to him in disbelief. "Unbreakable? If Alfgar's prophecy is true, then it will be Satan who comes in that whirlwind. I am quite sure he will find no difficulty in breaking down a door."

"What will be will be when the world ends," Godric said patiently. "We mean to keep ourselves safe from people around the Abbey, who may go wild with fear. We . . . need to protect ourselves." He glanced away, and I knew he felt ashamed to admit such a thing. "Elfric's orders."

"Does he not fear God's judgement?"

"He says God will not save sinners and so we must fear them."

I nodded, my eyes counting the blankets. "And are all the brothers invited down here, should the worst happen?"

"Yes, and you. Although . . . you do understand there will be no privacy."

"A small price to wait out the storm. And to be among God's servants when the end comes." I shuddered, dropped my voice low. "Do you actually think it possible?"

"I don't know," he said. "I fear it." He looked back the way we came. "But let us take some fresh air. My lungs feel tight in here."

I followed him to the door, which he pulled hard. It didn't shift a hair.

"What is it?" I asked.

Godric banged on the door. "Hoy. Hoy. Let us out." He turned to me. "The door has locked behind us. The Abbot did not realise. He has the key."

My blood cooled. "We are locked in?"

"Do not trouble yourself. I will be missed quickly, and Elfric knows where I am."

I was unsettled to my marrow. Being trapped in the crypt seemed to me some kind of live burial. I began to tremble.

Godric took my hand in his and squeezed it. All my fear fled. I looked across at him, very aware of the warmth of his skin against mine, and my body suffused with heat. Oh, I was happy in that instant. Achingly happy. Happy as I had never been before.

Then he let my hand go. "Come and sit. You look as though you might faint." He walked ahead of me and placed the candle on the floor. His shadow grew long as he hefted down a sack of grain and laid it down for me to sit on. I inched up my hem and sat, and he settled next to me. The only sound was our breathing, and a faint *drip-drip* noise from somewhere above. The candlelight illuminated my hands, the folds of my dress, and less clearly Godric's face and hawkish expression. The intimacy was at once too much for my senses to bear, and the very height of joy. We were awkward and silent with each other for a long time.

Finally, I boldly asked, "You said you feared that Alfgar speaks truth."

"I do."

"Is it death you fear? Or judgement?"

"One cannot fear death," he said. "For it is merely passing through a threshold. One fears only what is on the other side."

"So you do fear judgement?"

He inclined his head. "Yes," he said. "Or nothing."

"Nothing?"

"No God. No heavenly host." He spread his hands. "I suppose, though, that I will not know there is nothing."

I had never heard a brother or sister express the slenderest doubt in God's glorious afterlife before, and it shook me. "Nothing," I whispered, and even the word sounded tissue-thin.

"You have never wondered?"

"No," I said. "Nothing would be . . . a relief. Do you not think?"

"Ah," he replied. "You must fear judgement if the thought of no afterlife comes as a relief."

I sighed deeply. "I do."

The silence drew out, and still Elfric did not return. Then Godric asked, as I knew he would, "What did you do, Eadwyn?"

The secret strained against my ribs and throat. It wanted it to be free. But words would not form.

Godric placed his hand over mine again. "You will feel better if you tell me."

"You will think so ill of me."

"How could I? It is for God to judge. Not me." He dropped his voice. "I could not think ill of you, Eadwyn. Never."

I opened my mouth once, twice, then on the third attempt I spoke. "I ended a child's suffering," I said quickly, so quickly the words blurred together.

"That is a good thing."

"I ended his suffering by hastening his death," I continued, as though I hadn't heard. "I did not trust to God to take him in His own time in accordance with His plan. That is, I killed him. I killed a child."

Godric was silent and I knew he must despise me, but the words were flowing now and could no longer be stopped. "The boy was an orphan. His lungs were not working and every breath was savage pain. He begged us to end his misery. Sister Patience said no. Sister Alberg said no. Five sisters in a row said no to this poor child, who was little more than skin stretched over pain and bones. His death was certain but far too slow in coming. I dismissed them all. It was night. Cold. His little body . . . " I took a breath. "I kissed him and prayed for him and said it was time to go. He smiled at me."

Godric's fingers squeezed mine tightly and, emboldened, I told the rest. "I turned him on his stomach and said if he counted in his head to fifty, he would be with God. I pressed his face into the blankets and held him down fast, even when his limbs twitched and his animal instinct to survive came alive in him. It took longer than fifty seconds. It took four minutes. The longest four minutes of my life. Then he was still, and all was quiet. When Sister Patience returned . . . they all knew. They all knew."

I withdrew my hand and palmed away the tears. "That is why I lost my post at Hundley Vale. I destroyed the Abbey. The sisters could no longer be ruled by one who had murdered a child. One by one they began to leave, until the Archbishop ordered the Abbey to be disbanded. There was no fire, except perhaps the fires of Hell, waiting for me."

Godric chuckled. "You will not go to Hell for an act of mercy."

"Mercy? Do you not mean murder?"

"You acted from kindness and love, not hostility and hate. God knows your heart. He knows how you've struggled and he knows how brave you had to be in that moment. But you did the right thing; I am sure of it."

"How can you be sure?"

"Because the God I feel in my heart is gentle and forgiving and good. He is not a God to damn you for acting out of mercy."

His words soothed me, and I was so grateful that tears blurred my vision.

"Do you think God will forgive me?" Godric asked then, with a chuckle and a shake of his head.

"Forgive you for what?"

"For my disenchantment with monastic life? For my wish for something beyond these walls?"

I was so shocked by his sudden confession that I hadn't managed to gather an answer before the door ground open in its frame and a voice called out, "Godric?"

Godric shot to his feet, a guilty gulp at his throat. "Here. We were locked in."

Elfric's figure appeared in the threshold. "Come along then," he said, as though nothing had happened. "Alfgar is safely back in the refectory, the rain grows heavier, and Eadwyn should return to her quarters where she will be safe."

Like that, our moment of intimacy dissolved and I could not believe that I had told him about the boy. And I could not believe how relieved I felt to finally have confessed that burden to a forgiving heart.

❀

The sky was still a slate sheet above me, but Elfric was right that the rain had stopped. The idea of being cooped up back in the room was more than I could bear, not now that my soul had stirred to such a degree. Godric saw me off at my door and I waited for his footsteps to recede before I emerged, made my way up the rough wooden steps to the second floor, then along the hall past rooms that stood open and empty. In the corner room, the shutter was not properly closed and I moved inside to close it.

From up here, I could see over the whole northern side of the Abbey grounds. The corner of the plot looked as though it had dropped into the stream. The mill pond had joined the river and the water was easily six inches deep. I took a deep breath, stilled my hands. The slate sky lowered over it all, and it felt as though the world may very well be plunged into final chaos. I glanced over the Abbey wall and into the forest, and a blackened tree caught my gaze. An oak, split in two, its uppermost bough hanging about to fall. Charred down the centre from the lightning strike on the day we had taken Alfgar up to Helis Hill.

What force God had. It would take two men working for hours with axes to cut down such a tree, but God had done it with one brush of His mighty hand. I felt small. Insignificant. My deeds, my fate, they did not matter much to someone so powerful as God.

And if there was no God, then they did not matter at all.

❄

For the next three days, Godric brought me my supper after Vespers, and lingered until the Compline bells rang. What bliss it was to be with him, even as the clouds continued to unburden themselves with cold rain from one end of Cerneli to the other. Our sharing of secrets in the crypt had made us candid with each other, and I found myself telling him about my thoughts and feelings even as he told me his. Deeper and deeper we went, listening to the whispers in each other's spires rather than listening to our own fears about doomsday.

On the fourth night, however, he did not come. A thin-faced brother of nearly eighty brought my turnip soup and he did not stay. He left the wooden tray and returned to the rain.

I ate by the window, which I left open despite the rain, alert for Godric's arrival. When the Compline bells rang, I closed the shutter and prayed and went to bed. And so it was the next night, too, but then the rain began to ease and the clouds shredded apart on hesitant stars. Perhaps it was over, I thought.

I woke to the sound of rushing water. I rose and went to the window to open the shutter. Blue sky above. But below, I could see that the river had broken its banks and thundering brown water carved through the middle of the abbey. The ground either side eroded and fell in tumbling chunks into the flow. The way between the guesthouse and the rest of the Abbey was cut, and the floodwater was easily a foot deep. I thought of all the people of the village, their houses filled with the muddy river. I thought of the crypt, full of grain and stores that were now, without a doubt, inundated. I packed my satchel and rolled up my blankets and ascended the stairs. If the water kept rising, I would soon find myself knee-deep in it. Upstairs at least I had a chance to stay dry.

Nobody came to me that day. I ate some leftover bread and nursed an empty, growling stomach, and waited for the water to recede. When the evening drew in, I lay down on the hard floorboards and closed my eyes, wondering if I was to be all alone at the end of the world.

❈

That night, the wind came. It howled through the wood and over the roof, and blasted open my shutter deep in the night. I woke, heart thudding, and the heavy horror of the moment was upon me. Satan coming in his whirlwind. A prophecy that had not seemed possible was now unshakeable truth. I fell to my knees and prayed and prayed, my hands clasped so hard against each other that I could feel my bones and joints under my soft skin.

"Eadwyn! Eadwyn!"

I lifted my head, was on my feet a moment later. It was Godric. I ran to the top of the stairs and called down.

"Here. I am up here."

He appeared below me, his face turned up, his brow furrowed. "It is time," he said.

"The crypt must be flooded."

"It is, but we have saved most of the goods and they are stored on benches in the abbey church. That is where we will gather."

"Is it not flooded?" I asked, hurrying down the stairs.

"Ankle deep. You will get wet," he replied, taking my arm. "But nobody promised the world's end would be comfortable."

I boldly slipped my hand into his, and he glanced at me. His eyes were sad.

"I wish I had lived differently," he said, and his thumb moved back and forth over my knuckles.

"All joys will be available to us in Heaven," I said.

We waded through the cold brown water and out towards the church. The wind caught my scarf and whipped it off my head. It disappeared into the night and the damp. My steel-streaked hair whipped at my face. I could hear shouting, crying.

"What is that?" I asked.

"Villagers," he said grimly. "They have been gathering outside the gates since the rain stopped."

"Can we not let them in?"

He shook his head. "The Abbot has forbidden it."

I heard the wail of a baby, and my heart felt raw. On I went, beside Godric, my dress dragging in the floodwater, my bare toes sinking into the sodden ground. The church door opened as we approached, and inside was lit with torches that reflected amber in the water that covered the floor. The wind gusted in, sending all the flames dancing. Then the door slammed behind us and everything was still again. The porter dropped a bar into place, barricading us in. The wind bellowed over the roof and found cracks in the brickwork through which to screech. The benches in the nave were heaving under the weight of the stores. Some of the brothers had taken up space in the cracks between barrels and bags. On the other side of the stone arches, the other monks were crammed into the elevated space in the chancel, lying wrapped in blankets or kneeling and praying. The Abbot braved the floodwater, wading from place to place checking on the monks, holding his candle beneath their faces and barking their names as he did, as though listing them all in his head could keep them safe.

He turned, then, and saw Godric and me. His eyes narrowed, and he strode towards us as fast as the water would allow him. "No!" he shouted. "No, no! Godric, we have spoken of this. She may be here, but she may not be near you. Not so close to your judgement."

"And I have told you—" Whatever Godric was about to say was cut short by somebody calling out to the Abbot from the chancel.

"Alfgar is missing!"

The Abbot turned away from us, and snapped, "Then he meets his own doom alone!"

Godric seized my hand and dragged me away, back towards the door and towards a dim corner where one of the benches was pushed up against the cold stone wall. There, behind a tall stack of crates, we found a narrow corner to sit in.

"He'll find us," I said.

"He is busy. We are the least of his worries."

"What did he mean? About you not being near me so close to your judgement?" My throat constricted with heat and hope as I said this.

Before he could answer, there was a huge cracking noise and part of the roof lifted away. The wind gusted in and with it a shower of broken beams. They fell behind us, on the other side of the arches. Shouting and screaming filled the air.

"Stay here," Godric said. "I will be back for you."

I nodded, and shrank against the wall. I had never heard a noise like the wind that night. Louder than thunder and more constant. The sound of the world ending.

But beyond it, faintly, I could hear a voice shouting for help, on the other side of the church door.

I glanced around, but all the monks had moved to the chancel where part of the roof had fallen in. The porter was nowhere in sight. I approached the door and leaned my ear against it, straining to hear over the shriek of the wind.

"Help! My little girl!"

Somehow one of the villagers had entered the Abbey grounds. Or maybe more of them. The Abbot would not want the door opened.

"Help us! Please!" The voice snatched by the wind.

I closed my eyes and asked God, but he did not need to answer me. I knew the right thing to do. I lifted the bar and the doors blew open, sending me staggering back. Dawn light glimmered in the sky. Outside, a group of eight or ten people waited, ragged and wet and bloody. In the arms of the man at the front was the limp body of a child of three or four, whom he offered to me with a mournful expression on his face. "Is she dead?" he asked.

I leaned forward, still holding onto the door. The wind battered my body. I could see in the dim reflected light that the child's face was bloody.

"What happened?"

"We climbed over the wall," he said. "She fell."

I took the child from his arms and folded her against me. "I am sorry," I said, closing my eyes. "We should have let you in."

One of the women in the group began to sob hysterically. I sat on the threshold, hip-deep in water, and held the child. I wanted to sob too, but instead I chose to use my last moments in the world using the special gift God had given me. I summoned all the calm in my heart and blood and bones, and I enveloped her in it. Beyond the circle of her and me, there were horrendous noises. Trees cracking, roofs peeling, buildings falling. But I held her and I bathed her in God's love and we were warm and still here at the end of everything.

She began to move and the spell was broken. She raised her head and said, "Papa?"

Her father bent to scoop her up and I became aware that the wind was dying off. The sky brightened. And the Abbot was shouting at me.

"Get her out! Lock the door!" He roughly pulled me by the shoulder so I was on my feet, his face close to mine and twisted with anger. "What have you done? Why did you let them in? Get out!"

Then I was thrust outside and fell forward in the floodwater. I put out my hands to stop myself from landing on my face, but my dress was now soaked. One of the small party of villagers helped me to my feet. I looked around. The air had stilled. Half of the refectory was intact, but the rest was a mound of splintered wood.

"God be with us," I breathed. My eyes went skywards and I said a prayer of thanks, then instructed the villagers to go and shelter in the guesthouse.

"We heard the devil is coming," one of the younger men said.

"Perhaps he changed his mind," I replied, setting off towards the refectory. I could see bare white feet protruding from beneath the rubble.

I was halfway to the body when the door of the church opened, then slammed again.

"Wait, Eadwyn!" It was Godric.

I kept walking. I suspected who the body belonged to, but I wanted to make sure. I reached the wood pile and began pulling broken timber pieces off him. Godric joined me a few moments later, and between us we managed to wrangle the Alfgar's corpse from the ruins.

"Perhaps it was his own end he saw," I said, as Godric knelt to pray over Alfgar.

Behind us, a small group of monks had emerged, the Abbot among them.

"The weather has cleared. You must leave Cerneli," he said to me.

Godric's eyes looked up, met mine. He smiled sadly.

"I will," I said.

✳

Two weeks have passed since that terrible storm. I have been staying all this while with a family in Minterne, where the rain was gentler and the wind did not come at all. Life has been more still and calm, but more flat and grey. I told myself, when I set out this morning, that I only came to see how Cerneli had fared in the aftermath. Were the floodwaters gone, had the village cleaned up the layers of mud, had the Abbey repaired its church roof? But rather than investigating any of those things I walk straight through the village and find myself here, at the well, wishing for an end to this dull, sweet ache of longing.

I close my eyes. The sunlight makes patterns on my lids, and I take a deep breath of the soft air. A breeze moves in the branches, and I am suddenly aware that I am not alone. I open my eyes and turn. It is Godric.

At first I do not trust my own sight. But then he smiles at me and hurries forward. "I thought it was you," he said. "I saw you in the village and came after you as soon as I could get away."

I rise, guilt and shame on my face. Did he see me tie the ribbon? Did he hear my wish? "God be with you, Godric," I manage.

He laughs, seizing my hands. "You are back and it is the very sign I hoped for," he says.

"Sign?"

"Eadwyn, what if Alfgar was right and the end is coming? Will you be happy to die, knowing only what you have known?"

I try to say something godly, something righteous, but instead I simply shake my head.

"I am leaving the Abbey," he says.

"You are?"

"I am leaving the Abbey . . . for you."

Speechless, I feel my knees unhinge beneath me. He catches me, and I smell lemons and meadowsweet. The world can end whenever it pleases.

I do not mind.

The Giant

Autumn, 44 AD

THEY OUGHT NEVER HAVE RETURNED a spear to my father's hand, for he was ruined and no longer fit for war.

I knew by the boot marks in the mud that Senorix and Loxi were with him. I trudged up the slope from the gate house with Catria's little hand in mine and the dogs at my heels, when our round thatched roof came into view. One set of prints before me were heavy and cumbersome, the other sharp and light. Each man's personality distilled in their gait.

Senorix and Loxi had each been to visit Pa separately since the accident, but never together.

"Catria," I said, releasing her hand and turning her gently towards the village. "Go to see Gwyra and ask her for some fresh eggs for dinner."

"But Gwyra is so old and so boring and slow," Catria protested, turning her freckled face up to mine.

"Hush now. We must respect our elders. They are slow because they are wise. Tell her I will pay her tomorrow."

Catria slouched off reluctantly towards the granary, which was beside Ria's little hut. Catria preferred horses to people. I picked my way around the mud with the dogs and opened the door to our house. My eyes took a moment to adjust from the cool, autumn light outside to the dim, smoke-filled interior.

"Pa?" I asked.

Pa, who sat by the fire on a wooden stool, looked up at me and smiled. He never smiled much before the accident. In his hands was his spear, no doubt returned to him by Senorix who loomed over him. Loxi stood back, one foot propped behind him on the rough earthen wall, wiry tattooed arms folded across his chest.

"Ah, here is my Iona," Pa said, letting the dogs lick his face. "Where is Catria?"

"I sent her to get some eggs. Greetings to you, too," I said with a nod towards Senorix and Loxi. "Will you be staying for supper?"

They glanced at each other, clearly uncomfortable. "We need to speak with your father in confidence," Senorix managed at last.

I did not want to leave them alone with Pa.

"Away with you, Iona," Pa said kindly. "They won't stay long."

"I will go within," I said, indicating the rough woollen curtain hung from the beams that separated our living area from where we all slept on a straw mattress with the dogs.

Loxi looked dubious but Senorix said, "She's a girl. It doesn't matter what she hears."

Not a girl. Not anymore, as Senorix's eldest son Mato knew only too well. I leaned over and gave Pa a kiss on the head, next to the deep scar. He gave me that smile again. Soft. Slightly empty. I slipped behind the curtain and lay down on the blanket, eyes fixed on the thatching, and listened to every word.

"They have settled at Pol," Senorix said. "Their general's name is Vespasian. Now the Adrebads have submitted, he turns his eye to us. He has established a supply chain. There is no doubt he will come after Dwr-y-Trig holdings."

"The Romans want our iron. Our cattle. Our money."

"Wherever they go, they extract heavy taxes. Gold and grain.

The submitters starve. We cannot submit."

"We must form a tribal confederation," Loxi said. "We can no longer be a chain of unconnected hill forts that notice each other's watch fires only idly."

On they went, and Pa said nothing. Not two seasons past, my father was a leader of men, a thrower of spears. Vernico of Caern Helith was known for having brained a westerman with his slingshot from one-hundred yards away. Pa had a long red moustache plaited into his beard, a war horn always hanging from his belt. He had been fierce. I was frightened of his ferocity.

"Are you listening to us?" Senorix huffed, exasperation finally breaking into his voice.

"Yes. Yes I am," said Pa. "I will need to think. To seek good counsel."

"We *are* your good counsel," Loxi said. "Or at least we once were." Senorix and Loxi had their smaller forts on adjacent hills. It was their watch fires we saw the clearest when trouble was at hand. But until now trouble had always meant westermen, or failed trader tribes from across the channel trying their luck with small settlements. Not the mighty war machine of the Roman army.

"Do you understand, Vernico, that neither Loxi nor I will make terms with the Romans. You will be swept into war, one way or another. That is why I have had your spear repaired. That is why we have come here together this day. The wheel already turns."

A long silence, then Pa's voice, pleasant and unperturbed. "I will let you know my decision soon."

Moments later, their furious feet had left the house.

I emerged, came to sit with Pa by the fire. One of the dogs had his head in Pa's lap. Pa stared at the fire thoughtfully, humming the sweet melody that he returned to again and again.

"I heard everything," I said.

"I know. I don't mind."

"What shall we do?"

He looked up and smiled again. "You are not to worry about the Romans."

"But they will come. There is no doubt."

"Since the accident I can't always think straight," he said, gently touching the scar on his head. "I will need to ask advice."

"Who will you ask?"

He shrugged as if the answer was self-evident. "The piskies of course."

❄

It happened in the coombe. The chieftans of Caern Helith, Black Rock, and Meadow Hill had brought their war bands together for practice. The Romans were on their minds. Pa took the threat seriously then. Mato saw everything and told me later. Pa's foot stuck in the mud. He fell forward, holding out his spear to break his fall. The spear snapped and one of Loxi's nephews thought it a joke to slash out with his practise sword; that family had always resented Pa's power. The dull iron edge was not enough to kill Pa, but it was enough to cut the flesh, crack the skull. His brain swelled and for a week he lay between Catria and me, his head wrapped in bloody woollen bandages, breathing like he might die at any second.

He didn't die, but when he woke, he was changed. I still hoped he would recover, stop seeing piskies and trolls and spriggans, and lead the Dwr-y-Trig tribes in triumph against the Romans. But it seemed the Romans might not wait for him to recover. And it seemed I was the only person who knew how far the mighty Vernico had fallen.

❄

Preparations for the harvest blessing drove thoughts of Romans out of my mind for two days, and Pa didn't mention piskies again. At dusk, Pa led the villagers down the hill and through woods of elm, elder, and ash. Down in the little clearing we arrived at the Silver Well, where we always celebrated our blessings. We had brought with us a panel of hazel weave, which two of the men erected behind the well. Then the women, including me and Catria, began to decorate the panel with evergreen branches and leaves: juniper and holly, box and yew.

As the sky grew dark, the men built bonfires and the piper played and Pa sang. Pa's voice was deep and rich and sonorous, and we said our blessings and danced and threw, one by one, a year's worth of collected pinecones on the fire. Sweet smells filled the air. Embers danced on the breeze. The drummer played a faster beat, and a small group from Senorix's tribe arrived, Mato among them.

His hand was softly on my hip before I saw him. I whirled around, and he caught my hands. I smiled, he smiled. And we danced.

The music and the revels went on for another hour before the sky was fully dark, and then the pipers slowed and played a melancholy tune, and Pa stood before us to sing the harvest blessing song. He looked so handsome, tall and broad shouldered, with his checkered pants and his green tunic and a thick gold torque around his neck. We gathered, sitting on the ground, with our hands raised to the heavens as the pipers played and he sang our thanks and our hopes.

Mato had his arm around my waist. My face was warm. My heart beat happily. A feeling of settled contentment, a feeling that all would be well.

Then Pa stopped singing. In the middle of a line. His gaze went up and slightly to the left, and he looked for all the world as though he was listening to somebody talking.

The piper went on. The blessing remained unfinished.

I shot to my feet. I knew all the words of the blessing; I had listened to my father sing it every year since I was a baby. I sang, my voice soft and hesitant, but I sang. Pa heard and woke, as if from a dream, and joined me. We finished the song together. Catria looked up at me with eyes full of admiration; Mato looked suspicious.

The blessing song marked the end of the event, and slowly the villagers began to pack and make their way back up to Caern Helith.

Mato's lips were at my ear. "Find a reason to stay behind," he said.

I smiled up at him, excitement ringing in my heart. And lower. "I will," I replied.

He moved off with his family, and I found Pa and Catria.

"I will not leave with you," I said. "Gwyra is very old and uncertain on her feet. As the first daughter of the tribe, it falls to me to help her home."

Pa smiled down at me, his face gentle in the firelight. "You are a good woman. How proud I am of you."

These were things he never would have said before his injury, and worry took the shine from them.

"You forgot your lines," I said to Pa, in a quiet voice so nobody else could hear.

"No I didn't. I was listening to something . . . "

He didn't finish. One of the merchant's sons, who fought alongside Pa, approached and slapped his shoulder, laughing merrily about some nonsense. Catria gripped Pa's hand hard, and they walked away together.

"Gwyra!" I called, hurrying my footsteps after her.

She paused and looked around. She leaned on a thick, straight branch that had been cut for her. "Young Iona," she said with a smile.

"The hill is steep and you are slow and will be left behind. Let me help you."

"How kind," she said, and I did not correct her.

I slid my arm around her waist and she leaned into me. Her old bones weighed nothing.

"Your singing was beautiful," she said.

"Thank you."

"Is Vernico losing his memory?"

I chose my words carefully. "He's distracted," I said. "Thinking about Romans."

We walked in silence a little while, having reached the bottom of the winding path that cut through the vertical steepness of the hill.

"I'll need to rest," Gwyra panted.

"Of course." I stopped and we sat down. Others walked past us, laughing and talking. The night air was chill, damp.

"Romans are enough to drive happy thoughts out of anyone's mind," Gwyra said when she'd caught her breath. "We are very lucky to have Vernico to lead us against them."

A spear of guilt and worry pierced my heart. Gwyra deserved to live out her days in peace and contentment. I formed replies but none of them made their way out of my mouth. Instead, I said, "Let's get you home. It grows cold."

We slowly made our way up the hill in the dark, every minute weighing an hour. Finally, I left her by her door and hurried off, back down the hill to the Silver Well.

The fire still burned low, barely taking the chill off the air. Mato was nowhere to be seen. I sat on the grass by the well and dipped my fingertips into the freezing water. I heard a faint whispering sound, and startled; then realised it was simply the breeze in the trees.

It was said that the well was a portal to the Otherworld, that if a mother dipped a newborn baby in it at dawn then good fortune would follow, that the faces of the soon-dead appeared in the water at nightfall on Samhain.

It was said the well could grant wishes.

With swift fingers, I unpicked the leather strap that held my shoe together. I closed my eyes, trying to frame my wish. The sound of footsteps close by made me hurry.

"Keep the Romans away," I said quickly, binding the strap to the nearest branch of hawthorn.

"Iona?"

I turned, a guilty flush on my cheeks. "Mato. There you are."

"Are you wishing? Like a little girl?" He laughed good-naturedly.

"No, I'm . . . " I stood, abandoning my explanation. "Come here and kiss me."

He was with me a second later, lips on my mouth, chin, cheeks, and hands around my waist and sliding down to my bottom. He gathered up my skirt and my knees shook and heat flared deep inside me.

"Over there," he whispered against my cheekbone, and we walked—kissing, hands in each other's secret places—towards the bed of thick grass in front of the well. The grass was cold and damp against my bare backside, but I didn't care. Half in and half out of our clothes, Mato and I joined our bodies hungrily, fire and youth and recklessness.

When our hearts slowed, when our breathing evened out, when our clothes were smoothed, Mato lay with his head on my breast and said, "What did you wish for?" He propped himself up and grinned down on me, "Did I grant it?"

I tried to laugh, but his question brought all my problems back to my mind. "It was nothing."

"Go on. Perhaps I can help."

The poor lad. He thought it was about him.

"It's Pa," I said. "He's not . . . right. Ever since that blow to his head."

"Not right?" His eyebrows lifted.

I tried to read his expression. He was curious, but was he concerned. I reminded myself he was Senorix's son, that his loyalties were not guaranteed. "I'm probably imagining things," I said brightly.

"Iona, if there is any doubt that your father can help in the war with the Romans, you need to say something."

"No. Of course he can fight. His spear arm is legendary."

Mato sat up, pulled his boots back on. "Aye, that it is. When will I see you again? Tomorrow my father and mother travel to my uncle's farm for three nights. I will be cold by myself." A wicked grin.

My heart flipped over. "I will come if I can."

He crooked his index finger and touched my cheek. "You are so beautiful," he said. He kissed me, helped me to my feet, and set me on the path up the hill.

❧

I woke late the following morning, to the sound of my father humming that strange melody. I lay for a while listening. Catria was sound asleep next to me, a dog either side of her body, her hand in a loose fist beside her cheek. She was seven now, but I could still see her baby softness in her face. I had raised her after Ma died of a spotted fever when I was ten.

The humming intensified, and I heard the clatter of weapons, so I rose and parted the curtain to peer out at him. Pa was assembling weapons on a sheet of coarse-woven fabric by the fire pit. Spear, axe, sling, shield, five or six good sized rocks.

My heart lifted. He was preparing to fight the Romans after all. Then he folded the material over the weapons and wrapped them tightly, reached for a rope and began to wind it around and around, binding up the lot into a package.

"Pa?" I ventured.

The humming abruptly stopped and he turned to smile at me. "You and your sister have slept so late! Too much fun last night?"

I thought of Mato and heat prickled my cheeks. "Yes, perhaps." I indicated the package. "What are you doing?"

He lifted the wrapped weapons and deposited them in a wicker basket. "Collecting these things and leaving them where I will need them." He stood, opened the little back entrance where we kept our well buckets, and hefted the wicker basket out there.

"For the Romans?" I realised my pulse was thick in my throat. *Please say the Romans.*

He closed the door, took my hand, and pulled me down next to him to sit by the fire pit. "My daughter, can I be honest with you?"

"I hope that you always are, Pa."

"The piskies have told me a giant is coming."

My tongue felt leaden in my mouth. I could not bring myself to speak.

"I see from your expression you don't believe me."

"Who are the piskies, Pa?"

"The spirits."

"Which spirits?"

"Of the air, the water, the trees. They are everywhere. The unseen world teems with them. But the strongest ones are at the well, and last night they told me."

The unseen world teems with them. I had a flash of memory, a dream I'd had. Russet darkness, shadowed faces. It tickled at the base of my neck then was gone, leaving me fearful. "That is why you stopped singing?"

"Yes. To listen."

"And they said . . . " I could not bring myself to repeat the word "giant".

Pa had no such qualms. "There is a giant coming. He will come from the well and he will stalk up the hill and come for our homes, our children."

I thought perhaps if I asked some reasonable, rational questions, it might cause him to see sense. "Why have the piskies told you? Why do they care what happens to us?"

"They don't. The giant will destroy them too. For giants and piskies have fought over this land since the rocks were born." His voice grew urgent. "We stand on the land of an ancient battle. And as to why they have told me: am I not the mighty Vernico? Who else but me could defeat a giant? Loxi? His arms are like twigs. Senorix who moves like a bull?" He laughed, and it was so unexpected amid the dark thoughts and feelings that I almost laughed too.

"Piskies and giants, Pa? You never used to believe in such things."

"I believed in the gods. You honoured them alongside me at the harvest festival. If I believe in their unseen power, why not the power of other creatures?" He leaned close and I noticed his eyes were perfectly clear. Not clouded at all by ignorance or madness. "You must know this, Iona. In your heart. Surely you know this."

His words aroused a superstitious fear, and I pulled away from him. "I must go wake Catria," I said, not looking back.

I withdrew to the bedroom and fell to my knees on the blankets. One of the dogs raised his head and sniffed the air. Catria looked so young, so vulnerable. What would the Romans do to her? I had to look after her. Look after all of us.

I did not believe Pa about the piskies and the giant. These things were stories told to children. And if their magic was imaginary, so too was the magic of the well. I knew then that my wish could achieve nothing. If I wanted the Romans to stay away, I had to make them stay away myself.

Loxi and Senorix had said the general Vespasian wanted our gold. Pol was three days of walking from here.

I wondered how much gold Vespasian would need to leave us alone.

❋

Guilt is a strong emotion, but it cannot win out over fear.

I knew everyone in the village, and where all their roundhouses were within the high woven walls that enclosed it. I had seen last night that Alorax, our most successful merchant, was absent from the harvest blessing; I had seen, too, that his wife Dwinova, was dancing with her sisters by the evergreen weave. This meant that Alorax was away, and not ill and in need of nursing.

Alorax's house would be full of treasures, I was sure.

I took Catria, and for that I felt the most guilt. She didn't know what I intended, and nor did she question me when I told her what she had to do. With deft hands, she unpinned Dwinova's goose pen, with sure feet she ran to Dwinova's door, and with a clear voice she called out, "Dwinova! Dwinova! Your geese are loose!"

I lurked in the shadows by the granary, which stood in the middle of the village. When I saw Dwinova run out with Catria, and heard the flapping and honking of stubborn geese resisting being rounded up, I hurried around the back way, past three other roundhouses, to Alorax's home. He had a shuttered window facing the west, and I prised it open from the outside and wriggled my way in.

A moment as my eyes adjusted to the dark. Then I glanced around. A wooden chest. I flipped it open, heart pounding, and the dull gleam of gold caught my eye.

A cup, a torque, four brooches. And that was it. I shoved them all into the front of my dress, closed the box and was out the window while the honking continued.

I sat for a moment, my back leaning up against the rough thatching of the roundhouse, my hand pinned over the treasure in my dress. It wasn't much. It wasn't anywhere near enough to pay off Vespasian. I had hoped for so much more. A sack of treasure. A pile of gold. Something that would make him catch his breath and say, yes, I will stay away from your small, quiet fold of the world.

But I would have to do this again and again.

❋

That afternoon, I was grinding millet for bread when Pa dressed himself, hung his second-best spear at his hip and his second-best shot around his shoulder (his best were tied up in the package in the wicker basket) and told me he was heading to the coombe for training.

"Training?" I squawked. "With the other tribes?"

"Yes. You aren't to worry. I know it's my first time back since the accident, but I will be safe."

"I . . . " Lost for words, I grasped his hand. "I will come. To keep an eye on you."

"I don't need an eye kept on me."

I forced a smile. "You are right. I'm worried. I want to be there. Besides, I would like to watch."

He shook off my hand, so brusquely he almost seemed like his old self. "Suit yourself then, but it may be a long afternoon."

I left the millet half-ground, calling out to Catria that she should finish it. Pa was a few steps ahead of me, but I caught him just before the gate house and he was cheerful enough on the walk to the coombe, pointing out the clouds on the horizon and not mentioning piskies or giants.

The others were already there, setting up targets and pacing out distances. The young men, Mato among them, play-wrestled on the slopes, shirtless and bursting with excited aggression. I took a seat on the slope in the shade of an ash tree that had not yet lost all its leaves, and Pa joined them. They spoke to him and he to them, but their voices were snatched away from me on the wind. Could he get through training without mentioning creatures from the otherworld? So far, all seemed normal. Shield and spear practice. Drills with the shot. Mato glanced up at me repeatedly, swaggering, lifting his shoulders with exaggerated pride. He was glorious to look upon, with his smooth white skin and muscular arms. I settled, I relaxed. I even enjoyed myself. Pa was sluggish but otherwise normal, and who could blame him for being a little slow when it had been weeks since he last trained?

It was only in the last hour of training that Pa began to behave slightly out of the normal. He took a sudden intense interest in the tree I sat beneath, glancing up at it as though someone sitting in the branches had called him. He paused, arms going slack at his side, listening. Loxi's nephew, having learned his lesson from last time, tapped his shoulder gently with the edge of the sword.

Pa looked at the sword, shrugged, and brought his mind back to training.

Five minutes later, he paused and looked up again.

"Please, no," I said under my breath. "Don't let them notice."

Perhaps the others did notice, but nobody seemed to care. They were busy with their weapons, with their pounding hearts and aching limbs. Loxi called an end to training, and the coombe began to empty. Loxi's steward collected the targets, the young men wrestled again then left one by one. Only Pa stood there, shot in his hands, gazing up at the ash tree.

I stood. "Pa!" I called, waving. "Time for us to go?"

He said nothing, but he shook his head, and kept watching. By now, everyone had left except Mato and one of his friends, who lingered. Mato had his eyes on Pa.

"No, no, no," I muttered. I took two steps towards Pa, intending to collect him, when suddenly he sprang into life.

All traces of sluggishness were gone. He bolted up the hill fast as a hare, loading his shot. *Crack.* The rock hit an uppermost branch of the tree. A half-moment later another hit. The rocks thudded to the ground one after the other. I stood aside as Pa raced towards the tree, his rope in his hands now, and began to run around it in circles, winding the base of the trunk in rope.

"Pa?" I called, but he gave no indication he heard.

Around and around, the rope tighter and tighter until finally he pulled on it so hard I thought he might yank his arms out of their sockets. Then he released the rope, lifted his arm, ran up the hill and released the spear. It landed vertically, tip in the ground, quivering.

I became aware of laughter behind me. Mato and his friend, thirty yards below us.

"He certainly showed that tree," Mato's friend said.

Mato said nothing, but he fixed me in his gaze and I knew what he was thinking.

I turned my back on him, trudged up to the hill to where Pa had collapsed, panting, on the ground. "Are you all right?" I asked him.

He nodded. "I think all will be well," he said, and he stood and went about winding up his rope, humming all the while.

✳

I had chores in the village that afternoon, picking up leeks and turnips from the market and taking Catria's shoes to the leatherworker to fix a seam. Wherever I walked—past the smith or the stalls or the small roundhouses of the merchants—it was as though I saw another version of Caern Helith: the version left by the Romans. Burnt beams and piles of bones. All of us were merely playing our parts as though the future was not coming, but it most assuredly was unless I pulled together enough of a levy to keep Vespasian away.

My woven sack was full of vegetables and a bloodless goose, when we made our way to the edge of the village where the leatherworker's stall stood. Another woman was ahead of us, the corpulent sister of one of the merchants, and she haggled mercilessly with the leatherworker over a rain mantle. I placed the bag at my feet, readying myself for a long wait, when the door of one of the houses opened and a tall man strode out. He locked his door with an iron key, pocketed it, then disappeared off into the village.

But there must have been a hole in his pocket because his key dropped in the muddy grass, bounced once then lay there. He didn't see it.

I recognised him, of course. I knew most people in the village but especially the warriors and the merchants. He was a merchant named Airic, who traded with the northern tribes. Wool for silver. His house would be full of treasure, surely.

"Good afternoon, young Iona," the leatherworker said, clearly relieved to be rid of the demanding woman.

I glanced from the key, to the leatherworker. Then I quickly leaned in to Catria's ear and said, "Fetch the key in the grass and keep it. Don't let anyone see you."

She looked up at me with trusting eyes and nodded once. I applied my smile and showed Catria's shoes to the leatherworker.

✿

I waited an hour then went back. The sunlight was weak and grainy and the sky had grown cold. The market stalls were mostly shut, and the village smelled of smoke as one by one hearth fires were lit. I walked as boldly as I could to Airic's house, knocked once on the door and waited. Nobody answered. He wasn't home.

I took a deep breath, and withdrew the key from my apron. It was the size of my index finger, with a curled end and three prongs jutting from it. It fitted in the lock and turned with a snick, and I was about to lift the latch when I heard a voice calling, "Hoy! Iona?"

I whirled around, my heart thudding. Airic approached, followed by two men carrying a large casket. Treasure, perhaps. Enough to keep the Romans away. But none of Airic's treasure was coming to me now. I thought fast.

"Airic," I said, holding out the key. "You dropped this today. I tried to follow you, but—"

He snatched it from my hand. "And why are you lurking at my door?"

"I came to return it."

"By using it in the lock?"

Words tripped over my tongue. "I was going to leave it inside for you because you weren't home when I knocked."

His eyes narrowed, and he pushed a strand of his long silver hair behind his ear. "You are either stupid or a liar, but given what I heard your father did this morning, perhaps it is the former."

"Pa is not stupid, he's—"

"Away with you. I have known you long enough to know you are not a thief," he said grudgingly. "Go home and tell your father there are those of us in the village who doubt him. That we need to see strong leadership again, and soon."

I was so grateful to escape punishment that I actually said, "Thank you," even though he had offered such wild insult to my father, to me.

I hurried home, despair sending black roots into my bones.

❊

I could not sleep that night. My thoughts chased each other and their edges did not soften. My eyes would not lie closed. I listened to Catria's breathing, the dogs'. I listened to the autumn breeze in the treetops. I thought about Pa and giants and piskies and Romans.

Just before dawn, I rose quietly.

Mato had said to come to him, and I hadn't yet obeyed. I admit part of me longed for his hot kisses, but the reason I went was I needed to know what he thought of Pa now, what his friend thought, if others were talking.

I slipped out of the bedroom. Pa lay asleep on the floor next to the fire, one of the dogs curled against the crook of his legs. I held my breath a moment to make sure he wouldn't wake. He snored lightly. I cracked open the door and a breeze came in and lifted flakes of ash from the fire pit. I froze.

But Pa didn't stir. Perhaps he was dreaming of piskies.

I closed the door behind me and the autumn cold caught my lungs. I thought about Mato's warm house, his warm arms, and I hurried my feet. I slipped past the gate house and the huge standing stone that marked our village boundary, and off the stone steps to the grass, my toes curling to keep my balance down the steep slope.

I wound down into the sycamore wood and passed near the path to the Silver Well. Here my footsteps slowed. This was where Pa had heard the piskies, and I remembered the time I had been here and heard the whispering of leaves, echoing in the vale, and believed them voices too.

I turned and headed down towards the well, past hazel and linden and alder and rowan, until I arrived. I stood and closed my eyes, listening. If I could convince Pa that the whispers were simply the noises of nature.

A breeze picked up. Gooseflesh rose on my arms. The leaves rubbed and tickled against each other, a soft shushhh-shushhh sound in the dark.

"A sssssson . . . . A sssssson . . . ."

My eyes flew open. I glanced around. The leaves were moving, shushhhing. I had imagined it.

Hadn't I?

I hurried away. A son? It didn't even make sense. Not piskies. Wind in the leaves. I grew angry at myself for being so easily fooled. I trudged up the slope and then my feet struck the path, and I began the five-mile journey to Black Rock, pushing the imagined voices out of my mind.

The sky was indigo. Distant light flushed the horizon to dull pink. The riot of morning birdsong had not yet begun. Instead, a few forlorn calls in the woods; early wakers looking for company. The path narrowed into the woods, between the ancient trees, unruly and never coppiced. Hazel and hornbeam. Ash and oak. These trees had stood when my grandfather and his grandfather had lived at Caern Helith; my family *was* Caern Helith. The Romans wanted what we had drawn from the land: the copper and tin, the centuries of refining breeding cattle and growing grain, the tribal bonds through which our methods of pottery and ironwork had been perfected and passed down. Our land, our families, had done all the work and now they came, with their stronger weapons, and sought to take it all from us. The thought made me terrified and enraged all at once.

I walked on as the birds woke and dawn came to the sky. The hill where the village of Black Rock stood came into view, and soon I was making my way up it, heart pounding from the steep slope. I opened the gate in the hazel fence and went through into the village. It was much smaller than Caern Helith, and the ground was rocky and uneven. An old woman was up early, washing her clothes in a bucket. Chickens pecked at the ground, clucking softly. I followed the path to Senorix's roundhouse, and cracked open the door.

"Mato?" I could see him squatting by the fire pit.

He looked up, smiling broadly. With that smile, my body relaxed.

"Iona," he said. "You came."

I slipped inside and closed the door behind me. Smoke caught in my throat. He stood and came to me, took my hand gently and led me to the blankets by the hearth. We laid down together. The blankets smelled of him: wood and smoke and spice. Slowly, little by little, we stripped off each other's clothes until we lay naked. As his hands explored me, my body ran with desire and pleasure. He turned me on my side, and he lay behind me, hands on my breasts, to enter me. It was then I saw the gold.

Glimmering softly in the firelight, half-covered in a blanket, tucked beneath a bench. Mato's parents must have hidden it there before they went away. I would not have seen it had I not been lying down.

My mind and body were no longer with Mato. I was figuring a way I could take the gold and add it to my paltry collection, to convince Vespasian not to come to Caern Helith. Mato's breathing grew faster, I realised I hadn't made a noise for a full minute. I made the noises I was supposed to make, and he finished and rolled onto his back.

I turned over, laid my head on his chest. He stroked my hair. My thoughts sped: how would I get the gold?

Then Mato said, "I need to piss."

He rose and pulled on his trousers, then opened the front door and went out. He left the door open, a wedge of pale daylight.

I was on my hands and knees in an instant, flicking off the blanket and finding a gold torque, a handful of gold brooches, and a gold statue of a man about three inches high. I threw on my underdress, pulled the gold against my body, then tied my overdress over it to keep it in place.

And then Mato was back. "Dressed? Going home already?"

"I'd better—"

"It's early. Lie with me a little while. Sleep." He grasped my hand, pulled me against him. I held my breath.

Of course he felt it.

"What have you . . . ?" Curiosity bled into anger, as his fingers plucked at the ties on my dress and the golden objects fell out at my feet, the torque bouncing painfully off my toes.

"I'm not stealing!" I said, even though I was, of course, stealing. "I'm gathering treasure to take to Vespasian. To tell him not to come here."

Mato shook his head in disbelief. "You think you can just go to visit the general of the Roman army?"

"He's at Pol. I heard your father say—"

"A young woman from the tribes turning up with gold? They'll take it and then they'll all take turns raping you and you'll probably be glad when they slit your throat."

I felt a fool. A stupid girl with no knowledge of the world.

"You're mad," he said, bending to pick up the golden statue. "Like your father."

"There's nothing wrong with Pa."

"There is and you know it. What was that he did at training yesterday? Tying up a tree? Spearing the ground? He's lost his wits, and he can no longer lead the Dwr-y-Triges."

"Please don't tell Senorix," I gasped, pulling my dress around me and retying it.

"Get out, Iona."

"Please."

"Get out."

※

All day, my stomach swirled with guilt, shame, fear. I could not eat or think or settle. I went about my chores with only half a mind on what I was doing. My barley bread was dry and hard, my mutton stew was chewy. Pa and Catria ate it without a murmur of complaint. Catria asked me a hundred times what was wrong, why was I pacing, why I wasn't answering her questions. Finally, I settled her in bed and returned to the fire pit to sit beside Pa.

He was humming his tune, and carving a wooden man out of a stick.

"Do you think Catria will like this to play with?" he asked, holding up the carving. "I think I might make a few of them and she can have them talk to each other."

"You never used to carve poppets or wonder about what Catria would like to play with," I said on a rush of breath. "You have changed."

His eyebrows rose. "That I have. For the better, wouldn't you agree? I was a rough, unkind man before."

"But at least you didn't see things that weren't real."

He shrugged and turned his face away. Firelight glowed in his red beard. "I know what I see."

I sank to my knees in front of him and grasped his hands. "Pa, the Romans are real."

"Yes, Iona, I know."

I chose my words carefully. "Nobody has reported seeing a giant. Whole towns are falling to the Romans."

He continued as though he hadn't heard, his voice matter-of-fact. "And when the Romans see that we have killed a giant, they will know to fear us and stay away."

I searched his eyes, but could not see the barest flicker of understanding. Despair unhinged all my joints. "Oh, Pa," I said. "Whatever happens I love you."

He lifted his hand and twined a strand of my hair around his fingers softly. "And I love you, Iona. And your sister. You do not need to—"

Then the door burst open. I saw Senorix's bulky outline, a group of men behind him. I heard Mato's voice.

It happened so quickly, with such noise and violence, that I did not have time to try to protect Pa. They had him on his knees, his hands pinned behind his back, and a blade pressed at the side of his throat.

"Do not protest and all will be well, Vernico," Senorix said.

"Why are you doing this?" Pa asked, bewildered.

Mato marched past me towards the bedroom, and I cried out and tried to stop him but two rough men grabbed my arms and held me.

"My old friend," Senorix said to Pa, "for all the love I bear for you, I cannot let you lead the Dwr-y-Trig tribes against the Romans. It has to be me. I am taking over Caern Helith, your war bands, and your chieftan duties."

Catria shrieked and ran out of the bedroom, ploughing into me. I got an arm free to curl around her thin shoulders. Mato emerged with the cup I had stolen from Alorax and Dwinova. "Thief!" he spat at me, throwing the cup at my feet.

Pa struggled against Senorix. "Don't do this," he said. "There is a giant coming to Caern Helith and only I can defeat him."

I had never thought that laughter could sound so merciless. Mato laughed loudest of them all.

Senorix shook his head sadly and did not laugh. "Lock them all in the granary for the night," he said. "We will decide what to do with them in the morning."

❋

Pa fought like a demon until they threatened to hurt Catria. Then he went limp and quiet. They lifted him up to the opening of the granary and shoved him in, but Catria and I chose to climb in after him. They shut the door and then I heard them fasten it tight with ropes through the latch. It was cold and very quiet. Catria cried softly, cold in her shift, but Pa was silent.

When I heard their footsteps withdraw, I sat heavily on a sack of grain. My eyes had adjusted a little and I could make out Catria's white face, Pa's red hair, sacks on the floor and threshing tools hung on the walls.

I waited for Pa to speak. He didn't.

"What are we going to do?" I asked.

"Wait," he said.

My temper flared. "You seem little concerned. We have lost our place in the village, we have lost our home, our dignity. And we will simply wait?"

"Iona—" Catria started, alarmed by the fire in my voice.

"Yes, we will wait," Pa said, squaring up his shoulders, his voice booming. "The piskies will come. You will see, daughter, and when you do, perhaps you will trust in me as a daughter should."

Piskies. I groaned, slumped to the floor. Perhaps it was for the best that Senorix had taken control of Caern Helith and the Dwr-y-Triges. Perhaps Catria and I would be safer if the tribes combined and organised a defence against the Romans. Pa could not be helped any further.

He began to hum and I said, without heat, "I wish you would not hum that music."

"You will wish I did very soon," he said, then spoke no more.

Catia and I curled on the floor between sacks of grain, shivering despite our shared body heat. Pa sat on watch. I saw him with his head cocked, listening, just as I drifted off into a hard, miserable sleep.

❆

I woke to thin light, to the sight of Pa pacing across the few feet of wooden floor. Back and forth. Catria slept on.

"Pa?" I asked.

"It is dawn and the piskies haven't set us free."

I rose and went to him, put my hand up to his shoulder and stilled him. "That is because there are no piskies," I said, and I was almost relieved. The voices at the well had not been real.

He opened his mouth to reply, but then stopped suddenly, cocking his head.

"No, Pa. It's over."

He began to hum that strange, sad melody.

"Please, Pa," I said. "We have fallen so far. Make good with Senorix and fight the Romans."

"Stand aside, Iona," he said. "They are here. They will open the door, but you are in the way."

I planted my feet. "No."

He stepped forward and his hands locked around my waist like iron. He lifted me aside. I turned.

The door blew off its hinges. The gust of air rattled my clothes and tore at my hair. Catria sat up in shock.

"What . . . ?" I started.

Then the rumbling. Like thunder, but lower, closer.

"There is no time," Pa said. "Fetch my weapons and meet me on the eastern side of the hill."

"What is happening?" Catria shouted.

Pa went to the door, and the humming turned into a full-bodied song with mysterious words I did not know, and it rang out sweet and strange in the cool morning air.

"Stay here!" I shouted at Catria. "I'll come back for you."

I jumped down from the granary and turned towards home to fetch Pa's weapons. The sky was burnished copper as the sun rose, and the air was cold and crisp. Then the ground shook. The thumping, thundering noise grew closer. It sounded for all the world like huge, heavy footfalls.

Giant's footfalls.

A shadow fell.

I froze, turned. Lumbering up over the crest was a naked man. Forty feet high. Maybe fifty. His skin was baggy and almost grey. He had long, ragged hair and a beard to his chest. In one hand he held an enormous club, and when he saw the village he pounded the ground with it and howled. The earth shook beneath me.

My field of vision seemed to turn white and my ears rang. Beneath me, my knees began to buckle. These were sensations beyond any kind of fear I'd known. I thought I might die from fright. I heard screams. People ran in all directions, sleep abandoned just moments before. Panic made me want to flee.

But then I heard Pa's voice, strong and melodious, ringing out over the village.

His weapons.

I had to be brave. I uprooted my feet and I dashed, nearly colliding with a family running the other way. Outside my house I saw Senorix, gazing up at the giant with an expression of horror on his face. He called out to me but I was already past him, around the other side, grasping the bundle of weapons and dashing back towards the other side of the hill.

"Bring the warriors!" I shouted at Senorix as I ran past. "He can't do it alone."

I could see the giant at his full height now, his shadow stretching out a hundred or more feet on the ground. Pa was leading him away from the village with that sweet, strange song. But it hadn't soothed the giant or lulled it into a stupor. Rather, it seemed to enrage him.

I redoubled my speed, over the crest. Pa had stopped thirty yards away, and the giant thundered up to him, raised the club and roared. A smell like the depths of an old cave, faintly laced with sulphur, washed over the village.

I ran, nearly tripping and rolling. The club hit the ground, but Pa sidestepped at the last moment. The giant raised the club again. I flung Pa's weapons on the ground and Pa ducked away from the club with the agility of somebody much leaner and younger. He rolled under the giant's legs and, with one sweep of his muscular arm, unhitched the knot on the rope.

The sling was in his hand as the giant raised the club again, blocking the pale light of the sky. I backed as far away as I could. Voices up on the ridge drew my attention: Senorix and Mato and six warriors.

"Pa, they've brought help," I shouted. I should not have. The giant heard me and turned and snarled.

"No," I said, under my breath.

Crack.

The giant stopped in his tracks, reaching down to rub his shin. Pa had got him with a rock from his sling. Then another crack, and this time the rock hit the giant directly in the eye. He bellowed, losing his balance.

Crack. The other eye. The giant dropped his club, making the ground shudder. It missed me by only a few feet. His hands flew to his eyes, and Pa was under him, sprinting, winding the rope around his huge, hairy legs, just as he had done with the tree.

I watched in horror. The giant would fall, Pa would surely be crushed. But then Pa ran out, away from the giant and pulled the rope.

Over the giant went, crashing to the ground so hard that a boom went sounding out to the horizon, crushing against my ears. I was momentarily deaf, then the silence evaporated, leaving my ears ringing. Pa flung his spear, and it landed directly in the giant's heart.

Senorix and the others were advancing down the hill, battle horns barking and spears raised. Pa approached the fallen body of the giant. I thought it was dead. Perhaps Pa thought it was dead too, but then the giant lifted his massive hand and swiped at Pa.

Pa went flying. Ten yards or more.

I ran towards him just as the others brought their spears and swords and arrows down on the giant's head, its neck, its heart. A substance like blood, but grey-green, gushed forth. Senorix gave a victory cry, but I barely heard it through the thump of my pulse.

"Pa!" I cried. "Pa!"

I skidded to my knees next to his poor, broken body. His arms were twisted unnaturally behind him, his legs bent awkwardly. A trickle of blood—warm, red human blood—made its way from the corner of his mouth down to his chin. My hands went to his face, came away bloody. "No, no, no," I said, over and over. "Please, Pa, no. Don't die. Don't die."

I don't know how long it was before Mato came, his torso streaked with the grey-green giant's blood. He kneeled next to me, pulled me into his arms. "I'm sorry, Iona. I'm so sorry."

"Pa won't speak to me," I managed to say.

"I'm sorry."

I leaned into him, my eyes going over his shoulder to where the giant's corpse lay, stretched out on the hillside. As I watched, a fog began to form around his huge shoulders and ankles, spreading over him and making Senorix and the other warriors cough and leap backwards. The ground began to shake. Deafening. A million grains of earth rattling against each other. Mato released me, turned and gasped. The giant's body was sinking into the ground, as if being swallowed. Only moments later, the earth had closed over him. The grass was as green as it had ever been. Birds sang. The only sign the giant had been there was a wisp of grey fog on the hillside.

Once Pa was gone, the piskies began to talk to me in earnest, their little soft whispers rubbing against my ear. They told me I was to leave the hillfort to Senorix so that he could organise the defence against the Romans. I was to take Catria and build a little house for myself in the woods near the well. And so I did, while the tribes carved and chalked the shape of the giant—as tall as the shadow he had cast—on the hillside to warn the Romans that the Dwr-y-Triges were giant killers. My belly swelled and my son was born, and I named him Dwairin after the bright well that had seen his conception and birth. My sister and I gathered a reputation as the witches of the bright well, and the world left us alone. It changed. Conquerors came. A village was built in the coomb and Dwairin married a Roman lass. In the end, we fought for nothing.

But the giant stayed on the hillside, and Vernico's deeds became eternal.

Epilogue: The Past is Not Dead

March – June 2017

THE PAST IS NOT DEAD, ROSIE," MY father used to say.

It lives within us, entwined into every cell of our bodies.

When I was little, I was fascinated by butterflies. I used to draw them all the time, colouring in their wings carefully and then cutting them out. My father hung them all from a hoop above my bed, and they used to spin and twirl about in every breath of air.

My father knew a lot about insects, though spiders were his speciality. He told me that butterflies began life as caterpillars, and that they tasted with their feet and smelled with their antennae.

Our favourite thing to do together on the weekend was go to the Butterfly House at Melbourne Zoo. It was there I learnt about monarch butterflies. Like most winged insects, they only live a few weeks. But as the summer begins to turn to autumn, a new batch of butterflies are hatched that will live for months. They rise together and fly south, millions and millions of them, travelling as much as two hundred and fifty miles a day. By the time they arrive in the warmer lands, those vast flocks of butterflies will have travelled more than two thousand miles. None of them had ever flown that way before.

The butterflies mate and lay their eggs, and then fly home to die. A month later, the new generation of young butterflies follow them. Each will only manage a quarter of the distance of their parents, each laying new eggs that hatch into new butterflies that then continue their grandparents' voyage. It takes four generations of Monarch butterflies to complete the journey home, but they always return to the exact same trees that their great-great-great-grandparents left the previous autumn.

"But how do they know where to fly?" I asked my father that day in the Butterfly House.

"They remember."

"But how can they remember when they've never done it before?"

"It's a mystery," my father replied. "But, somehow, the memory of their ancestors' flight is born within them."

As I climbed Giant Hill and stood in the patch of earth called the Frying Pan, where my grandparents had once danced long before I was born, I thought about the monarch butterfly. And spiders who know instinctively how to spin a web, and baby robins that know to hide at the shadow of a hawk. How do they know? I wondered. Are they told in dreams and visions? Is it just a kind of intuition?

In the twenty-four hours since I made my wish at the well, I had started drawing. I could not explain why: perhaps it was my encounter with Isobel from the historical society. But it seemed that since I made the wish, if I shut my eyes, I could still see snatches of vivid images. A young woman curled in her bed, a tide of red creeping over the white of her sheets. A little boy in dressing gown and slippers, clutching a cat made from a peg, staring at a ghost of a dripping wet girl. Laughing figures dancing about a maypole. A face falling away under water. A young man crouched in an iron cage, lightning splitting the sky. A monk and a nun embracing.

A girl stealing gold. I took the notepad from my B&B room and scribbled them all down . . . no, I *drew* them all. The first sketchy lines seemed to prompt more details, and I tried to capture them as fast as I could. It had been so long since I had been creative. And it felt so very good, if not a little strange. The images resumed in my mind's eye on waking, and I anticipated another day of compulsive drawing, of cabin fever. Which was why I was out on the hill now, stepping decisively yet unknowingly in a mud puddle.

I withdrew it with an unpleasant sucking noise. My white Converse sneaker was now filthy-brown and sodden. I could feel the cold creeping up my legs. I huddled my hoodie closer around me and decided:

I needed coffee

I needed a decent breakfast

I badly needed shoes better suited to the English countryside

And a proper waterproof jacket. Preferably lined with fur.

I could do with some nice herbal tea before bedtime instead of those pills, because I suspected they were making me a little crazed.

I decided that hot coffee was first on the agenda. I found a café that served a full English breakfast with as much coffee as you could drink, and sat in the window watching the town come to life. A girl in jodphurs and a velvet hat rode past on a tall brown horse that gleamed like satin. Two mothers pushed prams along, the children inside so muffled up against the cold only their eyes could be seen. A man jogged past in shorts and a singlet, his breath huffing white before him. School children waited at the bus stop, enormous backpacks threatening to topple them over backwards.

Beyond the roofs, I could see the high line of the downs, lit with sunshine.

Gradually the unsettling memory of my dream faded away, and a new buoyancy filled me. I thought of Christopher, and wondered how soon I could turn up at Winterthorne Gardens without seeming too eager. Then I thought of the girl who he thought might be a relative. Poppy Brightwell, her name was. My father had said it was the custom in our family to name children after flowers and plants. He had been called Ashley, and his father had been Rowan, and his grandfather had been Perry, which apparently meant pear tree.

I paid my bill, and walked along the high street, hands shoved inside my pockets, my shoes squelching at every step. I had only walked a few hundred metres when I saw the green-painted shop with the big Brightwell's sign. I hesitated only a moment, then pushed the door open and went inside.

It was warm and bright and sweetly scented. Small posies of herbs and flowers were set in jars and jugs on an old paint-chipped table, with hand-dipped candles hanging from their wicks over a rail above. Shelves along the walls were laden with all kinds of products—jars of fresh herbal teas, pots of honey, gauze sacks of scented bath salts, containers filled with vitamins, tubs of skin cream, and bags of organic nuts and dried fruits.

A young woman was stacking shelves. She wore a bright green dress with an A-line skirt, daffodil yellow stockings, and a pair of gold high-heeled clogs. Her hair was tied up in two little buns on either side of her head, and her face was dramatically made up with black eyeliner and red lipstick. As I came in, she looked up and smiled. "Hello! Welcome!"

"Hi . . . er . . . thank you."

"Are you looking for anything in particular?"

"Um . . . something to help me sleep . . . jetlag . . . "

She rushed into talk, clattering around the shop and showing me different teas and drops and pastilles and explaining the benefits of each one. I chose a few, wondering how on earth I was to bring up the topic of whether or not we were related. She did not look much like me. My hair was so blonde it was almost white, and turned greenish if I spent too much time in a chlorinated pool. Her hair was dyed black as a crow's wing. My eyes were bright blue. Hers were brown. I was tall and curvy, while she was tiny, even with her clogs on.

As she chattered away, I wandered the store, picking things up and putting them back, feeling my usual paralysing shyness.

Then I saw something which stopped me in my tracks.

A row of eccentric gumboots. One had sunflowers on them, another had strawberries, and yet another was bright red with white rabbits. A row of little ones were decorated to look like ladybirds, or bees, or dinosaurs. And there, right on the edge, was a sky-blue pair decorated with butterflies.

I exclaimed with pleasure, despite myself.

The young woman smiled at me. "Aren't they divine?" she enthused. "If you must go tramping about in the mud, you might as well wear something cute, don't you think?"

"Surely they're just for children?"

"Why should kids have all the fun?"

Why, indeed. It was not long before she had coaxed me out of my sodden mud-besmirched sneakers and into the pair decorated with butterflies. They were lined with cosy fleece, and my feet felt warm for the first time in days.

"I look ridiculous," I moaned.

"You do not," she replied warmly. "You look fantastic. You'll be able to take the pig for a walk in the forest in those, and light up the day of everyone who sees you."

"Take the pig for a walk?" I repeated, bewildered.

"Or feed the llamas. Whatever it is you do all day."

Laughter bubbled up in me. "Llamas? Really?"

"Llamas are perfectly lovely creatures," she protested. "Or so I've been told. I've never met one myself. But I can tell you one thing. You won't care if you fall in a mud puddle while wearing those boots."

"I don't know . . . "

"Answer me one thing," she demanded. "Do they make you smile?"

I had to admit they did.

"Then what are you waiting for? You need to do one thing every day that makes you happy." She pointed to the wall behind the counter, and I saw the slogan was painted there, in large curling letters. "So why not wear boots that make you smile."

"You are a very good saleswoman," I said as I fished out my wallet.

"I know," she answered complacently.

I passed over my credit card, then said awkwardly, "you might notice . . . my name . . . it's the same as the shop . . . and my grandfather grew up here in Cerne Abbas . . . " She looked at the name on the card and then at me, her eyes round with surprise.

"What was his name?"

"Rowan Brightwell."

She laughed, ran around the counter and threw her arms about me. "Then we're cousins! Or second cousins. Or is it first cousin, once removed? I never know the difference."

"We are?"

"Yes indeed. Your grandfather Rowan was the little brother of my grandfather, Basil. Oh this is so exciting. My father will be thrilled."

"He will?"

"Oh yes. Because you're the long-lost daughter of his cousin. Or his second cousin. What does it matter? You're family. What are you doing here? Tell me everything."

And, much to my surprise, I did. Everything came pouring out— my broken engagement, my broken heart, my dead parents, my dead grandparents. I began to cry. Poppy passed me tissues, made me hot herbal tea, and every now and again gave me a hug. At last I was spent. I tried to apologise, but she hugged me and told me not to be an idiot.

"What else are family for?" she asked chirpily, opening up a bag of chocolate coated goji berries and pouring some into my hand.

It seemed strange to me that I could confess so much to her—a complete stranger—when I had kept up a relentless mask of cheerfulness to my friends back home. Perhaps it was because she was a stranger. Perhaps it was because she was family.

People began to come in, and Poppy had to go and serve them. I stood up shakily and said I must go.

"Meet me at the Giant for a beer later?" she asked. "Say 5.30?"

"Okay."

She grinned at me and shoved all my purchases into a bag for me, as well as my mud-caked sneakers. I was still wearing the butterfly gumboots. As I went towards the door, I saw another motto had been painted above it, twin to the one on the opposite wall.

Do something every day that makes you scared.

I went out into the thin spring sunshine, determined to be brave, determined to be happy.

I stopped at the general store and bought a sketchbook and a pencil set.

✳

We didn't drink beer when we met at the Giant, we drank champagne. To celebrate our family reunion, Poppy said. We drank it a little fast, too, and it loosened my tongue enough that I matched Poppy's galloping talking pace. I surprised myself by telling her all about Zac and the chilling mortification of being jilted, but instead of adopting the pitying expression most people wore when I told them (which I found added another layer of embarrassment), she raised her glass and laughed and said, "Congratulations on dodging that bullet."

"Dodging a bullet?"

"Imagine if you'd married him, never knowing he was the kind of man who could be so cruel."

I raised my glass, feeling light. Maybe it was the champagne. "I'd never thought of it like that," I said. "Cheers."

"Here's to perfect timing," she said.

"Perfect timing."

The Giant soon grew rowdy. A tall gentleman with a musty beret and a long-legged dog had just become a grandfather, and a small happy gathering were noisily drinking in celebration. At our table in the front window, we could barely hear ourselves think.

"Let's go to my house," Poppy shouted over the noise. "Much quieter. And I do believe I have a bottle of red wine in the cupboard under the stairs."

A small part of my brain warned me that I'd already drunk too much champagne, and that throwing red wine on top of it would almost certainly make me sick, but I told that part of my brain to shush.

After the noisy, close atmosphere of the pub, the street was quiet and cool. All the way to Poppy's, she regaled me with a story of a boyfriend who had treated her abominably: she'd let him move in too soon because he was broke, and gradually her things went missing. He was selling them to pay off his debts and when confronted, protested that they were just old things she didn't use.

"A box of my grandmother's jewellery!" she exclaimed. "Can you imagine? Just old costume jewellery mostly, but still."

"What did you do?"

"I kicked him out, of course. He was lucky I didn't call the police."

"Were you broken hearted?"

"For weeks!" she exclaimed, leading me down a street of old houses, some in the half-timbered style of centuries ago. "Months, maybe. I loved him, but he wasn't who I thought he was. It was a shock, you know. I was in shock."

In shock. Yes, I understood that feeling. Looking at Poppy now, so bubbly and chatty and so very comfortable in her own skin, I thought perhaps I would get over Zac after all.

Poppy's house behind and above the shop was as charming and eclectic as she was, cluttered and smelling like sandalwood. Downstairs a cosy living room with a fireplace, a narrow kitchen with French doors to an overgrown garden, and a messy nook with an ageing PC and overflowing inboxes of bills and invoices for the shop.

"Go have a look upstairs too if you like," she said as she opened the door under the staircase. She had to duck to get into the space. "I'll see if I can scare us up some wine."

I ascended the creaking stairs and found a bathroom with a claw-foot tub, a messy bedroom with an unmade four-poster bed strewn in clothes, and a second bedroom that was being used as an artist studio. I stopped here, gazing in. Two desks, a tall chest of drawers (none of the drawers were closed properly, and coloured paper spilled out of all of them), a couch stained with glue.

Poppy was beside me a minute later with two glasses of red wine.

"Here you are," she said, handing me one.

I took a sip. It was watery and thin. "Not Australian red wine," I said.

"You can tell?"

"Australian red wine is much better than this. I'll buy you a bottle while I'm in town."

"How long are you in town?"

I leaned on the threshold and sighed. "I don't know. I have nothing to go home to, really. I don't even know . . . " I trailed off, unsure how to finish. Not even sure who I am. It sounded so dramatic, like a teenager. I didn't want Poppy to think me an idiot.

"You like art?" I said instead.

"Yes. Well, craft really. I hand make birthday cards and so on, and sell them in the shop." She scooped up a handful of them from one of the desks to show me. Pretty layers of coloured card and paper, with curly paper flowers and cut-out letters.

"I draw," I said. "I mean, I like drawing. I started again . . . recently."

Her eyes rounded. I noticed one of the points of her winged eyeliner had worn off, making one eye look smaller than the other. "You do? I'd love to see your drawings."

I quickly explained what had been happening lately, about the well and the constant feeling that I was drawing pictures from the past, finishing on an embarrassed, "I suppose you think I'm an idiot."

"Not at all," she said, sipping her wine. "'There are more things in heaven and earth, Horatio, than are dreamed of in our philosophy.'"

Then when I stared back at her blankly, she said, "Shakespeare. Hamlet. I simply meant, keep drawing. Why question inspiration?"

"I suppose you're right."

"You're a serious little thing," she said, giving me a light punch on the shoulder.

I wasn't sure if it was a compliment, an insult, or just an observation.

"See that couch?" she said. "It folds out into a bed. Bring your stuff over tomorrow."

"Really?" I thought of the B&B, the sixty pounds a night it was costing me.

"Of course. You're family."

＊

The next two weeks spun away quickly.

Poppy let me stay on her couch as long as I liked, in return for giving her a hand in the shop. I could take my time deciding about going home or staying. She helped me apply for a work visa, and I began to look for a casual job in the local pubs and cafés. I went with her to meet the rest of her family, at her parents' cosy cottage on the river. Poppy had an elder brother called Linden who was a doctor. He was married with two little girls called Daisy and Lily. Within five minutes of meeting them, I was on the floor playing dolls with them, and had promised to babysit them the following Saturday night. Poppy's grandfather Basil was there too, his vivid blue eyes so much like my own grandfather's it made me choke up.

I had drawn up a list of things that made me happy and another list of things that frightened me. It had been a surprisingly difficult task. The first list embarrassed me. It sounded like an advertisement for an internet dating site. *I like walking barefoot on the beach, baking cakes, and watching classic old black-and-white movies . . .*

But I had persisted, adding things when they occurred to me. Then I tried to cross them off the list. I went to Lyme Regis, and braved the icy sand to walk along the water's edge. I baked Poppy a thank-you cake, and borrowed a pile of old movies, and we sat and watched them all, eating cake and laughing and painting each other's toenails. I visited Corfe Castle which is said to be the inspiration for Kirrin Castle in the Famous Five books, then spent a few days reading through Poppy's entire Enid Blyton collection. I emptied out my suitcase and got rid of all the things I hadn't worn since I'd arrived in Dorset. Too tight jeans. Too high stilettos. Sexy bras that hurt. In my head I called them my Zac clothes. I replaced them with vintage dresses and skirts I bought at op-shops, which I wore with sturdy boots and one of Poppy's hand-knitted scarves.

I had adopted Poppy's rule when buying clothes. Did it make me smile?

After feeling sad for so long, it seemed I was at last learning how to be happy.

❉

I found it much harder to write the second list. The list of things that frightened me. It took me a long time to write just a few words.

Dying alone.

Being unloved.

Being unlovable.

I tore the list up, and shoved the pieces deep in the bin, then wrote another.

Deep dark water.

Clowns.

Pitiful, I thought.

When two weeks had passed, I went to Winterthorne. The gardens were just as beautiful as Christopher had said, surrounding an old Elizabethan manor house that had—I was surprised to hear—been in the Beaufort family for centuries. The house had been turned into a kind of museum, with lots of art works and antique furniture. I paid the entry price, and spent a few hours wandering about and marvelling at the history of the place. Gloomy portraits of ancestors, stag antlers mounted on walls, suits of armour, a library of battered leather-bound books locked away behind grilles, and a tiny chapel with a midnight-blue domed ceiling studded with gold-painted stars. It was like something out of a book. Moonacre Manor in Elizabeth Goudge's *The Little White Horse* or Misselthwaite Manor from *The Secret Garden*, two of my all-time favourite books. How I wished I had grown up here.

It was late afternoon by the time I began wandering through the gardens. A riot of spring flowers against old stone walls. A parterre of sweet-smelling herbs. Cabbages and cauliflowers planted in pretty patterns. I loved it.

The café was in a round building with a very steep pointed roof like a witch's hat. I ordered tea and lemon drizzle cake, then managed to get up the courage to ask after Christopher. It was his day off, I was told. My disappointment must have shown in my face, for the woman serving me murmured an apology and suggested I return the next day. I shook my head, feeling my cheeks heating. "No, that's OK." I hesitated, then said diffidently, "he said that there was a bluebell wood . . . "

"There is," she answered cheerfully. "Go out the gate at the end of the garden and turn left. Just follow the path into the woods. The bluebells are beautiful at this time of year."

I thanked her and paid my bill.

"You should come back tomorrow," the woman said. "Christopher will be here all day, and we are hosting a cooking class in the afternoon, with a local celebrity chef. It'll be fun."

I nodded and smiled, and took my afternoon tea to sit by the window, looking out on to the garden. I'll do it, I decided. I'll come back. I've always wanted to do a proper cooking class.

When I had finished my tea, I went to the woods. The late afternoon sun was striking through the tree trunks in pale silver shafts of light. God's fingers, my grandmother used to call them. It was cold, but I had my new boots and jacket, and a hand-knitted scarf. I snugged my hands in my pockets and walked along the woodland path. A pale blue mist covered the ground as far as I could see, and the air was sweetened with a delicate scent. Overhead fresh new leaves rustled in the wind. A red squirrel darted across the path and up a tree, then paused in the perfect position for me to snatch a photograph on my phone. A blackbird sang from a budding cherry tree.

I realised that—although I was alone—I was perfectly and wonderfully happy.

※

"Nice boots," Christopher said.

I looked down at my butterfly gumboots. "Thanks," I said, lifting one and waving it back and forth. "At least my feet are warm now."

"And pretty." Christopher always seemed to have an undercurrent of amusement running under his vice. It was not unkind, however. It was a smiling voice. And very English. He sounded like a BBC announcer. I kept expecting him to say "goodness gracious me" and "golly gosh".

"Pretty feet are very important," I informed him.

"Perhaps not in my job," he answered, indicating his own very dirty gumboots.

"Poppy says my boots are perfect for taking the pig for a walk. If only I had a pig."

He laughed in surprised delight. "That sounds like Poppy."

"Thank you for sending me to her. She's a sweetheart, just like you said."

"It must run in the family."

I pretended to misunderstand him. "Oh yes, her parents are darlings too. And her grandfather. And her brother. And his little girls." I realised I was babbling, and stopped.

"I'm glad you've found them." He took a step closer, and his voice deepened. "And I'm glad you came back."

I went red and looked down at the ground. "I wanted to do the cooking class. And walk in the bluebell woods again. They'll be gone soon."

"They will," he agreed. "You've got to seize the day with bluebells."

Christopher was standing in the middle of a garden bed, leaning on a spade, his silver-streaked hair tied back in a messy ponytail. He was wearing grubby trousers, a laden tool belt, and a faded blue shirt that brought out the colour of his eyes. I felt a familiar warm, prickly, uncomfortable feeling.

"I might go . . . you know, walk in the woods." I waved in the general direction.

"Hang on a sec, I'll come with you." He took off his tool belt and heavy leather gloves, and hung them both from the spade, then walked over to a tap and washed his hands. I waited, feeling hot and self-conscious, yet also pleased. We walked together through the gardens, Christopher naming the flowers for me and telling me about some of his plans for the summer plantings. I had thought I'd be ill-at-ease with him, yet there was no need for me to worry. We talked as easily and naturally as we had done the first time we met.

In the warmth of the midday sun, the bluebells were not as ethereal as they had been the previous evening but the delicious scent was stronger. I sniffed rapturously.

"Why can't you buy bluebell perfume?" I asked. "I'd wear it every day."

"You can't distill bluebells, unfortunately," Christopher said. "And it'd be illegal to harvest them. Wild bluebells are under threat, you know."

"Really? But why?"

"Spanish bluebells. The Victorians brought them over and planted them in their gardens, but they escaped over the garden wall and into the forests. They thrive where wild bluebells can't, and the bees cross-pollinate them so that the wild bluebell stock is tainted."

"What's the difference?"

"Spanish bluebells are sturdier, and have no scent. They grow on upright stems too, instead of drooping over like little shepherd's crooks. If you ever see one, pick it. But never pick the wild ones. And never shake one."

"Why not?"

"Because you might die."

I gazed at him in astonishment.

He grinned at me. "They're fairy bells, and are rung to summon the fairy host. Any human that hears the bells must die. Or so the old folk say. It might just be a warning for kiddies not to pick them. The sap is highly poisonous."

"I'll take care never to ring a bluebell then."

"You might want to try turning one of the flowers inside out. Apparently if you can do it without tearing or damaging the flower, it means you'll win the one you love."

"Have you ever tried it?" I asked, even as I wondered if he was flirting with me.

"For sure," he answered, grinning. "I tried it when I was twelve and in love with Poppy."

"You were in love with Poppy?" For some reason the offhand comment rocked me back on my heels.

"Desperately. She sat in front of me in class and I was always throwing little pellets of paper at the back of her head. She absolutely hated me."

"So you tried to win her by turning a bluebell flower inside out."

"That's right. But I ripped the poor flower to pieces so that was no good. Then I tried pinning her plaits to the back of her chair with drawing pins, but for some reason that didn't work either."

"I wonder why."

"So did I. But then she broke my heart by kissing Peter Jacobs instead. It took me forever to get over it. A week at least."

"I didn't realise you'd known Poppy for so long."

"We went to nursery school together. I've known her since we were three. She hasn't changed a bit." He laughed, and an expression of nostalgia came over his face.

We walked in silence for a while after that. But then I caught him looking at me. He smiled, and a rush of tingles swept over me. I looked away, my cheeks heating. But I could not help the answering smile that curved my cheeks.

Then it was time for me to go to my cooking class, which was held in an old converted glasshouse that overlooked the gardens. It was great fun. We walked through the garden, choosing produce for our meal, and then learnt to cook it properly. The celebrity chef was lively and funny, yet could chop a carrot in perfect thin slices in seconds. At the end of the day, we ate the meal we had cooked together in the dovecote, with wines specially chosen by the chef. I made friends with a few of the other students, and we all signed up for the entire summer cookery course.

Poppy came to pick me up, there being no buses back to Cerne Abbas, and we drank more wine with Christopher and the celebrity chef and some of the other staff, and I found myself laughing and talking as if I had known them all my life.

I went to bed happier than I had been for a very long time.

❈

Yet something had been shaken loose in me.

I had recurring dreams of drowning. I'd wake with a gasp, finding it hard to breathe, my chest compressed as if in an iron vice. Other times I'd dream I was being chased, through smoking ruins, or through ancient shadowed crypts. Ghosts hung over me, touching my face with icy fingers. Poppy said I cried out sometimes in my sleep. I felt oppressed by the past, and not just my own. I returned to the well over and over, taking comfort in knowing others had been lost and found their way here. Centuries of people just like me, wishing for something more than they had. I drew my dreams, I drew my imaginings of other wishers. But if I tried to draw my future, I could imagine only a blank page.

Then, in June, I got an email from Zac. He said he was sorry, that he missed me, that he'd just freaked out with the wedding and everything. *I need to get away*, he wrote. *Where are you? Can we meet up somewhere?*

I could not believe it. I read the email over and over, and then spent an hour writing responses and deleting them.

In the end I shut down my laptop and did not reply. I went for a long walk on the hills, thinking and worrying. The path led me inevitably back to the old abbey graveyard, with the pathway that led down to the old well in its hidden corner. I went down and sat looking down at the pool, and then up at the twig where my green ribbon still fluttered next to Christopher's.

I stayed there a long time, letting the healing peace of that ancient place seep into me.

That weekend, after my cooking class, I went and found Christopher who was working away as usual in the garden.

"I need your help with something," I said.

"Sure. What can I do?" He leant on his spade, smiling at me.

"I've been trying to face some of my fears, but . . . well, I've been too scared."

He grinned. "Well, that makes sense. What are you scared of?"

"I don't like deep water, or water that's really dark. I have this recurring dream of drowning . . . "

"Maybe you drowned in a former life."

"Maybe. It made growing up in Australia hard, though. I wouldn't swim in the ocean. I'd only play around on the edges, where the water was shallow, or swim in a pool. But I think it's time . . . "

"Time to brave the deeps? Good on you."

"But I'm scared . . . so I thought if you came with me . . . "

"To hold your hand as you tiptoe into the cold dark depths of an English lake?"

"Exactly. If you don't mind."

"Oh, I don't mind at all." He grinned at me. "What other fears are on your list? I'm happy to hold your hand through it all."

"It's embarrassing."

"'Fess up. What else are you scared of? Spiders?"

"Oh no. My father was an arachnologist. When I was little he had tanks full of spiders in our house. And scorpions too. They're actually really fascinating creatures."

"I'll take your word for it."

I laughed. "And I grew up in Australia too, remember. Lots of spiders there. Big ones. Venomous ones."

He held up one hand. "All right, enough already. You've guessed I don't much like spiders. We're not talking about my fears but about yours. What else are you scared of?"

"Well, it's just . . . I really hate clowns."

"Clowns!"

"It's not so strange. Most people hate clowns. There's a word for it. Some kind of phobia. You must admit they're creepy."

"I love clowns. I had a clown perform at my twenty-first birthday."

"Well, you're just peculiar. What about last year? When those mobs of clowns were roaming round all over the world, freaking people out? You must admit you'd have been scared."

"Of a pack of clowns carrying chainsaws? Sure. I might be peculiar but I'm not crazy."

"So what can I do? I need to cross it off my list."

"I'll give that one some thought. The fear of dark water is easy, though. Some mates and I have got into wild swimming, and I know lots of great spots to go."

"Wild swimming? What's that?"

"Going swimming somewhere in the wild. You know, diving under waterfalls, swimming down rapids, skinny dipping in a forest pool."

I went red. "Do you do that often?" I managed to say, pretending not to be embarrassed.

"Not as often as I'd like to." He grinned, then said, "Are you busy tomorrow? If it's a nice day we could go to the River Stour. It's a lovely calm river, with some beautiful swimming spots. You can ease your way into it."

"Ok. But I'm not skinny dipping."

"Yet."

I shot him a warning glance, and he laughed.

Cheeky bugger, I thought.

The next day we drove together to the river. Christopher found a lovely spot with dangling willow trees, and a little sandy beach so I could go in step-by-slow-step. He didn't splash me or push me under, like most of the boys I had grown up with liked to do, but patiently encouraged me to inch deeper into the warm brown water.

He slipped in with me, the water rippling around his lean body. I'd been worried about exposing my body in a swimsuit but Poppy had helped me find a gorgeous vintage-style red one with big white spots that made me feel like Marilyn Monroe. Christopher certainly seemed to like it.

At one point, he made as if to lean in and kiss me. I thought of the email from Zac, and ducked away, striking back for shore. I felt embarrassed and uncomfortable. I sat on the beach and wrapped a big towel around me. Christopher swam alone for a while, then came out, shaking water from his long hair like a dog. "Lunch?" he said, in a rather cool neutral tone. "There's a pub just along from here that does great fish and chips."

"Ok," I said, not looking at him. "Sounds good."

Things felt a little strained between us. I was sorry. Maybe I should have kissed him. Maybe that would have helped me decide what to do about Zac. It didn't seem fair, though. I didn't want to overstrain these fragile new friendships of mine.

"Did Poppy tell you that I was jilted at the altar?" I said abruptly.

Christopher looked up at me. "No. Really? I mean she said you'd had a bad breakup . . . "

"It was not quite at the altar. But the wedding cake was made, I had my dress, my flowers, my veil." I was so humiliated that I could not look at him, but stared down at my plate instead.

"How awful. What a plonker."

"Yeah."

"Did he . . . did he say why?"

I was too needy, too clingy. I suffocated him. "He said he needed space."

"He couldn't have worked that out earlier?"

"My thoughts exactly." I looked up at him. Then, to my surprise, I laughed. "So I gave him all the space I could. Half a world. I ran away here."

"Why?"

"Because . . . because my grandparents had been so happy here. Because I'd always wanted to come." I gave a helpless shrug. "It just felt right."

He put out his hand and took mine. "I'm really sorry about your wedding, Rosie, but better before than after, I guess."

"Yeah, that's what I keep telling myself."

"And if you hadn't run away, we wouldn't have got to meet you."

"No. And I've been happy here. Happier than I've been in years."

"Well, that's good." He released my hand and picked up the menu. "Pudding? I think you deserve it. Being so brave and all."

"I do deserve it," I said. "I deserve it so much."

"Do you want to try swimming a little further downstream next week? Somewhere a little colder and darker?"

"That sounds good." I smiled at him, then said with difficulty. "Thanks. You know."

"My pleasure," he answered. "Anytime."

❋

I didn't have a nightmare that night. Indeed I felt so well and energised the next morning that I went for a long walk, cooked a batch of brownies, and cleaned the whole flat. Poppy was very impressed.

"You'll have to go on a date with Christopher more often."

"It wasn't a date."

"Really? You could have fooled me."

I grinned at her, shrugged my shoulders and went to reply to Zac. *Don't ever email me again*, I said.

The weeks unspooled quickly. I got a job in a café, and joined Poppy's knitting club, finding much to my surprise that I loved making pretty things with my hands. I learned how to make eggs benedict and cheese soufflé, and the difference between lemon balm and lemon verbena. Our cake-and-classic-movie night became a tradition, and Christopher turned out to be a Humphrey Bogart fan.

Or perhaps he just said so to please me.

Every Saturday I went walking in the countryside, and saw all the stone circles and fairy hills and devil's chairs and haunted castles that I could find. Both Christopher and Poppy worked on Saturdays, and so this was something I did on my own, gladly.

One day Christopher surprised me with a ticket for a workshop with "The Sacred Clown".

The brochure said: "Sacred Clown Training—emotional healing to help you reconnect to the joy and simplicity of childlike innocence. Through mime, play, improvisation, dance, movement, mindfulness, and the mask of the clown's nose, find the lost child within you."

"You are kidding," I said, staring at him in dismay.

"I'm not. What better way to overcome a fear of clowns than by becoming one?"

"Oh, Christopher. A whole day . . . "

" . . . with other clowns. I know." He tried to hide the mischief dancing in his eyes, but failed utterly. "I'll take you to dinner afterwards."

"Somewhere nice?"

"The nicest place I can find."

Reluctantly I dragged myself off to clown school, only to find myself enjoying it hugely. It was like being a kid again, playing and pretending all day long. A lot was said about living in the moment, and becoming fully aware and alive in the world. I felt they were wise thoughts.

"So?" Christopher said, when he picked me up.

"It was good," I said, unable to keep the huge grin off my face. "Look!"

I pulled out the red clown's nose we had all been given and put it on.

Christopher broke into laughter. "Okay, another thing crossed off your list. What's next?"

I thought about the list I had screwed up and thrown in the bin. I couldn't share that. It was too private, too hurtful.

I shook my head. "That's it. No more fears left."

"That's a shame," he said. "Maybe we can start work on mine."

I looked at him in astonishment. I had never met someone so easy and confident in everything he did. "What on earth are you afraid of?"

He looked me in the eyes. "Dying alone. Being unloved."

It knocked all the breath out of me. After a long moment, I said with great difficulty, "Well, yes. Me too. And . . . and being . . . unloveable."

He leant forward and kissed me very gently on the mouth. "Rosie, you are so loveable. The most loveable girl ever. No-one could help loving you."

Well, what could I do after that?

Kiss him back, of course.

❀

It took me four days to realise that I'd stopped having the dark dreams, stopped being easily able to conjure the vivid flashes of images that had been waiting just beyond my field of vision. I had a free afternoon and I took my sketchbook and pencils up onto Giant Hill. Sitting up there, breeze in my hair, looking down on the village. Bees. Birds. Blue sky. Sunshine. Deep breath. Happiness.

I began to draw. A picnic blanket. The stone slab of the well. Branches and ribbons. Two hands, fingers intertwined. His and mine.

I realised I was drawing the future.

❀

On Midsummer's Eve, I put together a picnic and we went to eat by the Silver Well, where we had first met. I packed cold chicken and salad and champagne, with a Dorset apple cake for afterwards.

It was a luminous starry night, and the air was sweet with the smell of the linden blossoms. The water of the pool glimmered darkly.

"Can I ask you something?" I looked up at Christopher's face, my head cradled in his lap.

"Anything."

"What did you wish for? That day we first met. When you gave me the green ribbon."

He bent and kissed me. "I wished for you, Rosie. Though I didn't know then that you were the one."

"So your wish came true."

"It did." He hesitated. "What about yours, Rosie?"

I smiled up at him with real joy. "Oh yes. My wish came true too, Christopher. In more ways than I could ever have imagined."

also by Kate Forsyth

also by Kim Wilkins

AVAILABLE FROM TICONDEROGA PUBLICATIONS

978-0-9586856-6-5 Troy BY Simon Brown
978-0-9586856-7-2 The Workers' Paradise EDS Farr & Evans
978-0-9586856-8-9 Fantastic Wonder Stories ED Russell B. Farr
978-0-9803531-0-5 Love in Vain BY Lewis Shiner
978-0-9803531-2-9 Belong ED Russell B. Farr
978-0-9803531-4-3 Ghost Seas BY Steven Utley
978-0-9803531-6-7 Magic Dirt: the best of Sean Williams
978-0-9803531-8-1 The Lady of Situations BY Stephen Dedman
978-0-9806288-2-1 Basic Black BY Terry Dowling
978-0-9806288-3-8 Make Believe BY Terry Dowling
978-0-9806288-4-5 Scary Kisses ED Liz Grzyb
978-0-9806288-6-9 Dead Sea Fruit BY Kaaron Warren
978-0-9806288-8-3 The Girl With No Hands BY Angela Slatter
978-0-9807813-1-1 Dead Red Heart ED Russell B. Farr
978-0-9807813-2-8 More Scary Kisses ED Liz Grzyb
978-0-9807813-4-2 Heliotrope BY Justina Robson
978-0-9807813-7-3 Matilda Told Such Dreadful Lies BY Lucy Sussex
978-1-921857-01-0 Bluegrass Symphony BY Lisa L. Hannett
978-1-921857-06-5 The Hall of Lost Footsteps BY Sara Douglass
978-1-921857-03-4 Damnation and Dames EDS Liz Grzyb & Amanda Pillar
978-1-921857-08-9 Bread and Circuses BY Felicity Dowker
978-1-921857-17-1 The 400-Million-Year Itch BY Steven Utley
978-1-921857-22-5 The Scarlet Rider BY Lucy Sussex
978-1-921857-24-9 Wild Chrome BY Greg Mellor
978-1-921857-27-0 Bloodstones ED Amanda Pillar
978-1-921857-30-0 Midnight and Moonshine BY Lisa L. Hannett & Angela Slatter
978-1-921857-65-2 Mage Heart BY Jane Routley
978-1-921857-66-9 Fire Angels BY Jane Routley
978-1-921857-67-6 Aramaya BY Jane Routley
978-1-921857-86-7 Magic Dirt: the best of Sean Williams (hc)
978-1-921857-35-5 Dreaming of Djinn ED Liz Grzyb
978-1-921857-38-6 Prickle Moon BY Juliet Marillier
978-1-921857-43-0 The Bride Price BY Cat Sparks
978-1-921857-46-1 The Year of Ancient Ghosts BY Kim Wilkins
978-1-921857-33-1 Invisible Kingdoms BY Steven Utley
978-1-921857-70-6 Havenstar BY Glenda Larke
978-1-921857-59-1 Everything is a Graveyard BY Jason Fischer
978-1-921857-63-8 The Assassin of Nara BY R.J. Ashby
978-1-921857-77-5 Death at the Blue Elephant BY Janeen Webb
978-1-921857-81-2 The Emerald Key BY Christine Daigle & Stewart Sternberg
978-1-921857-89-8 Kisses by Clockwork ED Liz Grzyb
978-1-925212-05-1 Angel Dust ED Liz Grzyb
978-1-925212-16-7 The Finest Ass in the Universe BY Anna Tambour
978-1-925212-36-5 Hear Me Roar ED Liz Grzyb
978-1-921857-56-0 Bloodlines ED Amanda Pillar
978-1-925212-45-7 Crow Shine BY Alan Baxter
978-1-925212-54-9 Ecopunk! EDS Liz Grzyb & Cat Sparks

WWW.TICONDEROGAPUBLICATIONS.COM

LIMITED HARDCOVER EDITIONS

978-0-9806288-1-4 The Infernal BY Kim Wilkins
978-1-921857-54-6 Black-Winged Angels BY Angela Slatter

EBOOKS

978-0-9803531-5-0 Ghost Seas BY Steven Utley
978-1-921857-93-5 The Girl With No Hands BY Angela Slatter
978-1-921857-99-7 Dead Red Heart ED Russell B. Farr
978-1-921857-94-2 More Scary Kisses ED Liz Grzyb
978-0-9807813-5-9 Heliotrope BY Justina Robson
978-1-921857-36-2 Dreaming of Djinn ED Liz Grzyb
978-1-921857-40-9 Prickle Moon BY Juliet Marillier
978-1-921857-92-8 The Year of Ancient Ghosts BY Kim Wilkins
978-1-921857-28-7 Bloodstones ED Amanda Pillar
978-1-921857-04-1 Damnation and Dames ED Liz Grzyb & Amanda Pillar
978-1-921857-31-7 Midnight and Moonshine BY Lisa L. Hannett & Angela Slatter
978-1-921857-44-7 The Bride Price BY Cat Sparks
978-1-921857-60-7 Everything is a Graveyard BY Jason Fischer
978-1-921857-64-5 The Assassin of Nara BY R.J. Ashby
978-1-921857-78-2 Death at the Blue Elephant BY Janeen Webb
978-1-921857-82-9 The Emerald Key BY Christine Daigle & Stewart Sternberg
978-1-921857-57-7 Kisses by Clockwork ED Liz Grzyb
978-1-925212-06-8 Angel Dust ED Liz Grzyb
978-1-925212-17-4 The Finest Ass in the Universe BY Anna Tambour
978-1-925212-37-2 Hear Me Roar ED Liz Grzyb
978-1-921857-38-9 Bloodlines ED Amanda Pillar
978-1-925212-37-2 Crow Shine BY Alan Baxter
978-1-925212-37-2 Ecopunk! EDS Liz Grzyb & Cat Sparks

THE YEAR'S BEST AUSTRALIAN FANTASY & HORROR SERIES EDITED BY LIZ GRZYB & TALIE HELENE

978-0-9807813-8-0 Year's Best Australian Fantasy & Horror 2010 (hc)
978-0-9807813-9-7 Year's Best Australian Fantasy & Horror 2010 (tpb)
978-0-921057-98-0 Year's Best Australian Fantasy & Horror 2010 (ebook)
978-0-921057-13-3 Year's Best Australian Fantasy & Horror 2011 (hc)
978-0-921057-14-0 Year's Best Australian Fantasy & Horror 2011 (tpb)
978-0-921057-15-7 Year's Best Australian Fantasy & Horror 2011 (ebook)
978-0-921057-48-5 Year's Best Australian Fantasy & Horror 2012 (hc)
978-0-921057-49-2 Year's Best Australian Fantasy & Horror 2012 (tpb)
978-0-921057-50-8 Year's Best Australian Fantasy & Horror 2012 (ebook)
978-0-921057-72-0 Year's Best Australian Fantasy & Horror 2013 (hc)
978-0-921057-73-7 Year's Best Australian Fantasy & Horror 2013 (tpb)
978-0-921057-74-4 Year's Best Australian Fantasy & Horror 2013 (ebook)
978-0-925212-18-1 Year's Best Australian Fantasy & Horror 2014 (hc)
978-0-925212-19-8 Year's Best Australian Fantasy & Horror 2014 (tpb)
978-0-925212-20-4 Year's Best Australian Fantasy & Horror 2014 (ebook)
978-0-925212-47-1 Year's Best Australian Fantasy & Horror 2015 (hc)
978-0-925212-48-8 Year's Best Australian Fantasy & Horror 2015 (tpb)
978-0-925212-49-5 Year's Best Australian Fantasy & Horror 2015 (ebook)

THANK YOU

The publisher would sincerely like to thank:

Kate Forsyth, Kim Wilkins, Kathleen Jennings, Lisa L. Hannett, Liz Grzyb, Donna Maree Hanson, Pete Kempshall, Karen Brooks, Jeremy G. Byrne, Marianne de Pierres, Jonathan Strahan, Peter McNamara, Ellen Datlow, Grant Stone, Sean Williams, Simon Brown, David Cake, Simon Oxwell, Grant Watson, Sue Manning, Steven Utley, Lewis Shiner, Bill Congreve, Janeen Webb, Jack Dann, Amanda Pillar, Angela Slatter, Garth Nix, Anthony Panegyres, Anna Tambour, Joanne Anderton, Alan Baxter, Deborah Biancotti, Stephen Dedman, Jason Fischer, Dirk Flinthart, Kim Gaal, Stephanie Gunn, Robert Hood, Jane Routley, Martin Livings, Rivqa Rafael, Kirstyn McDermott, Jason Nahrung, Lucy Sussex, Kaaron Warren, the Mt Lawley Mafia, the Nedlands Yakuza, Shane Jiraiya Cummings, Angela Challis, Kate Williams, Andrew Williams, Talie Helene, Kathryn Linge, Al Chan, Brian Clarke, Alisa and Tehani, Mel & Phil, Jennifer Sudbury, Paul Pryztula, Helen Grzyb, Debbie Lee, Hayley Lane, Georgina Walpole, Rushelle Lister, Nerida Fearnley-Gill, everyone we've missed . . .

. . . and you.

IN MEMORY OF
Eve Johnson
Sara Douglass
Steven Utley
Brian Clarke